MIDNIGHT HUNT

MIDNIGHT HUNT

WOLVES OF MIDNIGHT

BECKY MOYNIHAN

BROKEN
BOOKS

Published by Broken Books
www.beckymoynihan.com

ISBN-13: 979-8-9883737-4-2

Cover design by Becky Moynihan
Cover model by www.depositphotos.com

*To anyone who's wished their canine best friend
could become a gorgeous man . . .*

This one's for you.

PROLOGUE

7 Years Ago

GRIFF

She came in hot, just like I knew she would.

My bedroom door banged open so violently that it smacked against the wall, no doubt leaving a dent in the plaster.

"Griffin Hayes O'Neal!"

She's fixin' to tan your hide, boy, drawled a voice in my mind, one that had adopted a heavy southern accent.

I didn't respond to my wolf familiar, continuing to rinse the shampoo from my hair as the irate female stormed across my room. Not even bothering to knock, she barged into the bathroom where I was taking a shower.

"What the hell did you do?" she barked, undeterred by my naked state.

Cracking an eye open, I peered through the fogged glass at the angry sixteen-year-old brunette. Her fists were clenched at her sides, and her normally dark amber irises were glowing a bright purple from the colored contacts she always wore. She was pissed, all right.

"Vi..."

"Don't *Vi* me, Griffin. Jeremiah won't even *speak* to me, let alone come near me."

"You're really cute when you're angry. Your mouth does this adorable little—"

"GRIFF!"

Sighing, I finished rinsing off my hair and switched off the shower. "He started it."

"I don't care. You didn't have to publicly *humiliate* him."

Yeah, you should have just killed that no good son of a—

"I was defending your honor," I spoke before Whiskey could finish the sentence. As I stepped from the shower, a towel flew at my head. I nimbly caught it but took my time wrapping it around my waist. The girl's blazing eyes didn't stray once from my face.

"And what could Jeremiah have possibly done that would make you beat him up until he *wet* himself in front of his friends?" Vi demanded.

Recalling the memory, I couldn't quite hide a smirk.

"This isn't *funny*, Griff."

"Ah c'mon, Vi. That jerk deserves a whole lot worse for what he said."

Heat practically shot from her eyes. "What. Did. He. Say?"

Pursing my lips, I snagged a hand towel from the counter to dry my hair. "I overheard him at the bar bragging to his friends about his plans to defile you tonight after your date. The details were explicit."

I watched in the mirror as her mouth slowly fell open. Blinking rapidly, she cleared her throat and muttered, "Oh. Well, that was kind of dickish."

"It was disgusting. He's lucky I didn't rip his tongue out." I dropped the hand towel and roughly jerked a comb through my blond hair, styling it so the bleached tips stood up in spikes. "Just because he's a member of Midnight Pack doesn't mean he's honorable. I thought you'd learned that lesson after the last two scumbags you hooked up with cheated on you."

Her eyes flashed hotly once more, and she popped her hands onto her hips indignantly. "I didn't 'hook up' with them. I didn't even let them get to second base, not that my love life is any of your business."

"It's my job to make sure you don't date creeps."

"Why, because we had sex? It was *one time*, Griff, and only because I was in heat."

A sudden ache pierced me, her words like a dagger through my heart. Ignoring the feeling as best I could, I turned to her and drawled, "Well, it was more than one time. I recall you begging for my cock at least a dozen times before your heat started to fade."

Her gaze finally dropped below my chin, taking in my lean muscular frame and the dark tattoos winding up both arms. Water still dotted my golden skin, and her eyes followed their downward path to my waist. When they dipped lower, I thought about letting the towel slip and revealing the goods. Before I could, she looked away.

"That was six months ago, Griff. I was in a vulnerable state, and a lot has happened since then. Kolton appointed you as his third, and you live across the hall from me now. I don't think we should complicate that with sex."

I kept my tone casual, but tension lined my body as I dared to ask, "What about when you go into heat again? What will you do then?"

Her shoulders fell. "I . . . I don't know."

"It's okay, Vi," I reassured when her expression turned troubled. "You don't have to decide anything right now. Just know that if you need help again, I'll be there for you. It doesn't have to affect our friendship."

Worrying her lip, she whispered, "Promise?"

"Cross my heart. We're family. That will never change."

She nodded but still wouldn't look at me.

"How about this," I continued. "Let's make a promise to always be there for each other, no matter what."

She finally looked up at me, her eyes suspiciously wet. "Even if I date dickish guys?"

I smiled at her despite the persistent ache in my chest. "Even if you date dozens of dickish guys. Which I'll beat to a pulp if they dare disrespect you."

She rolled her eyes, her anger from earlier gone. "Fine. I promise."

When she stuck out her hand, it was my turn to roll my eyes. "You know me better than that, Violet Jane. Come here."

She immediately rushed forward to accept my embrace. Just like that, my tension evaporated. Over the years, we'd hugged each other more times than I could count, but hugging her felt different now. Maybe not to her, but it sure as hell did for me.

We'd been intimate, our bodies exploring each other in every way possible. When I touched her now, every inch of me became hyper-aware of her. And when she touched me, my body yearned for more.

But she'd made it perfectly clear how she felt about me. Even if she allowed me to help with her heat again, we were only friends.

Still, I didn't let that stop me from tightening my arms around her. She might never see me as anything more than her brother's best friend, but I would always be there for her.

No matter what.

CHAPTER 1

VIOLET

The crowd erupted into chaos. I joined the excitement, rising from my seat to clap and holler at the top of my lungs.

"Yeah, Reid! Woohoo!"

It was the first football game of the season, and we'd won by a landslide—not surprising, considering who the quarterback was.

For four years running, Reid Zimmerman had led the New England Rebels to Super Bowl victory. Never before had the NFL seen a quarterback throw with such speed and accuracy. He'd taken the industry by storm, quickly rising in fame and securing the adoration of millions.

Girls fawned over him at every opportunity, all but willing to donate a kidney for one of his megawatt smiles. Charities loved him, benefiting from his giving nature, and fellow players respected him for his down-to-earth attitude.

Reid was the epitome of an all-American hero. Friendly, kind, hot as hell, and to his female fandom's chagrin . . .

Taken.

That's right. The six-foot-three, twenty-five-year-old quarterback with golden hazel eyes, dark brown hair, and gorgeous light brown skin was my boyfriend.

Oh, and did I mention he was a werewolf?

That part wasn't common knowledge, though. In fact, no one in the packed stadium but me and a handful of others knew that he could transform into a massive black wolf. Hiding his furry side from the public wasn't always easy, but he somehow managed. He usually only needed one night a month to wolf out, often choosing to head home to his pack in Maine for the occasion.

Constantly being in the spotlight held risks, yet Reid fit into the human world with an ease I couldn't help but admire. I wasn't too bad at it myself, but Reid blew my efforts out of the water. He truly was an impressive male, and I was lucky to call him my boyfriend. Perfect strangers reminded me of that fact on the regular—and not always in a nice way.

I was dating a superstar, and with that reality came a fair share of jealousy. I could feel eyes on me even now as Reid scored the final touchdown of the game. His teammates rushed into the endzone to celebrate their victory, and I forced my eyes to remain on them instead of the excited crowd around me.

Reid had offered to buy me a private box seat on the second level, but I'd turned it down in favor of being closer to the action on the sidelines. Although we could both easily afford the VIP seats, I didn't want to stand out any more than I already did. The sister of a New York billionaire dating the most popular quarterback in the NFL got quite enough attention already.

As the players became a bobbing pile of navy-blue jerseys, Reid suddenly turned my way and blew a kiss into the air. Girly screams pounded my sensitive eardrums, but I just smiled and blew him a return kiss. He grinned a mile wide, holding my gaze a moment before turning back to his teammates.

I continued to watch him celebrate, a small smile playing about my lips. He made it easy, *so* easy to like him. Being with him was like filling my lungs with oxygen. Simple. Automatic. Effortless.

Hmph.

As the disgruntled sound filled my mind, I replied back through our telepathic connection, *Don't start, Sable.*

What? I didn't say anything.

Yes, you did. You said a thousand things with that little sound.

My wolf familiar let out another harumph. *You're the one with the loud thoughts, Vi. At least I know how to keep mine to myself.*

Yeah, well, keep your sound effects to yourself too. I'm having fun, and you promised you wouldn't spoil it for me tonight. Please, Sable. Don't start another fight.

She huffed again, but it was more of a sigh this time. *Fine. Have your fun tonight, despite how much I'm going to hate it.*

Rolling my eyes, I started gathering my things. This wasn't the first time I'd been at odds with my familiar, but she'd never been this mopey for so long before. Despite the fact that we shared a special bond rarely seen in the supernatural world, the celestial being and I often wanted very different things. The moment she'd chosen me at birth to house her essence on the earthly plane, I'd been gifted a sliver of her spirit. The connection allowed me access to her powerful abilities and innermost thoughts, but that didn't mean I always understood or agreed with her.

The past eight months had been a constant battle of wills with the strong-minded demoness. She hated being away from her pack. *Our* pack. And every time I took her away, even for a day or two, she complained the entire time. Even worse, she didn't like Reid and reminded me of that fact every chance she could. Whenever he tried to kiss me, she would push to the surface and effectively separate us.

It was getting old. *Really* old. Especially since she refused to let us have sex.

As I finished collecting my things and headed for the stairs, I recalled what had happened when I'd gone into heat earlier this summer. Grimacing, I firmly locked away the memory. Tonight would be different. I was *finally* going to have sex with my boyfriend after eight long months of abstinence. Reid was a saint for being patient this long, but I knew he wanted to take that next step in our relationship as much as I did.

With the high from his win and the freshly waning moon, he was no doubt filled with testosterone and more than ready to seal the deal. Although we had a long distance relationship, I'd spent the past week with him at his upscale apartment in downtown Boston. He'd wanted some quality time with me before the official start of the football season, and I'd enjoyed several evenings of sightseeing the city with him. But as each evening had come to a close, Sable had asserted her presence between us like a frickin' cement wall.

Not tonight, though. My familiar and I had finally come to an agreement after hours of arguing, and there would be no celestial cock-blocking this evening. One uninterrupted night with my boyfriend in exchange for returning home tomorrow. Knowing that she'd only have to endure this city for one more day had done the trick.

For one night only, I was free to tackle the quarterback with no interference. Her words, not mine.

I could work with that. It was a step in the right direction, at least. Besides, Reid would win her over eventually. He *had* to. I couldn't stand much more of this tug-of-war.

With thoughts of hot, dirty sex on my mind, I started up the steps already crowded with fans. Although I wore a baseball cap over my dark brown hair, my straight bangs further acting as a shield, I heard my name whispered several times while ascending the stairs.

"Look! That's Violet Rivers, Reid Zimmerman's girlfriend."

"Oh, wow. Isn't she, like, a billionaire?"

"Yeah. Some people have all the luck in the world."

"Man, I would *kill* to be her."

I decided against reminding the gossipers that comparison was the thief of joy. I loved my life, but it wasn't all sunshine and rainbows. The world I lived in was dangerous, and I'd almost lost everything more times than I cared to remember. The humans in this stadium wouldn't survive a day in my shoes.

Distracted by the gossiping, I almost bumped into a huge guy standing like a road block a few stairs up. As I skirted around him, I could have sworn he leaned over to inhale my scent.

Sable pushed to the surface in sudden interest. *Werewolf*, she said, even before I could finish confirming with a sniff of my own.

Curious, I peeked over my shoulder at the male, only to find his dark eyes already on me. At the way he openly stared, the hairs on my body slowly stood on end. Probably in his late twenties, he looked for all the world like a Russian mafia hitman.

I don't recognize him, Sable said, her interest turning wary.

Neither do I, I replied before breaking the stare and facing forward again.

Normally, I'd stare him down to ascertain his dominance level, but the crowd was restless around me, their fight or flight instincts kicking in from being so close to two predators. I allowed the sea of bodies to sweep me up the stairs and shook off the encounter. Although this territory wasn't mine, all werewolves were allowed to attend certain public events no matter their location. Professional sports was one of them, so I was technically standing on neutral ground.

If the black-haired werewolf didn't like me in his territory, then he could take it up with his alpha. I personally knew Alpha DeRosa, and he was a decent guy as far as alphas went. Even though Reid belonged to a pack in Maine, allowing him in his territory was profitable for business. He didn't even mind that the quarterback owned a Boston apartment.

Soon, my thoughts were back to anticipating the evening ahead, an evening spent having hot sex with my boyfriend. The sun was already low in the sky, so I wouldn't have to wait much longer. When I reached the top of the stairs, I used my supernatural agility to slip through the crowd with ease. Reid and I had planned ahead of time to meet up at his apartment after the game, but I needed to pick something up first.

In no time, I was exiting the stadium and hurrying toward my purple Jeep. Reid had said I could use his town car while I was here, but I much preferred the independence my Jeep offered.

The second I hopped in and started her up, I rolled down the windows and cranked up the music. A popular country song blared through the speakers as I slowly navigated the busy parking lot and took the exit toward Boston. Once on the highway, I took off the Rebels hat to let my hair fly free in the wind, enjoying the smells of late summer.

"Any man of mine . . ." I loudly started to sing, knowing the song lyrics by heart. "Better walk the line . . ."

Finally caving to the carefree moment, Sable howled to the music. With a laugh, I threw back my head and let the howl belt from my lungs. The passenger in the car next to me gave me an odd look, but I just kept singing. Life was too short to care what other people thought of my car karaoke.

Twenty minutes later, I was hustling into a lingerie shop before they closed for the night. As I placed several lacy little nothings on the checkout counter, the female clerk asked, "Hoping to surprise your man?"

I slid her a sly grin. "Yeah. Hoping he'll take one look at me in these babies and beg me to take them off."

She winked and handed me the bag with my receipt. "Best of luck to you."

"Thanks!" I sang and hurried from the store.

I was nearly to my Jeep when the hairs on my nape suddenly lifted. Slowing, I took stock of my surroundings with my heightened senses. It was a Sunday night, and the sidewalks weren't nearly as busy as they'd been half an hour ago. This particular stretch was especially quiet, but traversing city streets after nightfall didn't usually trigger my instincts. Humans mostly kept to themselves, and they rarely recognized me outside of the stadium.

Still, something felt off. It almost felt like I was being . . .

Stalked. I feel it too, Sable commented as I threw a glance over my shoulder.

Paparazzi, maybe? They've hounded us before, I replied, trying to shrug off the unsettling feeling. Being chased by cameras was annoying, but they were harmless.

I don't know. This feels different. I sense danger.

At Sable's words, my guard went up. I might be a dominant hybrid werewolf, but I wasn't invincible. I was alone in a strange city without my pack, and I was keenly feeling their absence at the moment.

I was just about to look over my shoulder again when I spotted a lone figure up ahead standing near my Jeep. Immediately recognizing him as the werewolf who'd been blocking the stairs at the stadium, I went on high alert. Without a moment's hesitation, I encouraged Sable closer to the surface, hoping to intimidate him with my suddenly glowing purple eyes.

Regular werewolves couldn't shift at will, but hybrids could. Even if the male ahead was more dominant than me, I could call on Sable's strength in a heartbeat, not to mention my claws and fangs.

As the spirit familiar within me eagerly rose to my aid, I allowed my hybrid identity to poke through my human facade. My eyes flashed brightly in warning, and I curled my upper lip back to reveal a set of lengthened canines.

It was too dark for most humans to see the slight transformation, but I knew the werewolf could easily see me with his night vision. In response to my clear warning, he tipped his mouth into a faint smirk. Scowling, I opened my own mouth to tell him off. Before I could utter a single word, something rushed me from behind.

Vi! Sable barked, but it was too late.

In a flash, black fabric fell over my head, making the world go dark. I whirled around with my claws extended, but they caught nothing but air. A rough shove from behind sent me sprawling onto the sidewalk. I managed to tuck and roll, but I lost my purse and shopping bag in the process. As I yanked the black fabric off my head, hands grabbed my arms and legs and hoisted me up.

"Let go!" I snarled, fighting like a feral beast to break free. One of my legs slipped from their hold, and I struck out. This time, I made contact and was rewarded with a pained masculine grunt.

"Subdue her," a male growled, probably the black-haired one who'd been standing near my Jeep.

Still gripping one of my legs, the other male withdrew something from his pocket. When it caught the light of a nearby street lamp, my eyes widened. A syringe. He was trying to *inject* me with something.

Outraged, I kicked at his head with my freed foot. When my shoe made contact with his chin, he swore colorfully, dropping the needle and my other leg. Before I could wrestle my arms free, he stepped forward and punched me square in the face. The hit caught my cheek, nearly shattering the bone. Bright stars burst in my vision, the pain immediately dulling my senses. I'd been hit in the face plenty of times by werewolves, but being punched point-blank always sucked.

As I struggled to regain my eyesight, the male still holding my arms started to drag me away. I quickly blinked the stars from my vision and spotted a black SUV with its back door open. When I realized that they planned to shove me inside, fear coursed through my veins.

Sable! I cried, and my wolf immediately answered my call with a fierce, protective growl.

Familiar heat spread throughout my body as she took control and began to force the change. Not *all* the way into animal form, but just enough to give us an edge. My muscles swelled and hardened, stretching my skin taut. I gladly welcomed the bite of pain, knowing that I couldn't win this fight without Sable's help.

With another growl that ripped from my throat this time, Sable used my body to lash out at the males. A well-aimed knee to the groin sent one of them staggering back with a groan. The other one who'd followed me from the stadium managed to avoid a head butt. But when I twisted in his grip, his fingers slipped.

Sable immediately took advantage, ripping my arms free to whirl around and punch him in the throat. We stayed long enough to watch his eyes bug out in shock, then dashed away before either of them could catch us. Pausing a split second to scoop up my purse and shopping bag, I quickly unlocked my Jeep and scrambled inside.

Each movement was swift and precise, my senses firing off on all cylinders. The second the engine rolled over, I peeled away from the curb and floored it, the tires squealing loudly against the asphalt. For several minutes, I drove like a maniac, repeatedly glancing in the rearview mirror to see if I was being followed. When I reached Reid's apartment complex, I circled the block a few times just to be sure, then hurriedly parked and all but sprinted inside the building.

Only when I was in the relative safety of Reid's apartment did the shaking begin. It started in my fingers, then swiftly spread to the rest of my body. No longer able to stand, I sank to the hardwood floor and rummaged in my purse for my phone. With trembling fingers, I selected a number on autopilot, my breath coming in short spurts as I waited for him to pick up.

"Please, please, please," I whispered, feeling lightheaded as the phone rang and rang. "Please, pick up. Please, pick—"

The ringing abruptly stopped, and a familiar voice flooded the speaker. "Vi? You okay?"

A sob got stuck in my throat.

"Griff," I replied in a trembling voice. "I need you."

CHAPTER 2

VIOLET

I knew I wasn't thinking clearly. Knew I'd basically just committed relationship suicide.

But all I could focus on was the need pounding through my body. A need so intense that I could barely function when Reid found me half an hour later still sitting on the floor of his apartment.

I told him about the attack, but it hadn't made me feel any better. I knew he was worried and confused. Knew that I'd completely ruined our romantic evening by making that one call. A call I should have made to *him*.

Still, all I could think about was the fact that Griff was coming. Three little words, and he'd rushed to my aid, just like he always did. I waited for the guilt to hit, but the only thing I felt was relief.

He was coming. Nothing else mattered right now.

Forty-five minutes later, my keen hearing picked up the sound of footsteps approaching the apartment. When I heard more than one pair, I leapt to my feet, ready to fight again.

Reid turned toward the door as well, instinctively putting himself between me and the threat. He knew that I'd called Griff, but he shouldn't be here yet. The drive from Lake Placid was over four hours long. There was no way he could have—

I nearly jumped from my skin when a loud bang rattled the door. "Open up, Vi. It's Kolton."

At the unexpected sound of my brother's voice, some of my panic faded, but I continued to shake as Reid strode forward to open the door. The second he did, a tall figure barged inside, forcing him to step back.

"Where is she?" the blond male demanded, even as his brown eyes quickly scanned the room and collided with mine.

"Griff. She's—" Reid started, but the male shoved past him before he could finish.

A second later, I was being crushed in an impossibly tight hug, one that lifted me clean off my feet.

When his spicy clove and cinnamon scent surrounded me, the desperate need that had plagued me for over an hour immediately started to fade. I gripped the back of his shirt, relieved that my hands no longer shook. Sable heaved a sigh, one that warmed my insides and chased away the last of my terror.

Finally, she whispered, contentedly settling into the embrace.

Neither Griff nor I said a word, but we didn't need to. All we needed in this moment was each other's touch. For as long as I could remember, it had always been this way between us. One hug, and everything bad just slipped away.

Even though our relationship was strictly platonic now, his closeness soothed my nerves like nothing else could.

"What happened?" I heard Kolton question Reid.

"She was attacked by two males on the street, both werewolves. Apparently, one of them followed her from the stadium, but I don't recognize him from her description," Reid answered Midnight Pack's alpha. "I was still at the stadium when they—"

"Why weren't you with her?" Griff interrupted him, lifting his head from the crook of my neck to glare at my boyfriend.

"We decided to meet back at the apartment after the game. She had an errand to run."

"And you let her go, just like that?"

"Of course."

"But we entrusted her to you. It's your job to keep her *safe*. She shouldn't be wandering the city by herself."

"Vi is a grown woman and doesn't take orders from me," Reid replied, a slight edge to his voice. "I don't know how you do things in the Midnight Pack, but in the Lunar Falls Pack, we allow our females to come and go as they please."

"Even the unclaimed ones?"

"Yes."

Griff scoffed. "Some alpha you'll make some day."

"Okay, *enough*," I finally interjected before things could escalate.

When I started to pull away, Griff reluctantly let go of me. At the loss of his touch, Sable released a low whine. Ignoring her, I faced the guys, surprised to discover that Jagger had come as well. I took in his familiar light brown skin and serious blue gray eyes, noting that he must have given his black hair a fresh shave while I was away. He stood just inside the apartment like a silent sentinel, the diamond studs in his ears contrasting sharply with his black attire.

"Reid isn't to blame for what happened," I continued, relieved when my voice remained steady. "It was my idea to meet back here after the game. Besides, he's right. I'm a grown woman and can take care of myself."

"We know that, Vi," Kolton calmly replied, even as his dark amber eyes narrowed on the tear in my Rebel's jersey. "Griff was just worried. We all were. We're not used to you being so far away from home, and this attack has us all on edge."

At his confession, I deflated like a balloon, realizing just how homesick I'd been now that they were here. I hurried across the room to hug my brother, and as he folded me into his arms, I soaked up his steady strength before murmuring, "Please don't tell me you guys took the jet."

"Of course we took the jet."

Groaning, I stuck out a fist behind Kolton's back. "Hey, Jag." The pack's second in command silently bumped my knuckles. I knew better than to attempt a hug with him. "Sorry I freaked you all out. You really didn't need to come. I'm perfectly fine."

"I smell blood," Jagger quietly remarked.

"Where?" Griff demanded. In an instant, he was across the room and tugging me from Kolton's arms.

"Griff," I groaned again, batting his hands away as he tried to find my injuries. "It was just a few cuts and bruises, and they've already healed. No need to fuss."

Peering around him, I gave Reid an apologetic look. He'd seen the guys in protective mode before, but this was excessive. Still, my heart warmed at the realization that they'd missed me too.

"I've already contacted Alpha DeRosa, but I'll need to see him while we're here," Kolton said, his tone all business. "I could use your help if you have time, Reid."

"Sure," my boyfriend immediately replied. "He'll want a full report anyway. I was about to contact him myself."

"Good. If Vi's attackers are members of his pack, I have no doubt that he'll properly punish them, but I need assurances that this won't happen again while Vi is visiting his territory."

"I'll go too," I started, only for Kolton to shake his head at me.

"Reid, Jagger, and I can take care of this. Griff will take you home. Gather your things. The jet is already waiting for you."

"But you need me to describe what my attackers looked like to Alpha DeRosa."

"Reid can do that. Until we get to the bottom of this attack, I don't want you here any longer than necessary."

"But I'm *fine*," I pressed, frustrated that he was pulling both the big brother and pack alpha card on me. "Once Sable got involved, there was no way they were getting me into that SUV."

"They tried to *kidnap* you?" Griff roared, nearly making me jump. "That's it. You're not staying here another minute. Let's go."

He snagged my arm, but I jerked it free and shouted, "Wait!" When they all blinked at me in surprise, I inhaled a calming breath before saying, "Can we slow down here, please? I know you're all just trying to keep me safe, but if I leave the way you want me to, it'll make me look weak. Let me go on my own terms. I want to drive my Jeep home."

Griff looked ready to argue, but it was Kolton who shocked me by replying, "Fine, but you're not going alone."

"I'll go with her," Griff immediately offered.

"Done," Kolton said before I could protest. "Once Vi is packed, we'll make sure you two get to the Jeep safely before meeting up with Alpha DeRosa."

"Sounds like a plan," Griff replied with a nod.

When they all looked at me again, this time expectantly, I rolled my eyes and moved to collect my things. I was used to being bossed around by dominant males, but I didn't expect to be bossed around *here*. Although Reid was also a dominant male and would become alpha of his hometown pack soon, he was pretty chill.

He and Griff were alike in that way—except that Reid didn't go ballistic when another male messed with me. Griff, on the other hand, revealed just how dangerous he could be the moment a male even looked at me wrong.

He'd never made a jab at Reid before, though. Until now. It worried me more than I wanted to admit. Griff tended to chase off my suitors when he didn't approve of them.

Because none of them were right for you, including Reid, Sable butted into my thoughts.

Hush, I replied, entering the guest bedroom where I slept while I was here—since Sable wouldn't let me sleep with Reid. *You've never liked any of the males I've been with.*

Not true.

I snorted. *Fine. Name one.*

She didn't respond.

See? You're too picky.

Am not. You're just blind.

Okay, stop, I groaned, grabbing my suitcase to plonk it onto the bed. *Reid is amazing, and I have every intention of rescheduling our sexy evening. Once my attackers have been dealt with, I'm coming right back here to spend a hot night with my boyfriend. It's been way too long since I've gotten any.*

Yuck, she said with a disdainful sniff.

Get over it. You owe me. We're leaving for home even earlier than planned.

I felt her perk up at that.

Truth be told, I was excited too. This was the longest I'd been away from my niece and nephew, and I couldn't wait to breathe in their intoxicating baby smells again. Despite my reasons for leaving early, I was more than ready to be reunited with the rest of my family.

Five minutes later, I was packed and wearing a fresh plum-colored top with a deep V-neck. The scratches I'd received in the attack were scrubbed clean, and not a single mark marred my deep olive skin. Thanks to my supernatural healing, there wasn't even a bruise on my cheek from the brutal punch. I'd taken a few seconds to sweep my hair up into a high ponytail and rearrange my bangs so they fell perfectly straight once more.

Looking in the mirror, it was like the near-abduction had never happened.

Except that everything had changed in the blink of an eye. Reid and I were no longer going to take the next step in our relationship tonight, and I was running home with my tail between my legs.

Angry that the two male bastards had ruined my romantic evening, I swept from the room with my luggage and beelined toward my boyfriend. He was deep in conversation with Kolton when I interrupted by pulling his head down for a kiss. As our lips fused together, I felt him stiffen in surprise. Not caring that we had an audience, I stood on tiptoe and deepened the kiss. A moment later, he eagerly responded, raising his arms to pull me close.

True to her word, Sable didn't try to break us apart. Taking full advantage, I allowed the kiss to last for several long moments.

A throat suddenly cleared, and I broke the kiss to whisper against Reid's lips, "Sorry I'm leaving this way. I'll make it up to you."

He pulled back to meet my eyes. At the promise he saw in them, a slow smile stretched his mouth. "Looking forward to it."

Returning his smile, I pecked him on the cheek and stepped back. The second I did, a huge hand engulfed mine.

"Okay, we're out of here," Griff said, practically dragging me toward the door. When I stumbled a bit, he reached back and plucked the suitcase from my hand.

"Griff," I protested, trying to wiggle my hand free. His grip only tightened, so I gave up with a sigh.

Arguing with a male werewolf in overprotective mode was pointless. I usually did it anyway but didn't feel like putting up a fight at the moment. The attack must have taken more out of me than I cared to admit.

When we reached my car, though, I finally put my foot down. "I'm driving."

Griff opened the driver door for me without comment.

Pleased, I climbed inside my purple ride and started her up. As Griff placed my suitcase in the back and claimed the front passenger seat, Kolton said through my open window, "No detours, Vi. Head straight home. Call me if you think you're being followed."

"I will."

"I won't let anything happen to her, Kol. You have my word," Griff said as he shut his door. "She won't leave my sight for a second."

Sensing yet another dig at Reid, I pursed my lips. The minute the coast was clear, Griff and I were going to have *words*.

As we exited the parking garage, I opened my mouth to give him a piece of my mind. Before I could, a plastic bag rattled. I glanced over just as Griff pulled out the lacy little nothings I'd purchased a few hours ago.

"Griff!" I swiped at the lingerie and missed.

"A present for *me?*" he gushed, holding the apparel just out of reach. "You shouldn't have."

"It's not for you, dummy."

"Well, it was on *my* seat."

"I . . . Just give it to me, will you?"

Not surprisingly, he ignored me. Now that it was just us two, he was back to his usual obnoxious self. If there was an olympic medal for teasing, Griffin O'Neal would win gold every time.

Humming, he inspected the lingerie more closely before saying, "I like the strappy purple one best. You can see right through it. Which one do you like, Sable?"

"GRIFF!" I barked. "Don't you two dare team up on me right now. I'm not in the mood. Besides, this is totally inappropriate."

Sable snickered, clearly amused.

"I bet Reid the Steed hasn't seen these yet."

"Not that it's any of your business, but, no, he hasn't."

"What a shame."

At his sarcastic tone, I threw a sideways glare at him. "I thought you liked Reid."

"I do."

"Then what's with the verbal jabs and the nickname? You always give the guys in my life lame nicknames when you start disliking them."

Shrugging, he tucked the lingerie back into the bag. "Okay, fine. I'm pissed he wasn't there when you were attacked."

I blew out a frustrated sigh. "We've already been over this. It was *my* decision to leave the stadium without him."

"I know, but . . ."

When he didn't finish, I glanced at him again. "But what?"

"But," he slowly said, fisting the bag in his lap, "I should have been there for you."

I opened my mouth, only to snap it shut. Oh. He wasn't really mad at Reid, then. He was mad at *himself* for not being here.

"Griff . . ." Unsure what to say, I closed my mouth again.

Silence settled between us. After several moments, he quietly said, "You scared the hell out of me with that phone call, Vi."

Without thought, I reached between us and found his hand. "I'm sorry," I said, glancing down as he threaded his fingers through mine. A familiar warmth spread up my arm at the contact. We hadn't held hands in months, not since I'd started dating Ried. Although I knew it was nothing more than a friend's comforting touch, an instinct poked at me to pull away. Ignoring it, I focused on the road again and said, "I shouldn't have called."

"Yes, you should have. We made a promise to always be there for each other, remember?"

A slow grin tugged at my mouth. "Even if I date non-dickish guys?"

He lightly scoffed and squeezed my fingers. "Yes, Vi. Even if you date non-dickish guys."

CHAPTER 3

GRIFF

The nearly five hour car ride ended way too soon.

Vi and I spent the majority of it listening to her blaring country music, both of us loudly breaking into song on several occasions. It was like the past week apart had never happened and everything was back to normal between us.

Except that it wasn't.

She'd called me. She'd been scared and called *me* instead of her boyfriend.

What's more, she still hadn't had sex with him. I'd teased her earlier about the lingerie, but I'd already known Reid hadn't seen it. If he had, they would have definitely had sex, and I *definitely* would have scented it.

They'd been living in the same apartment for an entire week. I thought for sure she would come home smelling like him this time, complete with a fresh claim mark. I'd dreaded it. *Prepared* for it. And yet, when I'd swept her into my arms back at Reid's place, I'd inhaled nothing but crisp fall leaves and dark chocolate, a scent I knew better than my own.

I'd nearly crashed to my knees, beyond relieved at the discovery.

Still, I'd spent the past five hours making nothing but small talk. We didn't even bring up the fact that two males had tried to kidnap her. Vi didn't respond well to being pushed. The only reason why Kolton sometimes got away with it was because of his position as the pack alpha.

If Vi wanted to talk about Reid or the attack, she'd do it on her own terms. Although I outranked her in the pack, she was just as dominant—maybe more so in some ways. If I forced her to talk, it would put a strain on our relationship, a lifelong friendship we'd fought so hard to maintain.

So I kept silent, carefully bottling up the words that desperately wanted to spill free. I didn't bother to do this with anyone else in my life, but with Vi . . . things were different.

The second she parked her Jeep inside the family estate's five-car garage, she jumped out and beelined for the house. I could sense how homesick she'd been, and even though it was two in the morning, I had no doubt she planned to tiptoe into every bedroom just to catch a glimpse of her family.

Smiling a little, I stayed in the Jeep long enough to text Kolton: *Made it home safely. No one followed us. Any news on the two males?*

A few seconds later, he sent back: *No news. They aren't members of Alpha DeRosa's pack. We're heading back now. Be there in an hour.*

Cursing under my breath, I exited the vehicle and grabbed Vi's luggage from the backseat. I was just about to tuck her newly-purchased lingerie into the suitcase when an image of her modeling them for Reid popped into my head. I stuffed the bag into the back pocket of my jeans instead.

When I closed the garage and entered the three-story mansion a few minutes later, I found Vi upstairs in one of the nurseries.

"I think he grew while I was gone," she whispered as I silently came up behind her. I peered around her at the nine-month-old baby sound asleep in his crib, then down at her. Her lashes were fluttering, a sign that she was on the verge of tears.

The need to comfort her was like a swift kick to the ribs, but I didn't initiate contact. If she wanted my touch, she would come to me. When she didn't move, I replied in an equally soft voice, "Personally, I think Luca's getting a bit chunky. Too many people spoil him in this house now that he can eat solid foods."

When she muffled an amused snort, the ache in my ribs faded.

After a few more minutes of staring at her nephew, she crept back out and made for the third floor. I knew she was dying to see her four-month-old niece, but Lillian was still co-sleeping in the master bedroom with Kolton and his wife Nora. Luca had always been a calm baby who easily slept through the night. Lily, on the other hand, kept her parents up at all hours of the night. Nora was probably in there right now trying to nurse her fussy, night-owl daughter to sleep.

Not surprisingly, Vi peeked inside Melanie's room next. Her seven-year-old sister was sound asleep, gripping a stuffed blue unicorn as usual. Hovering at the door for a moment, Vi crossed the ultra girly room newly decorated in blue and stopped at Mellie's bedside to place a soft kiss on her cheek.

The girl rolled over in her sleep, mumbling something about dresses and tea parties.

Satisfied, Vi left the room, only to tiptoe to the next occupied bedroom. When she cracked open the door, though, a quiet gasp left her lips. My protective instincts surged to the surface, along with my wolf familiar's. Whiskey went on high alert, ready to attack at the first sign of danger. But as I crowded in close to Vi, prepared to whisk her out of harm's way, she whirled around and shot past me.

"Vi," I hissed, but she was already across the hallway and scurrying down the stairs. I went after her, trying to keep my footsteps light. By the time I reached the ground floor, she was nowhere in sight. Using my heightened sense of smell, I tracked her through the house. She'd rushed toward the back where the dining room was, but when her scent veered sharply to the left, I knew where she was headed.

As I approached the open doorway, freshly baked dough and warm chocolate teased my senses. Whiskey immediately started to settle, and I slowed my mad dash. Already knowing what I would find, I paused at the kitchen entrance to take in the scene. Sure enough, two figures stood at the massive kitchen island, the countertop covered in cooking supplies and freshly baked goods.

"It's the middle of the night, Mom," Vi gently said to the older female whose face and sleep t-shirt were streaked with flour. "You should be sleeping."

"I know, honey," Charlotte Rivers distractedly replied as she finished placing another batch of chocolate chip cookies on the cooling rack. "I was feeling restless, and you know how baking helps settle me."

"I understand, but I'd feel better if you were upstairs in bed. How about I get you a glass of milk and finish cleaning up here?"

Her mother paused to glance up at her eldest daughter. They looked so much alike. Same straight dark hair and deep olive skin. Same dark amber eyes, even though I rarely saw Vi's on account of her purple contacts. Tucking a premature white streak of hair behind her ear, Charlotte considered her daughter's words before saying, "Sure, honey. A glass of milk would be nice. But you should get some sleep too. You look tired."

Vi waved her mom's concern away with a small laugh. "I'm okay. It's just a long drive from Boston."

Charlotte set down her spatula with a slow blink. "Oh."

Vi didn't seem affected by the sudden blank look on her mother's face, but I knew better. It had been five months since Charlotte had come home, five months of slowly incorporating her back into society. We still hadn't reintroduced her to the entire pack, but they all knew she was alive, that Kolton and Vi had hidden her away after she'd succumbed to heartbreak over her husband's death.

Some of the members felt betrayed by the secrecy, but no one could really blame them for what they did. Their mother wouldn't be alive right now if they'd told the pack of her broken state. She was still recovering, still drifting off inside her mind, but she was lucid most days, thanks to Nora's healing magic.

Her short-term memory had suffered the most from the mental break, though. Sometimes, she forgot that she had a seven-year-old daughter. That she was no longer the alpha female of Midnight Pack. Keeping track of the household's comings and goings was also hard for her. She probably hadn't even realized that Vi had been gone all week. What's more, she constantly forgot about Reid. In fact, she thought Vi and I were—

"Oh, Griff!" she suddenly exclaimed, her eyes brightening in recognition as she spotted me in the doorway. "I should have known it was you keeping my daughter up so late. Not getting her into trouble, I hope."

At the adoring, slightly scolding look she gave me, my face split into an impish grin. "I promise I'm not getting your daughter into trouble, Mrs. R."

"Please, Griffin, I insist you call me Charlotte. I'm not blind, you know. I see what a strapping young man you've become. You're not that towheaded little boy anymore who used to pull on Violet's pigtails."

At the mental image the memory gave me, I burst out laughing. Vi rolled her eyes, but when she huffed a laugh of her own, my chest warmed.

"If I recall, Mrs—Charlotte," I teasingly drawled, "your daughter got her revenge for all that hair pulling by giving me my first black eye."

"Why, Violet Jane," Charlotte gasped in mock dismay.

"He deserved it," Vi muttered, throwing me a glare that promised retribution for outing her.

Ooh, tell another story, Whiskey purred, clearly enjoying the slightly dangerous banter. Dangerous, because Vi was probably going to beat me up after this.

My mouth curved into a wicked grin. Seeing what I was about to do, she opened her mouth to stop me. Before she could, I blurted, "She also stole a bottle of vodka from your liquor cabinet once and dared me to drink the whole thing. I was only fifteen."

"Hey, I didn't *force* you to drink it," Vi protested, her eyes practically shooting lasers at me. "I was twelve years old. I didn't know it would make you throw up like that."

"Yeah, and my mom's warned me of the dangers of alcohol ever since. Every Christmas, she gives me the stink eye before letting me touch even a drop of wine."

Vi snorted in amusement. "Really? I didn't know that. Serves you right, though. I still can't believe you drank the *whole* bottle."

"You dared me," I said with a shrug.

Shaking her head, she moved toward the cabinet where the glasses were kept. As she lifted an arm to grab one, her purple shirt rode up, exposing a sliver of smooth olive skin just above her favorite designer jeans. I'd seen that strip of taut flesh more times than I could remember, but my body reacted to it all the same.

Your screwdriver is showin', mate, Whiskey casually remarked, this time in an Australian accent. *Might wanna put him away before the lady sees.*

She won't notice, I replied.

I was talking about her mum.

Well, in that case, he had a point. Most evenings when her brain was tired, Charlotte's mind got stuck in the past. Seven years ago, to be exact, when she was still pregnant with Melanie and her husband Anthony was still alive. When things were happiest for her. When her son was in college and her eldest daughter had just been freed from a toxic relationship.

The calm before the storm. Before everything had changed. For *all* of us.

Charlotte was stuck in that happy place now, blissfully unaware of the seven hard years that had passed, years that had shaped us into different beings. Right now, all she saw was her nearly sixteen-year-old daughter, her son's oldest best friend, and the exciting possibility of a budding relationship. Not just lifelong friendship but something more, something deeper.

Apparently, deflowering her precious baby girl equaled wedding bells. Didn't matter that the intimate moment had happened while Vi was in heat at the tender age of fifteen. Charlotte was clearly waiting for me to make my intentions known—and reminding her about Reid didn't help. Whenever her brain was stuck like this, she only had one goal in mind . . .

Getting me to claim and mate Vi before Anthony Rivers promised her to another pack heir.

All these years, I'd thought Charlotte had approved of the betrothal, but she'd revealed some secrets to us over the past few months. Namely, her distaste for the archaic tradition of uniting two packs through an arranged marriage contract. Which was ironic, considering the deal her son had made last year with Nora, his fated mate.

But Vi didn't see me as something more. And the *last* thing I wanted was to push her into a relationship she didn't want.

The reality of our situation was like a bucket of ice water, effectively dousing the heat in my groin. She was with Reid now. A pack heir, ironically. Charlotte might be stuck in the past and hoping for a mate match between me and her daughter, but I couldn't afford to entertain that fantasy.

Vi was in a healthy relationship for once, and I wouldn't stand in the way of that. Not this time.

She deserved a good guy, and I couldn't deny that Reid was just that. He was kind, upstanding, and respectful, a male I could actually approve of.

There was no good reason to sabotage their relationship.

None, whatsoever.

My skin suddenly felt too tight. Needing something to do, I pushed off the doorframe and headed for the mess on the counter. A minute later, I was elbow-deep in warm water and soap suds, scrubbing bowls and pans so vigorously that they all but groaned in protest. Vi continued to chat with her mother as she too helped clean up, putting away the cooking supplies and wrapping up the baked goods while Charlotte finished her glass of milk. In no time, the kitchen was back to its pristine condition.

Charlotte looked around approvingly before nodding and saying, "Thanks for the help, you two. I'm off to bed now." Before leaving, she gave us both a kiss on the cheek goodnight, then paused and added, "And if you're going to have sex, be discreet. Anthony is still adjusting to the idea of you two being together."

With that, she gave me a final pat on the cheek and left the kitchen.

Vi and I gaped after her, our jaws slightly unhinged. Well, that was a new one.

"Did she just . . . ?" Vi whispered.

"Yup," I whispered back. "Your mom just got super cool."

She whacked my stomach, making me grunt. "Knock it off, Griff. I think she's getting worse."

Hearing the worry in her voice, I gently nudged her shoulder with mine. "Healing takes time, Vi. The mind can break in a second but take years to repair. With lots of patience and compassion, she'll get better. You'll see."

She released a tired sigh but didn't comment.

"Your mom's right, though. You should get some sleep too. You've had an exhausting day."

"But Kolton and Jagger aren't back yet. I need to know what they learned about my attackers."

"Kol texted me. Alpha DeRosa doesn't know who they are."

Her shoulders fell. "Great. Just great." Reaching up, she yanked the tie out of her hair. As the dark strands tumbled onto her shoulders, I had a sudden desire to feel them gripped tightly between my fingers. Oblivious to my inner turmoil, Vi added with another sigh, "Well, I'm off to bed, then. Night."

"Night," I murmured, watching as she left the kitchen.

She was still acting like everything was normal between us. Like she hadn't called me in a panic earlier and admitted that she needed me.

Needed.

I opened my mouth to call her back, to demand she explain herself. To *push*. Instead, I firmly shut my mouth and allowed her to go unchallenged, bottling up the unspoken words between us once more.

Only when I heard her reach the stairs did I move to follow, forbidden thoughts of touching her still dancing through my mind.

CHAPTER 4

VIOLET

"Rivers' residence. Vi speaking," I said in my most chipper voice despite the early hour.

"Oh, Vi, you're back! We missed you at the initiation last week," an all too familiar voice responded in an even more chipper tone.

"Yes, Mrs. Bailey, I was sad to have missed it," I replied to the pack gossip—aka my childhood nanny. Still groggy from barely getting any sleep last night, I picked up my mug of coffee from the study desk and took a sip. "Is Desirae settling in well?"

"Indeed, she is! I still can't believe I have a *hybrid* staying in my home. Brings back so many fond memories of nannying you and your brother. It was the biggest challenge of my life, you know, keeping your secret from the rest of the pack. Good thing everyone knows about hybrids now, because Desirae *loves* to shift. She takes off into the woods every night in wolf form and usually doesn't come back until dawn. Independent, that one is. Makes sense, since she's been living on her own for the past decade."

She finally paused but only to take a quick breath and plow on.

"Still, it's dangerous for an unclaimed female wolf to be alone. I was hoping that Jagger or Griff could accompany her on her nightly runs, seeing as they are both hybrids. It's why I called, since she hasn't come home yet, and I'm a bit worried. And, who knows? Maybe a love match will come of it. It's time those two bachelors found their mates and settled down."

I blinked, trying to process the whirlwind of words. My brain got stuck far too long on the fact that she was trying to matchmake Griff and Jagger with Midnight Pack's newest female wolf. Sure, she was young and pretty, but we still didn't know much about her. Besides Nora, we'd never initiated a hybrid into the pack before. Desirae had also grown up as a pack outcast because of her abnormal abilities, but she was an omega. I doubted Jagger or Griff would be interested in a non-dominant female.

Right?

Uncertainty squirmed in my gut, but I quickly shoved the feeling aside. No way would my boys be interested in an omega. They needed a *challenge*. A submissive, docile female wouldn't give them that. As I opened my mouth to set Mrs. Bailey straight, the rest of her words finally sank in. "Wait, are you saying that Desirae is missing?"

"Well, I don't want to cause undue alarm, but she's never stayed out this long before. She doesn't bring her phone, and I tried looking for her, but I can't get very far in my human form. I thought maybe Alpha Rivers, Jagger, or Griff could come out since they can shift at will and cover a lot more ground. It would mean so much to me. Desirae is still new to pack land and might have wandered off too far. Any number of things could have happened to her."

"It's okay, Mrs. Bailey. We'll head out right away and look for her," I reassured the distraught-sounding woman and pushed to my feet. After she thanked me profusely, I ended the call and strode across my brother's office to the door.

So much for catching up on the emails and paperwork that had piled up during my absence. Normally, I'd tell Kolton about the incident and trust him to take care of it, but the thought of a female wolf going missing so soon after my near-abduction had me on edge. Work would have to wait.

I found my brother and the rest of the family in the dining room, just finishing up with breakfast. My mother caught my eye first. She was bustling around the long table, busily collecting plates that had been picked clean. Now that she was back, we had no more use for our human staff and had let them go. From dawn until dusk, she kept herself busy with never-ending housework and feeding our growing family. Apparently, being strapped to a bed for seven years had given her boundless energy, and she hardly ever sat down for more than a few minutes.

Nora's parents were no longer staying with us, but there were still ten people living here full time. Plus, the current Rivers' nanny, Miss Gabby, was coming back to homeschool Melanie for another year. The house was always in motion, and I absolutely loved it.

A squeal drew my gaze across the table to Griff who'd just lifted Luca from his highchair and was in the process of tickling him. The dark-haired boy threw back his head and belly laughed.

"Griff, he just ate. If he spits up, it's on you. *Literally*," Nora said in exasperation, even as her aqua blue eyes twinkled with faint amusement. The curly-haired ginger sat on the other side of her son's highchair with a flower-printed cover draped over her. Even after living with us for over a year, she still wasn't comfortable with nudity and preferred to cover herself while nursing her children.

One of Lillian's adorable little fists poked out from beneath the cover, and I had to stop myself from hurrying around the table to nibble on her tiny baby fingers. Since I'd woken up before everyone else, I hadn't been able to properly snuggle with my niece and nephew yet. I'd decided to take a quick shower and jump right back into work, needing to distract my mind from everything that had happened yesterday.

Sleep had eluded me last night as I'd replayed the attack over and over again, fruitlessly trying to figure out what the two males had wanted with me. The only thing that made sense was that they could use me as leverage against Kolton. Challenging the most powerful alpha in America was practically impossible, and ever since the werewolf community had learned of his hybrid nature, challenges had pretty much been nonexistent. But we'd known it was only a matter of time before they started up again.

Kidnapping a member of his family would definitely throw Kolton off his game.

"Vi, you're back!" a little voice excitedly squealed, dragging me from my thoughts.

Everyone stopped what they were doing to focus on the newcomer. As all eyes went to me, I paused to bask in the attention. When I felt the love in each gaze, a lump formed in my throat.

I'd missed this. I'd missed this *terribly*.

Before I could respond, little arms wrapped around my waist and squeezed. "What did you get me? What did you get me?" that same excited voice chirped.

"Melanie," Kolton softly chastised the dark-haired girl clinging to me like an octopus. "That's not the proper way to welcome your sister home."

Mellie tilted her head back to look at me, her dark amber eyes rounding innocently. "Sorry, Vi. I can be patient. Do you want to see my new loose tooth?"

Several of the adults around the table chuckled as the seven-year-old opened her mouth and excitedly pointed inside it.

"Oh," I replied in mock seriousness, peering intently at the somewhat crooked baby tooth. "Looks like I came home just in time. That sucker needs to be pulled."

As my hand beelined toward her mouth, she jumped back with a petrified shriek. "No! It hurts when you do it."

"Ah c'mon, Mellie. If you want the souvenir I got you, that tooth is the price," I cajoled, crab-walking toward her with pincer hands.

"Kol!" she wailed, whirling to seek the protection of her brother.

At the mildly scolding look my mother threw my way, I shrugged and said, "What? That'll make her think twice about treating me like a gift shop."

Griff barked a laugh, clearly the only one amused by my twisted sense of humor. He tickled Luca again, who had no choice but to join in on the laughter.

Thoroughly distracted by the cuteness, I almost forgot what I came in here for. Just as I was about to speak, someone else stood from their seat to hug me.

"Welcome home, Vi," Brielle murmured, her tropical-scented, honey-brown hair brushing my face as she enveloped me in a warm embrace. Like most werewolves, the newest turned-werewolf of Midnight Pack showed affection through physical touch. The only exception to that rule was Jagger, who was still in his chair and silent as a tomb. I could practically count on one hand how many times he'd initiated physical contact with me. "Have you eaten yet? You feel thinner."

At her words, the laughter in the room abruptly stopped. I pulled back to wave a hand dismissively. "I was too busy catching up with work. I had coffee, though."

"There's leftovers in the kitchen. I'll go get them," Mom said, already moving toward the kitchen.

"No, Mom, it's okay," I hurriedly said, ignoring the looks everyone gave me. "I actually don't have time for breakfast right now. Kolton, I need to speak with you."

"Privately?" he asked, raising one dark brow.

Seeing the expectant faces around me, I sighed and shook my head. "No. It might not be a big deal anyway. Mrs. Bailey just wants us to check on her new ward."

"Desirae?"

"Yeah. She didn't come home this morning, and Mrs. Bailey's getting worried. Apparently, Desirae likes to wolf out every night and roam the woods. Something might have happened."

"I'll go look for her," Jagger finally spoke up, rising from his chair.

"Me too," Griff said.

"And me," I quickly said before Kolton could say anything. At the penetrating look he gave me, I stood taller and stared right back at him. Almost immediately, the weight of his dominance threatened to pull my gaze downward. Sensing my struggle, Sable pushed to the surface, and I gladly accepted her help in staring my brother down.

After several long moments, Kolton's mouth curved into a faint smirk. "Fine. But we're taking the truck."

"I call shotgun!" I sang, grinning when Jagger grunted his displeasure.

"I need to change my shirt first," Griff groaned, drawing my gaze to him once more. At the sight of spit up running down his shirt front, I snorted out a laugh.

"Told you," Nora murmured, struggling to keep a smile off her face.

"I'll clean him up," Brielle said and rounded the table to take Luca from Griff.

As soon as his arms were free, Griff yanked the soiled t-shirt over his head. Before I could stop them, my eyes dropped to the golden expanse of his chest and stomach. Every inch was familiar to me, a sight I'd seen countless times before. He didn't possess an ounce of shyness when it came to nudity, and he often walked the halls butt naked in the evenings. Still, I couldn't help but take in the hard, lean muscle, tracing each swell and dip until his jeans blocked me from seeing more.

Realizing too late what I was doing, I jerked my gaze away before anyone could notice.

As Griff left the dining room to change his shirt, I made sure to look everywhere but at him. In doing so, my gaze collided with Nora's. Something flashed in them, and I knew she'd seen. Quickly playing it off, I grinned at her and hurried over to give my baby niece a quick nuzzle goodbye.

"I'm so sorry you were alone during the attack last night," Nora quietly said before I could pull away. "You okay?"

The question was light and unobtrusive. A simple show of concern.

Although Nora was the alpha female of Midnight Pack, her dominance level equal to Kolton's, she didn't *push* for answers. That respect for personal boundaries was one of the things I loved most about my sister-in-law.

"A little shaken up," I admitted, knowing the others in the room could hear. I hadn't told her what happened, but Kolton had no doubt filled her in. News didn't stay hidden for long in our pack, so the entire household probably knew the gist of it all by now. Gently swirling one of Lily's fiery curls around my finger, I finished with, "I'm fine, though. I hurt them more than they hurt me."

Before she could question me more, I let go of the soft curl and straightened.

"Meet you in the car, boys," I called, forcing myself to leave the dining room and head for the front door. A pack member was missing, and that was all I wanted to focus on right now. Dealing with any trauma I'd experienced from last night would have to wait.

The boys joined me in the garage minutes later, Kolton hopping into the driver seat of the dual-rear-wheeled white truck while Jagger and Griff jumped into the back. Not a second after the engine roared to life, a hand materialized over my shoulder and dropped something onto my lap.

"You need to eat," Griff said, leaving his arm propped on the back of my seat while Kolton eased the truck from the garage.

I glanced down at my lap to find a blueberry muffin, several strips of bacon, and a handful of breakfast sausages jammed inside a baggie. "Thanks, but I don't think I can eat right now," I replied.

"*Eat,*" all three males said in unison.

I threw a scowl at them, but inwardly, my heart melted a little. Growing up with three protective males had been a headache at times, but I'd missed this. It felt like forever since just the four of us had done something together. So much had changed this past year, changes I was still adjusting to.

Knowing it was pointless to argue with the three bossy males, I opened the baggie and removed the muffin. After the first bite, my appetite returned in full force. Less than a minute later, I was licking my fingers clean and reaching for the sausages.

"Are you worried that Desirae was kidnapped?" Kolton questioned me while I ate.

Not surprised that he'd properly guessed my main reason for wanting to come along, I nodded and replied around a mouthful of sausage, "It could very well be nothing, but it just seems weird that a pack member would go missing so soon after I was attacked."

"I was thinking the same thing. You might not be their sole target, whoever 'they' are."

"My only guess is that someone is trying to challenge you. No werewolf has directly done so since finding out that you can shift at will. Maybe they're trying to get creative by taking pack members hostage. It gives them the upper hand, at least."

"It'll incite a manhunt if the entire pack finds out," Jagger commented.

"True. I wouldn't mind hunting the bastards down," Griff said almost directly in my ear. He was still leaning against my seat, his face practically even with the headrest. Realizing what he wanted, I rolled my eyes and held up a strip of bacon. He took it from me canine-style, using his teeth to swiftly snatch it from my fingers.

"Good boy," I crooned, reaching back to pat his head.

"Hair," he yelped and quickly retreated.

"I swear, Griffin, you're more obsessed with your hair than anyone I know."

"Hey, appearances are important to me."

I rolled my eyes again. "You look like a surfer straight from the beach, even during the winter. When's the last time you wore actual *shoes* instead of flip-flops?"

"Kolton's the suit-wearing businessman in this family. My job doesn't require me to wear a neck noose and overpriced shoes that pinch my toes."

"Or anything at all," I muttered under my breath.

"What was that, VJ? You saying I would look better in the nude? Because I will happily take off my—"

"NO!" we all shouted at him in unison.

He chuckled. "You protest, but I see you all checking out this godlike bod when you think I'm not looking."

I nearly choked on the bacon strip I'd just put into my mouth. Swallowing, I sassily replied, "You wish."

He suddenly leaned forward again to purr in my ear, "Don't be coy, Violet Jane. I know you like what you see."

Feeling a shiver work its way up my spine, I swiveled in my seat and pushed his face back with my open hand. "Get over yourself, Griffin."

He loudly laughed in reply. When I felt a sharp tug on my hair, I bared my teeth at him and growled, "Try that again and see what happens."

His puppy brown eyes sparkled with mischief . . . and challenge. When they briefly flashed yellow, Sable perked up in interest.

"You two bicker like an old married couple," Jagger quietly groused.

Just like that, the playful moment came to a screeching halt.

"Uh, hello? I've got a boyfriend, remember?" I snarkily replied. When all Jagger did was slowly raise an eyebrow at me, I stiffly turned around and lapsed into silence.

Thankfully, Mrs. Bailey's house wasn't too far away from ours, so we arrived before the silence became too uncomfortable. The second the truck rolled to a stop, I scrambled out. Our former nanny was already hurrying down her porch steps to greet us, her pale face creased with worry.

"Oh, my," she twittered, flailing her hands comically as she watched Kolton, Jagger, and Griff exit the truck. "I wasn't expecting *all* of you to come. Now I feel bad for making such a fuss."

"No worries, Mrs. Bailey," my brother said, stopping beside me. "We take disappearances in the pack very seriously, as you know. Even if Desirae is perfectly fine, it's better to be safe than sorry."

She bobbed her head enthusiastically, several strands of brown hair escaping her low bun. "I wholeheartedly agree. You can never be too careful. Desirae usually takes a northeastern route through the woods behind the house. I'll point you in the right direction."

Instead of chatting our ears off for several minutes like she usually did, the middle-aged woman swiftly turned and led us around the house.

"There," she said, pointing to a spot along the treeline bordering her backyard. "The trail is faint, but I'm sure you'll have no problem picking up her scent in wolf form."

When she turned to stare at us expectantly, Griff chuckled under his breath. "You heard the woman. Let's get naked."

For the second time today, I watched him whip off his shirt. But when he reached for the button on his jeans, I forced myself to look away. Kolton and Jagger started to undress as well, and I followed suit, not the least bit embarrassed to be stripping naked in front of them.

We'd been doing this for as long as I could remember, unleashing our wolves to run as a pack deep in upstate New York's Adirondacks. As children, we'd spent hours every day out in the woods, playing and honing our hunting skills. As soon as I'd been old enough to join them, I'd worked hard to prove that I was worthy of a spot in their inner circle.

Less than a minute later, all four of us were stripped bare. I chanced a quick peek at Griff, only to find his eyes trained on me. My breath caught. He looked away a second later, but not before I'd seen something in his gaze. Something old. Something familiar. Something . . .

I gave my head a sharp shake and banished the thought. I must have seen wrong. We were only friends now. *Friends.* We didn't look at each other that way anymore.

The cracking of bone brought me back to reality, and I quickly initiated my own transformation, silently encouraging Sable to take over. She gleefully rose to the surface and triggered the shift. A painful minute later, I stood on all fours. Rather, *Sable* stood on all fours, her nearly black fur glistening in the early morning sunlight.

She quickly shook off the shift, then full-body stretched with a satisfied groan. Since she'd missed the pack run during the full moon last week, I mentally prepared myself for her rebellious energy. She hated missing out on pack events even more than I did, and I knew she was feeling a bit resentful that I'd chosen to spend the time with Reid instead.

Stick to the task at hand, I warned her through our telepathic connection. I had no intention of wrestling control from her, but I really hoped she didn't do anything stupid like—

I sighed in exasperation as she whirled and sought out her favorite wolf. Standing taller than a human, Whiskey was a tawny brown color, his sleek coat littered with blond patches. When he saw Sable heading toward him, he yipped with excitement and met her halfway. Their massive bodies tangled together, and they playfully nuzzled and nipped at each other as if they'd been apart for months.

Although they couldn't speak mind-to-mind, they had no trouble communicating how much they liked each other. When the nuzzling turned into licking—on the *mouth*—I finally put my foot down.

Sable! I snapped. *Don't forget that I have a boyfriend.*

He's not my *boyfriend*, she replied, continuing to lick Whiskey's mouth like a brazen hussy. *My spirit and the spirit inside Whiskey's body—*

Used to be lovers on the celestial plane. Yeah, yeah, I know, I said with a mental eyeroll. *But Griff and I aren't a couple, so it's really uncomfortable when you and Whiskey get all hot and heavy.*

I have the perfect solution for that, she purred, shuddering when Whiskey bent his head to nip at her neck.

Don't say it, I quietly growled.

Start having sex with Griffin again.

I groaned, and she let the sound roll from her throat in an erotic way. The noise sent Whiskey into an excited frenzy, and he started rubbing the length of his body against Sable's. I groaned again, knowing from experience that they were about to hump. It didn't matter that they had an audience. Didn't matter that Griff and I had been telling them not to for the past several months. Whenever they were together, they just *did* it, and there was no stopping them.

In all honesty, it didn't really bother me that they were having sex or that I could feel it through my bond with Sable. What bothered me was that their horniness made *me* horny, and that feeling was always directed at the same person. Which wouldn't have been a problem a year ago, but it *definitely* was now.

Just as Whiskey prepared to mount Sable from behind, a low warning growl drew him up short.

Ha! You just got cock-blocked, I crowed, more than a little relieved. I watched with satisfaction as Kolton's massive dark wolf stared daggers at Whiskey. When Whiskey dared to bark at him in protest, Shadow snarled and bared his razor-sharp fangs.

With a huff, Whiskey backed down, but not before giving his alpha the stink eye. Shadow chose to ignore it. Turning toward the woods, he took off like a shot. Jagger's equally large black wolf loped after him, and Whiskey and Sable quickly followed suit.

All work and no play, Sable softly whined after several minutes of following Desirae's scent trail.

Although she'd been stopped from getting her freak on, I could tell she was enjoying the run with her demon boys. It had been ages since just the four of us had run together. We'd been so busy lately with our growing pack, family, and various responsibilities that this outing was a breath of fresh air. I'd felt a bit detached from the boys over the past several months, so it felt good to reconnect with them like this. I knew Sable felt the same.

Burgundy is so lucky, she said, referring to Desirae's wolf familiar. *I'd love to spend each night roaming the woods. Whiskey could join me.*

I barked a humorless laugh. *Nice try, Sabs. You'd spend the entire night* humping *him.*

Not true. Not every *night anyway. We can control ourselves, you know.*

Right. You just choose not to.

Hey, a girl has needs. Just because you're not getting any doesn't mean I *have to close up shop.*

I'm not getting any because you won't let *me.*

Also not true. I'll gladly let you hump—

La, la, la, not listening. You have seriously got to accept that I'm with Reid now.

Ha. You haven't even thought about him once today.

I started to protest, but nothing came out. I'd thought about him. I *must* have thought about him.

Right?

As I rehashed my thoughts for the morning, Shadow came to a sudden halt. The rest of us skidded to a stop behind him, barely avoiding a collision. When he lowered his head and sniffed at the ground, we did the same. Immediately, Sable scented what had caught his attention.

Blood.

A *lot* of it.

CHAPTER 5

VIOLET

To say that Sable was excited would be an understatement.

The blood immediately triggered her hunting instincts, and thoughts of jumping Whiskey's bones were pushed to the back of her mind.

It's not Burgundy's blood, she assured me, eagerly dancing in place. *Moose!*

When Shadow took off again, she bounded after him with a yip. Judging by the way he closely followed the blood trail, I assumed Desirae's wolf must have injured the big animal. It would take several regular wolves to bring down a moose, but hybrids were the largest-known werewolves in existence. Even if she hadn't shifted into her true form, Burgundy should be able to bag the moose all on her own.

A few miles later, Shadow started to slow. Sable could still smell the moose's blood, but the droplets had grown sparser. Burgundy must have attacked the moose and let it run off to slowly bleed out. Smart strategy. Easier to kill it that way without sustaining injury.

A sudden warning growl cut through the trees up ahead, alerting us to Burgundy's position. Even though we were her pack now, she was no doubt feeling possessive of her kill, especially since she'd been packless for so long.

Shadow stopped, silently communicating with us to do the same. He could easily take the moose from Desirae's wolf, but her position in the pack hierarchy had already been decided. Asserting dominance right now wasn't necessary.

The crack of bone announced Shadow's transformation into human form, and we followed his example, all four of us rising onto two legs moments later.

"We didn't come here to take away your kill, Desirae," Kolton called out, motioning for us to be ready in case she defended her prey by charging us. "But we need to speak with you and make sure you're okay."

When another growl rumbled through the trees, Kolton set his jaw and strode forward. The growl turned feral, but he didn't waver in his steps. I moved to follow him, and Griff ended up in front of me somehow. Realizing what he was doing, I rolled my eyes. Desirae was an *omega*. Even if she charged, she wouldn't get the best of me.

Jagger brought up the rear as we picked our way through the trees and entered a small clearing. At the sight of us, Burgundy snarled and snapped her jaws. I peered around Griff to see a massive dead moose on the ground and an equally massive wolf standing guard over it.

The wolf's coat was a deep red, so deep that it looked black in the absence of light. But a thin ray of sunshine had leaked into the clearing and was highlighting the red in her fur. Her eyes were a bright shade of blue, a sure sign that the celestial being residing inside the big furry body was angelic.

When she trained those glowing eyes on me and bared her bloodied fangs, Griff moved in front of me again. Annoyed, I stepped forward and nudged him aside. He allowed me to stand beside him but lifted an arm to keep me from going any further.

As Burgundy continued to growl at us, Kolton's voice boomed through the clearing, "Stand down, wolf. Give control back to Desirae."

His tone rang with alpha authority, and even I felt the need to submit. Burgundy immediately shrank back and lowered her head, allowing the shift to take over. A minute later, a young woman with medium brown skin and a cute pixie-cut slowly rose from where the wolf had been.

"I'm so sorry," she rasped, her voice slightly rusty from being locked away inside a wolf's body all night. "Burgundy is still learning to share. She wouldn't have attacked any of you, I promise."

"It's okay, Desirae," my brother calmly reassured her. "We know you both are still adjusting to pack life. Mrs. Bailey was just concerned when you didn't return by dawn like you usually do. I'm assuming the moose has something to do with it?"

She bobbed her head, her doe-brown eyes brightening as she surveyed her kill. "Yes. We were heading back when Burgundy scented the moose. It was too great of a prize to pass up."

Knowing that she'd grown up fending for herself and hadn't just killed the moose for sport, Kolton nodded his understanding. "We'll help you carry it back to Mrs. Bailey's. We should head back, though, before she needlessly worries anyone else."

"Of course," she replied, staring longingly at the dead moose for another moment before reluctantly stepping away. As Kolton and Jagger moved toward the moose, she spotted me and raised her hand in a shy wave. Before I could say anything, her gaze went to Griff and noticeably brightened. "Hi, Griffin"

At the rather adoring look she gave him, I raised both eyebrows.

"Hi, Des," he said, and my brows rose even higher.

Des? Since when had he given her a *nickname*?

That's what happens when you stop having sex with a male. They start looking for someone else to bone, Sable commented rather snidely.

Stop being crude, I chastised her irritably. *Griff isn't like that.*

He's a virile male in his prime. Of course he's like that.

A sudden image of Griff and Desirae passionately kissing popped into my head. Heat flushed up my neck, and I mentally tore the image to shreds.

Well, I'm dating Reid now, I responded, focusing on Kolton and Jagger as they hoisted up the mostly-intact moose instead of the flirtatious little looks Desirae kept sending to Griff. *If Griff wants to have sex with another female, he has every right to.*

And he should. Desirae seemed like a nice girl. If he wanted to pursue her as his mate, I'd be happy for him. He deserved to find someone amazing. Someone *worthy* of him.

If that happens, you'll lose him for good, Sable bluntly said.

I pursed my lips, feeling the flush return. *We're friends. Family. That will never change. We'll always be there for each other, no matter what.*

Sable barked a laugh. *Oh, like how he was there for you the last time you were in heat?*

Beyond uncomfortable, I swiveled on my heel and started back the way we'd come. The others followed, and I heard Desirae strike up a conversation with Griff.

"Thank you again for watching my back during the initiation."

"No problem. I was glad to help," Griff replied in that congenial way of his. "Hopefully the unmated males didn't freak you out too much. They get pretty excited when a new female enters the pack."

"It was intense being surrounded by so many, but you kept them from getting too close. I really appreciate that."

Oh, God, I inwardly groaned. *She's hero-worshipping him.*

Can you blame her? Sable continued to torture me. *He's always been very helpful and attentive. You know how addictive that kind of attention is.*

I did, all too well. Griff's attention was like being swaddled in a warm blanket. He was called the pack healer for a reason. If he couldn't fix what ailed you, his attention alone was enough to make you feel better.

Recalling how often he'd made *me* feel better, I picked up the pace until I was almost jogging. As the others continued at a more sedate pace and their voices faded to a low hum, some of the tension left my body.

Deciding to cut a straighter path toward Mrs. Bailey's, I veered off the trail we'd made and descended into a shallow gulley full of dead pine needles and leaves. Reaching the bottom, I prepared to quickly scale the other side. As I brought my foot down and sprang forward, a sudden *snap* cleaved the air, followed by an explosion of dirt and pine needles.

The pain was instant, streaking up my leg like a bolt of lightning.

Shocked, I crashed to my hands and knees. A bloodcurdling scream blasted my eardrums, the sound pure terror and raw agony. As it went on and on, I realized that it was mine.

I'd never felt pain like this before. A pain so wretchedly consuming that I was frozen in place, unable to do anything but scream.

Sable pushed to the surface, her need to protect me causing her to take over. The second my bones began to shift, the pain grew ten times worse.

"STOP!" I wailed, my consciousness flickering. When she obeyed my command, I promptly turned my head and threw up.

A frantic shout suddenly reached my ears, calling my name over and over.

Griff.

I tried to respond but only managed a small whimper.

As I heard him scramble into the gulley, the slight vibrations sent fresh agony tearing through me. I tried to lift my head, but something attached to my leg caught my attention. It was metal and shiny. *Too* shiny. The jagged teeth were viciously clamped around my ankle, digging in so deeply that I glimpsed bone through all the blood and ripped skin.

My bone.

Broken? Probably.

I shoved down the need to vomit again and managed to croak, "B-bear trap."

Griff crouched beside the trap, his face pale and horrified, so unlike his usual expression that I couldn't help but wheeze out a laugh.

He looked at me like I'd lost my mind. "You're *laughing* right now?"

"Your face," I gasped, the sound more sob than laugh. "It's priceless."

His horror only intensified, making me want to laugh all the harder.

"Kol!" he roared, so loudly that I coughed out another laugh.

I was suddenly surrounded on all sides, the tears filling my eyes making it impossible to see their faces.

Another figure crouched beside the bear trap, one that I recognized as my brother. He reached down to touch the trap and immediately pulled his hand back with a hiss. "Silver."

"A *s-silver* trap?" I sputtered, then burst into a fit of giggles. "No wonder it hurts so bad."

"What's wrong with her?" Griff asked, clearly panicked.

"She's in shock," Jagger said from somewhere above me. "Probably a good thing. The pain must be unimaginable."

"We need to take it off," a feminine voice exclaimed, one I couldn't place at the moment. Things were getting fuzzy, the world going in and out of focus every few seconds. Even the pain didn't feel as bad anymore.

Just as I had the thought, the trap shifted on my leg, and I was suddenly screaming again.

"You're hurting her!" Griff bellowed over my screams. "Don't touch it!"

"It has to come off!" Kolton bellowed back.

"N-no, please don't!" I sobbed, lashing out to knock aside any hands too close. The action shifted the trap again, and I belted out another bloodcurdling scream.

"Restrain her, Jagger," Kolton ordered, making me scream even louder.

"DON'T," Griff barked, with such authority that I forgot to scream for a second. "I'll do it."

Hands touched me, and I tried to jerk away. They snaked around me, and I was suddenly locked in a pair of strong arms.

"I've got you, Vi," Griff said in my ear, holding me so tightly that I could no longer move my upper body. "I'm here."

I struggled to break free, but his grip was ironclad. "Please don't do it," I whimpered, resorting to begging instead. Maybe if I sounded pathetic enough, they'd take pity on me and leave me alone. "It hurts. It hurts so much."

Griff made a pained sound but didn't release me.

"The silver is poisoning you, Vi," Kolton tried to reason with me. "It'll get harder and harder for your body to heal the longer you're exposed to it."

"But I *can't*," I cried, tears rolling down my cheeks as my body shook with fear. "I can't bear the pain. Don't touch it. *Please*."

The moment that trap shifted again, I would lose it. The pain was too much. *Too much.*

"Griff, put her under," Kolton quietly ordered.

Terror gripped me. Desperate, I began to struggle again. "P-please, Griff. Don't do it. I'm *scared*."

That should do it. I *never* admitted that I was scared.

"Oh, Vi," he groaned.

"Griff!" Kolton snapped.

With a sigh, Griff shifted his hold on me to place a hand on my forehead and murmur a quick spell under his breath.

Just like that, darkness pulled me under, and my pain blissfully melted away.

CHAPTER 6

GRIFF

She looked peaceful sleeping in my arms.

The spell had done what it was supposed to do, forcing Vi to remain unconscious while we pried the trap off her leg and set her broken bone. As I'd carried her back to Mrs. Bailey's, she hadn't woken up once.

The silver that coated the trap had leaked into her bloodstream, slowing down her healing ability and leaving her pale and weak. Even if she'd woken, her leg wouldn't be able to carry her yet, so I'd gladly volunteered to do it for her.

Kolton had yanked the trap out of the ground and attached it to the moose carcass, bent on studying it when we returned home. Questions were swirling through all of our brains, but we knew one thing for certain.

This trap hadn't been made to capture a bear. It had been made to capture a werewolf. Probably Desirae.

When we'd made it back to Mrs. Bailey's, Kolton had immediately ordered her and Desirae to stay out of the woods until further notice. Desirae had looked crestfallen, but one look at Vi's still form in my arms had kept her from commenting.

Someone was hunting wolves, and Vi had been hurt because of it. *Twice.*

Not wanting to further scare either of the females, I'd kept a calm outward appearance. But inside, I was seething. Without even saying goodbye, I'd made for the truck and carefully climbed into the back with Vi. A minute later, Kolton handed me a blanket, and I gently tucked it around Vi's naked body.

"She still hasn't woken?" he asked, fully dressed once more as he jumped into the driver's seat. With the silver trap securely tied down in the truck bed, Jagger opened the front passenger door and hopped in.

"No," I replied, watching Vi breathe for a moment before adding, "The exposure to silver, combined with blood loss and exhaustion, is keeping her under. Rest will help her heal faster, though."

The truck roared to life and lurched into motion, causing Vi's head to loll sideways. I gently caught it and rested her cheek against my chest once more.

"This can't be a coincidence," Kolton said. "We'll have to alert the rest of the pack about the danger. They'll need to be on the lookout for anything or anyone suspicious."

I looked up to ask, "Do you think the males who attacked Vi in Boston planted this trap?"

"I don't—"

"Yes," a female voice weakly confirmed.

My heart thudded at the sound, and I looked down just as Vi slowly opened her eyes. When they focused on mine, bone-deep relief shuddered through me.

"There you are," I said, my voice gruffer than moments before. Swallowing roughly, I brushed a stray lock of hair off her face. "How do you feel?"

"Tired." Her eyelids drooped closed again. "Do I still have my foot?"

Jagger snorted.

"Yes, Vi, you still have your foot. You'll be good as new in no time," I promised.

She hummed in reply, her breaths slowing once more. Right before she fell back asleep, she whispered, "I smelled them. Both of them. They're here."

Alarmed, I met Kolton's gaze in the rearview mirror. As anger flashed in his eyes, my own reared up.

Och, those scrotes are deid the minute I find 'em, Whiskey growled in a Scottish accent.

"Do you think Vi could be right?" Jagger asked Kolton. "Are they trying to kidnap pack members as a way to challenge you?"

"Only if they're cowards," Kolton replied, his clipped tone barely concealing his rage. "Now that we know the males are on pack land, I want to organize a search. Better yet, I want a bounty on their heads. Dead or alive—preferably dead."

Whiskey howled with satisfaction, but I swallowed the sound to say, "I'll organize the search."

"No, Jagger can do that," Kolton replied, glancing at me again in the mirror. "I need you to keep an eye on the females, especially Vi. She won't be happy when I announce to the pack that no females should be out alone until this is resolved."

I hiked up both eyebrows. "You're right. She's going to hate that."

"I know, but these bastards are serious, so we should be too."

"I agree, but we've finally settled into a sense of normalcy after everything that happened last year. This will be a hard pill to swallow, especially for Vi since she's been traveling so much lately."

Kolton flicked another glance at me. "Can you handle it?"

I immediately knew what he meant. Vi was a force to be reckoned with when she didn't agree with something, but he wasn't referring to that. He was referring to our history, the *closeness* we once shared. Not just as friends, but as lovers. I hardly ever talked about those moments with my best friend, but he knew how I felt about his sister. How I *still* felt about her. Probably more than I wanted him to.

"Of course I can handle it," I drawled, then added with a small smirk, "I just don't know if *she* can."

Both Kolton and Jagger shook their heads at my hubris but thankfully didn't call me out on it. Minutes later, we were pulling into the estate's roundabout, prepared to break the news to the females in the household. When I walked through the front door still naked and carrying Vi wrapped in a blanket, several voices bombarded me all at once.

"Is that *blood?*" seven-year-old Melanie blurted, looking more intrigued than concerned.

"Oh, my poor girl," Mrs. Rivers whispered, placing a hand over her mouth.

"What happened?" Nora and Brielle asked in unison, their hands empty of babies for once. Must be nap time.

"This," Jagger replied, holding up the silver trap now carefully wrapped in a blanket.

The females stared at it in horror. Well, except Mellie, whose amber eyes were wide with fascination.

"We'll explain everything," Kolton said, coming in last and shutting the door, "but Vi still needs time to heal. While she's sleeping, we'll fill you in on what happened and what we plan to do about it."

Knowing I couldn't hold Vi forever, even if I wanted to, I made for her bedroom on the third floor. As I entered her private domain decorated in varying shades of purple, I paused to drink in the air saturated with her scent. This was the first time I'd been in her room since the house had been rebuilt, and I took a moment to scan the space. The family photos that had been on her vanity when the house burned down couldn't be salvaged, but she'd printed new ones and reframed them. Among the photos were newly-added pictures of Nora, Luca, Lillian, and even Brielle. There was also an updated portrait of her mom.

I moved closer as one photo in particular caught my eye. It was a candid picture of me and Vi, taken at least a decade ago. She was riding on me piggyback style, and our faces were alight with laughter. Recalling the memory, a lump formed in my throat. That had been the morning of her thirteenth birthday. I'd showed up early and surprised her with a gift before driving her to school. She'd felt so grown up in the new outfit and shoes I'd bought her, and Mrs. Rivers had snapped a picture of us on our way out the door.

She'd been my best friend's little sister to me back then. The girl who was slowly becoming a young woman, trading in her torn overalls for designer jeans and her pigtails for chic bangs.

We'd been so innocent back then. So carefree. Little did we know that tragedy would strike only three years later, and that our friendship would become something more. Something . . .

Shaking off the memories, I finished scanning the row of framed photos, then froze. Everyone important in Vi's life was displayed on her vanity. Everyone but one. There wasn't a single photo of Reid.

She suddenly stirred in my arms, and I glanced down just as she buried her face in my chest and released a sigh, one that seeped into my bare skin to warm my insides. Loath to let her go, I took my time crossing the room to place her on the bed. The second I finally released her, she curled up on her side with the blanket tightly tucked under her chin. Smiling at the sight, I hesitated for a solid minute, then bent over and brushed my lips across her cheek.

Forcing myself not to linger, I straightened before she could notice and slowly backed away.

Forbidden. She was *forbidden*.

I'd told myself over and over today that every touch and stolen glance had been innocent, but I was treading a dangerous line, one I had no business crossing.

Vi was with someone else, and she needed space to be with him. All that would come of getting close to her was the harsh reminder that she only saw me as a friend. Once upon a time, she'd needed me to be more than that, but those days were over now.

If I didn't accept that, I wouldn't just be hurting myself.

I would be hurting her too.

CHAPTER 7

So *this* was what it felt like to be human.

I'd only ever been exposed to silver a few times in my life, and the encounters had been brief. Every occurrence had been while I was shopping, but accidentally touching a pair of silver earrings was nothing compared to the pain I'd felt this morning.

Having silver in my bloodstream was so much worse, and although I'd broken a few bones in my lifetime, I'd never needed to heal this long. It had been *hours* before I could finally get out of bed unattended to use the bathroom. Nora and Brielle had practically spent the entire afternoon taking care of me, which had felt strange.

I was used to taking care of *others*, not the other way around. I'd basically raised Melanie from infancy and supported Kolton as he'd become Midnight Pack's alpha at the tender age of nineteen. I'd become a secretary for our family's billion-dollar business at age seventeen and oversaw pack communication, making sure the two worlds didn't collide.

Taking care of others was my main responsibility in life, so being unable to left me feeling useless. My least favorite thing.

The attention was nice, though. Family members had flitted in and out of my room all day, and I'd spent quality time with each of them. Mom had made me a fresh batch of Snickerdoodles, and I'd eaten over a dozen. Nora and Brielle had helped me paint my nails while we watched a movie. When they'd left to feed the babies, I'd finally called Reid and told him what happened.

"Do you need me there?" he'd asked, his worry clear.

"No, that's okay," I'd quickly reassured him. *"I have a full house of people taking care of me."*

We'd chatted for a bit until his coach had called him back to practice.

When the afternoon dragged on, I started to get bored. Kolton and Jagger had set up a working station on my bed—so I could at least respond to some emails—but not before dropping the bomb that I wasn't allowed to go anywhere alone until further notice.

"But I plan to visit Reid again this coming weekend," I'd protested, feeling even *more* useless. They were going into protective mode again, and I understood why, but that didn't make this any easier.

I wasn't some fragile little omega who needed constant support from big macho alphas. Well, maybe at the moment, but I'd be all healed by tomorrow. I was perfectly capable of taking care of myself.

Seeing the frustration on my face, Kolton had only shaken his head and replied, *"You can still go, but you're not going alone."*

He hadn't said *who* would be going with me, but I already knew. Which was probably why the male in question had been avoiding my room all day. Everyone else had come to see me but him. I tried not to let it bother me, but by the time evening rolled around, his absence was all I could think about.

Had I done something to upset him? But even on the rare occasions when he was mad, it wasn't like Griff to avoid me. I must have said something during my pain-filled delirium this morning. I couldn't think why else he would stay away.

As my unease over his absence grew, I decided to distract myself with a much-needed shower. Choosing not to call anyone for help, I carefully got out of bed and slowly hobbled into the bathroom. My leg was still tender, but the pins-and-needles feeling had lessened. The break should be completely mended by morning. Still, by the time I finished showering, blow-drying my hair, and putting on fresh pajamas, I was more than ready to slip back into bed.

Limping back into the bedroom, I nearly jumped out of my skin when I saw a tall figure leaning against my door.

"*Jeez*, Griff," I said, placing a hand over my pounding heart. "A little warning next time."

"Sorry. Just wanted to check on my patient," he replied, taking in the way I favored my still-healing leg. A sudden frown creased his brow. "You shouldn't be out of bed yet."

"I'm fine. It's just a little tender," I began, but he was already striding across the room toward me. My words of protest fell on deaf ears as he scooped me up like I weighed nothing and carried me the short distance to the bed. "Really, Griff? It was like *three* feet."

Ignoring my grumbling, he set me down on the mattress and started cleaning up my mess. My jaw practically fell into my lap.

"What?" he said, spotting my expression.

I watched him place my laptop on my desk, along with the portable work station Kolton and Jagger had set up for me before replying, "You're cleaning."

"So?"

"Since *when?*"

"I did the dishes last night, if you recall."

"I do. I was shocked then too. You've just never been one to *willingly* clean something."

He shrugged and gathered up the blanket I'd been wrapped in all day to drop it by the closed door. "I clean now. I even do the laundry. Guess you've been too busy with Reid to notice."

The words were delivered lightly, but they still felt like a jab.

I watched him collect my dishes and start to stack them before murmuring, "Are we okay?"

He paused to casually lean on the desk. "Of course we're okay. Why do you ask?"

Hmm. Maybe I'd read his absence wrong.

I quickly waved his question away. "Forget it. I'm just tired."

He studied me for a moment, then straightened and picked up the dishes. "You should get some sleep."

"Yeah."

There was a moment of awkward silence, both of us staring at each other but refusing to speak. Something was definitely up. What had happened while I was unconscious?

Wait. Was it *Desirae?* Was he dating her and just didn't know how to tell me?

"So, Desirae seems nice," I blurted, then immediately wanted to kick myself.

Smooth, Sable drawled.

"She is," he replied, a line slowly bisecting his brows as if he was confused.

Swallowing a frustrated groan, I added, "She seemed sweet on you earlier."

The line between his brows immediately vanished. "Oh, that? She was just glad I kept the other pack males from trying to pursue her. She's not ready for that yet."

"You sure about that? I bet she'd be open to *you* pursuing her."

He huffed a laugh that sounded a bit nervous.

He's uncomfortable, you ninny, Sable growled. *Stop trying to force something that isn't there.*

Annoyed, I said, "Sable thinks you should ask her out."

WHAT? my wolf familiar barked at me.

Griff laughed again, the sound incredulous this time. "*Sable* said that?"

See? He's too smart to fall for your lies, Sable sniffed.

Feeling ganged-up on, I didn't answer, and the silence quickly became awkward again.

"You should get some sleep," Griff repeated, clearly wanting to be anywhere but here. Not knowing what else to say, I simply nodded. He turned toward the door with my dishes and somehow managed to open it, nudging the soiled blanket out into the hallway in the process. "Night."

I opened my mouth, but nothing came out. Without waiting for a reply, he shut the door, leaving me more confused than ever.

For the next two hours, I tossed and turned, unable to sleep. Every time I tried, nightmares swiftly invaded my mind, making me jerk awake. Just knowing that my would-be abductors could be plotting yet another attack was troubling me more than I cared to admit.

Being a Rivers came with many risks, and there were countless werewolves who would love to see our family fall from power. We held a covetous position in the werewolf world, one that many wanted and would kill for. We'd dealt with plenty of attacks from other werewolves over the years, but they hadn't known we were hybrids. Now that they knew—and chose to attack anyway—was extra concerning.

Beyond frustrated when another hour passed and I *still* wasn't asleep, I grabbed my phone from the nightstand and texted Reid, *You up?*

I waited several minutes but didn't get a response.

Sighing, I selected the TV app on my phone and flipped on my flatscreen. I browsed for a few moments, then selected a movie and turned the volume down low so it wouldn't wake anyone. Half an hour into the movie, a particularly funny scene made me laugh out loud.

A second later, I heard a sound outside my bedroom door. I immediately went on high alert, imagining the two male attackers bursting into my room. Sable surged to the surface, ready to help again if they tried to abduct me.

The doorknob turned, and I prepared to spring from my bed and go crazy on them. The door cracked open, and—

I flopped back against my pillows with a huff. "Griffin Hayes!" I hissed between my teeth. "You scared the crap out of me."

Sable settled back down with a chuckle.

"Sorry," he whispered, poking his blond head inside my room. "I heard something and wanted to make sure you were okay."

"I *laughed*," I whispered back, still annoyed. "What are you doing stalking the halls like a creeper anyway?"

He shrugged but didn't respond.

"Let me guess. Kolton put you on guard duty?" I rolled my eyes, but deep down, I was more than a little relieved that Griff was keeping watch while we slept.

Instead of answering, he said, "Can't sleep?"

It was my turn to shrug.

He opened the door wider and came all the way in, only to cluck his tongue in mock disapproval when he saw the TV. "You're watching a scary movie in the middle of the night? No wonder you can't sleep."

"Pfft. You know they make me laugh. It's *you* who's scared of them. You were terrified of closets for *months* after we watched that one slasher movie."

"I was twelve. I'm not scared of them anymore."

"Ha. Prove it."

When he raised an eyebrow, I scooted over and patted the

mattress beside me.

"Watch the movie or admit I'm right."

He quietly groaned and stared up at the ceiling, and I struggled not to laugh.

"Come on. It's time you faced your fears, Griff. Watch the movie with me. I'll even hold your hand."

He suddenly went rigid, then quietly barked a laugh, making me think that I'd imagined the tension. Closing the door, he silently crossed my room and flounced onto the bed beside me. Propping himself up on an elbow, he muttered, "Fine. Let's get this over with."

I grinned ear to ear and settled more comfortably against my pillows. "You won't regret it. Horror movies are hilarious. You'll see."

"Just shut up and watch the movie," he grumbled, making me grin even wider.

Only a few minutes in, he started to fidget. I kept peeking at him out of the corner of my eye, fighting back laughter every time he grimaced. At the next jump-scare scene, I waited for the perfect moment, then grabbed his shoulder and said, "Boo!"

He violently started, and I burst into a fit of giggles.

"You think that's funny?" he said.

"It's hilarious," I replied, batting my lashes at him not-so-innocently.

He scowled. Then, faster than I could blink, he grabbed one of my pillows and whacked me in the face with it.

"Hey!" I protested a little too loudly. Grabbing another pillow, I whacked him back. Or tried to anyway. He caught it and wrestled it from me, then whacked me in the face again. With a growl, I launched myself at him, only to end up flat on my back. When his gloating face appeared above me, it was my turn to scowl. "No fair. I'm still recovering."

"Excuses," he drawled, hovering over me a moment longer before sitting up. When he extended his hand toward me, I batted it away and scooted back against the headboard on my own. He just smirked and settled against the headboard beside me.

As we continued to watch the movie in companionable silence, my restlessness from earlier faded. My eyelids were beginning to droop when he abruptly said, "Did you tell Reid?"

Struggling to stay awake, I replied, "About this morning?"

"Yeah."

"I did. He asked if I needed him here."

Griff was silent for several beats, then asked, "And do you?"

"Hmm?" I yawned, losing the battle with sleep.

"Do you need him here?"

My eyes slid shut, the pull of sleep too strong. As it dragged me under, I mumbled out a reply. I meant to say yes, but what slipped out was, "I have you."

CHAPTER 8

I woke up in a warm cocoon smelling of cloves and cinnamon.

The spicy scent was *everywhere*, so intense that I wondered if Griff had left his shirt behind last night. I hadn't seen him take it off, though. Before falling asleep, he'd been wearing a white tee that hugged his chest and biceps, along with gray sweatpants that hugged, well, *other* things.

Wait.

Had I fallen asleep with him still in my bed?

Something abruptly shifted beneath me. Rather, *someone*. Long arms came up in a languid stretch, then lazily draped over my back. When I felt a large hand drift south to lightly cup my backside, my eyes sprang open.

I suddenly became painfully aware of my predicament. *Our* predicament. Griff was asleep in my bed, and I was lying on top of him. My cheek was pressed to his chest, and the rest of my body was perfectly aligned with his. Including my lower half, which meant that my pelvis was pressed to—

Oh, God. I could feel it. I could feel his *dick*. My core was right on top of it, my thighs slightly parted to accommodate him.

Just as I had that realization, his hand gripped my butt and ground me against him. Against his *dick*. Which was rock hard and growing larger by the second.

My body went wild at the intimate contact, exploding awake in excitement. In *recognition*.

Shocked by the eager response, I jerked my head up with a gasp. The second I did, Griff's eyes flew open. Our gazes clashed, and we stared at each other in horror.

Knock knock knock.

"Vi, you up? Reid's here."

At my brother's words, I burst into action as if I'd been set on fire. With an agile twist, I shoved Griff off the mattress. As he thudded to the floor, I jumped out of bed and frantically pointed at the bathroom. He got the message and quickly picked himself up to hurry out of sight.

Not a second too soon. Kolton cracked open my bedroom door to peer inside, and I whirled, squeaking like a rabid chipmunk, "Yeah, I'm up!"

Not suspicious at *all*.

Kolton stared at me for several long, torturous moments before calmly saying, "I know you're in here, Griff. I suggest you leave before Nora lets Reid into the house. You have thirty seconds."

Griff emerged from the bathroom and sauntered across my room, looking *far* too relaxed. When he reached the door, Kolton held it open for him.

"Morning, bro," he casually said as he passed through.

"Morning, Griff," my brother responded as if seeing his oldest best friend coming out of his sister's room first thing in the morning was completely normal. I stood there gaping like a fish out of water until Kolton focused on me again and said, "I suggest you take a shower before coming down."

With that, he silently closed the door, leaving me scrambling to scrub Griff's scent off my body before my *boyfriend* arrived.

I didn't know what was worse. The odd looks everyone kept giving me, or Sable's lack of protest when Reid pulled me into a tight hug.

You could have woken me up, you know, I hissed at her while returning Reid's hug and praying my quick shower had done the trick.

But it felt so good to be pressed up against him, she purred unapologetically. *That morning wood was all for you.*

No, it wasn't, I growled, beyond pissed at her. *You said so yourself. He's a virile male in his prime. He wakes up like that* every *morning.*

Maybe, but I felt how turned on you were when he rubbed you against his dick.

Barely able to suppress a frustrated scream, I pulled back from Reid to give him my best smile. "I can't believe you're here. You didn't have to come."

"I know, but I wanted to see for myself that you were okay," he replied, returning my smile. "It's just for today, though, unfortunately. Coach has us working on a new play, and we need a lot more practice before the next game."

"I understand. Thanks for surprising me." When I stood on tiptoe to kiss his lips, Sable didn't stop me.

Before I could pull away, Reid captured the back of my head to deepen the kiss. As his tongue softly stroked mine, I became hyper-aware of our audience. Namely, the blond male I'd been accidentally cuddling with only minutes before. He'd taken a shower too, and I couldn't help but wonder if he'd taken care of that *wood* at the same time.

Feeling guilty for having the thought, for even *thinking* about him while Reid was kissing me, I gently broke the kiss.

Oblivious to my reasons for pulling away, Reid glanced down to inspect my jean-clad legs. "Looks like you're all healed."

"Yeah. Good as new," I said, noticing that Griff was looking anywhere but at us.

"Any leads on who the males are?"

He directed the question at Kolton, who replied, "Not yet. I contacted my influential members yesterday who spread the news of the attacks to the rest of the pack. They were warned to be on the lookout for anything suspicious and to take necessary precautions, but I haven't heard anything yet. We'll be organizing a hunting party soon to see if we can flush them out."

"Good. I'd like to keep apprised of that."

"Sure thing. You could join, if you'd like."

"I just might," Reid replied, focusing on me again. "If you're okay with sharing me when I come visit."

I nearly swallowed my tongue at the word sharing. Reid definitely hadn't meant the word in the way my stupid brain was thinking, and I doubted very much he would ever be willing to share *me*, which made me feel even guiltier for how I'd woken up this morning.

"I'm okay with it," I readily said. "But I plan to join the hunting party as well, so we'll still see each other."

Kolton made a noise in the back of his throat, and I immediately stiffened.

"Don't say it," I quietly warned him, already knowing what that sound meant.

"Vi . . ." he began.

"Don't *Vi* me," I snapped, whirling toward him. "I agreed not to wander off alone, but I didn't agree to stay hidden away like a useless lump. I can *help*, and I want to find those slimy bastards probably more than anyone. So *let* me, Kolton. *Please*."

Used to my impassioned outbursts, no one looked shocked that I'd challenged my pack alpha. Well, maybe no one except Reid. He shifted uncomfortably on his feet as Kolton and I became locked in a silent staredown.

When I refused to back down, Reid broke the silence to say, "I can watch over her, Kolton. She'll have eyes on her at all times."

Without looking away from me, my brother replied, "Thanks for the offer, Reid, but I already have someone doing that."

My eyes narrowed to slits.

"I appreciate that, but she's *my* girlfriend," Reid bravely pushed back.

"Yes, but until she's been claimed and mated, Vi is still a member of Midnight Pack," Kolton said. "Therefore, she's my responsibility."

Ah, crap. That was *definitely* a jab. One that I'd expected *Griff* to make, not Kolton.

Feeling hot tears of embarrassment sting my eyes, I broke the staredown. An awkward tension settled over the group, and I suddenly wanted to crawl into my bed again.

"Well, *that* got heavy," Griff's voice cut through the tension. "I think we're all a little hangry and could use some breakfast. How about I help you in the kitchen, Mrs. R?"

"Charlotte," my mom corrected, smiling up at him as he offered her his arm. I watched them head toward the kitchen and couldn't help but wish she'd smile at *Reid* that way. She barely acknowledged his existence, even during the daytime when her mind was at its sharpest.

"Are you going to marry my sister?" Mellie abruptly piped up, staring at Reid with big innocent eyes.

I stiffened and threw Reid an apologetic look.

He just laughed good-naturedly and told her, "Well, that's up to your sister."

Mellie turned that curiosity to me next. "If you marry Reid, will you have to leave us for good?"

At that, everything in me went cold. I tried to respond, but my throat sealed shut. Unable to breathe, I murmured a lame excuse about needing to grab something and hurried up the stairs.

The second I closed my bedroom door, I sank to the floor and hugged my knees to my chest, willing myself not to fall apart. But Melanie's words continued to ring in my ears, filling me with more and more panic.

Leave us for good. Leave us for good.

Leave my pack. My *family.*

If I did end up marrying Reid, he would expect me to live with him. To join his pack. To become his alpha female one day.

Being with Reid meant that I would have to face my worst fear, a fear that I'd lived with every day for the past seven years. I hadn't fully realized until this very moment what dating Reid would lead to, but that reality had finally caught up to me, and—

"Vi? It's just me and Brielle. Open up, please."

At the sound of Nora's voice, I forced myself to stand and open the door. The moment I did, she and Brielle sandwiched me in a hug.

"You okay?" my sister-in-law asked, reaching back to close the door.

"Yeah, I just . . . I just panicked. My emotions have been kind of everywhere lately." I gratefully clung to them both, drawing comfort from their scents and closeness.

"For good reason," Brielle spoke up, then said in a soft whisper, "Did something happen between you and Griff? I heard him in your room last night and saw him coming out this morning."

I groaned, feeling guiltier than ever. "Yes. I did something terrible."

She pulled back to look at me, her green eyes wide like saucers. "How terrible?"

"I fell asleep with him in my bed last night."

One of her dimples flashed as she pursed her lips in thought. "Well, that's not so bad."

"I woke up on *top* of him."

Her mouth formed a large O. "Okay, yeah. That's kind of bad."

"Brie," Nora lightly chastised her best friend, who gave her an apologetic look.

"No, she's right," I said. "It never should have happened, and I feel awful. What should I do? Do I tell Reid?"

Nora stared at me but in a non-judgmental way. It felt more like she was *searching* for something. After a long moment, she quietly said, "I think you should be honest with him."

I closed my eyes with a groan that sounded more like a whine. "This sucks."

They both gave me sympathy squeezes but didn't offer further advice. Now wasn't the time for one of our soul chats, not that I usually unburdened my feelings to them even then. Brielle was the feelsy one in our girl's group.

We headed down a few minutes later to find Kolton, Reid, and Jagger in the front office, deep in conversation as they studied the silver trap that had almost taken my foot off. Feeling queasy the second I laid eyes on it, I immediately turned around and headed for the kitchen instead.

But the moment I entered and saw Griff in a frilly pink apron, sharing a laugh with my mother, I quickly backtracked again.

"Vi! Come and join us," my mom said before I could escape. As Griff looked my way with a big grin still on his face, I froze like a deer in headlights, recalling how he'd pressed me against his dick less than an hour ago. Something heated flashed in his eyes, as if he was thinking of the memory too, and I quickly looked away.

"Um, I'm really not that great at cooking," I replied to my mom, slowly stepping backward. "I should probably check my emails."

"Nonsense," she said, forcing me to halt once more. "You've just never had the *patience* for cooking. The boys were always better at following directions than you."

Griff snickered, and I threw my best glare at him.

"You just need to slow down a bit," my mom continued. "Here. Watch how Griff scrambles the eggs. He's not trying to hurry the process by *blasting* the heat. Cooking is a process, one that can't be rushed."

She gestured me over, and I reluctantly joined her and Griff by the stove. When I was apparently too far away to properly see the pan that Griff had just poured the whisked eggs into, my mom came around my other side and nudged me closer. My arm bumped into Griff's, and heat flushed up my neck. Another memory assaulted me, and I vividly recalled how it felt to be wrapped in his arms.

Sable made a happy little purring noise, and I ground my teeth together. Standing this close to him was torture, but I couldn't scoot away, not when my mother was practically pushing me against him while she explained the art of making light, fluffy eggs.

Too hyper-aware of my arm brushing against his, I completely tuned out her words. By the time the eggs were finished, I still had no idea how to properly make them and was desperate for some fresh air. When Griff reached around me to accept the bowl my mom handed him, I jumped, nearly making the bowl fall to the floor.

"Sorry," I blurted, stepping back the second Griff moved his arm. "I'm going to, um, set the table."

I hastily began to gather plates and utensils before my mom could torture me some more, putting much-needed distance between me and Griff.

You're being ridiculous, Sable remarked. *It's not like you had sex with him. A little pelvic rub is no big deal, especially with clothes on. You didn't even orgasm.*

Wanting to scream, I booked it out of the kitchen, almost dropping the plates in the process. When we all sat down to breakfast minutes later, my restlessness only worsened. Every time I glanced across the table, I'd find Griff's gaze already on me. He'd immediately look away, but I knew he was thinking about what happened between us just as much as I was.

We needed to talk, but I was already dreading the conversation, along with the one I needed to have with Reid. He was currently answering all of Melanie's incessant questions, still utterly oblivious to the tension between me and Griff. Guilt was my constant companion, made all the worse when I'd catch one of the others watching me.

They knew. They *all* knew. Well, maybe only half of them, but it sure felt like the whole table was silently judging me for cheating on my boyfriend. Even baby Luca was scrunching up his nose at me.

It's because his father is forcing him to eat squished-up bananas, Sable said with a disgusted snort. *And you didn't cheat. You were asleep, and so was Griff. You're not responsible for what your horny subconscious does.*

Thanks, Sabs. I feel so *much better*, I sarcastically replied, absently playing with the fluffy eggs on my plate.

You're welcome.

I made the mistake of rolling my eyes and once again found Griff's gaze on me. Unable to bear another second of this torture, I set down my fork and prepared to excuse myself from the table.

Before I could, Griff said to the room, "I think we should play some football." When everyone stopped what they were doing to stare at him, he added, "We could use a little fun after the stressful few days we've just had. Besides, we have an MVP guest in the house. So, what do you say? Who's in?"

"I'm in," Reid readily replied.

"Yeah, man," Griff said and stuck out his fist. When Reid reached across the table to bump his knuckles, I wanted to crawl under the table in mortification.

"I'm in too," Brielle replied, staring at the pair like she was watching a soap opera. She noticed my scowl and shrugged apologetically.

Jagger and Kolton volunteered next.

"Me too!" Melanie chimed in excitedly, even though she barely knew what football was.

"You have school, Mellie," Kolton firmly told her.

"Pleeease?" she begged, sticking out her bottom lip and adding a little quiver.

"Sucker," I muttered under my breath when I saw Kolton start to cave.

Sure enough, he replied, "Fine, but school right after. And no trying to weasel your way out of homework this time."

"Deal!" she sang, smiling like a cherub, even as her eyes twinkled devilishly.

"How about you, Mrs. R?" Griff asked my mom.

"Oh, not me, thank you. But Miss Gabby and I could watch the babies if Nora wants to play."

"Sure, I'll play," Nora said and slid her husband a sly look. "So long as Kolton and I aren't on the same team."

Kolton's mouth curved into a wicked smirk. "Sure you're up for the challenge, wife?"

"Are you?" she tossed back.

Griff barked a laugh, then focused back on me. "What do you say, Vi? We need one more player to even out the teams."

"Are you sure my leg is healed enough for that?"

"Definitely. Besides, some fresh air and exercise will do you good. Doctor's orders," he said with a wink.

"Well, if you put it *that* way, count me in."

Griff whooped and shot from his chair. "Meet you all out front in ten!"

He was out of the room in a flash, no doubt to rummage in the garage for a football. We rarely had time to play sports anymore, but letting off a little steam was just what I needed—even if it meant I'd have to carry around my guilt a while longer.

The eight of us who were playing met on the front lawn ten minutes later, each of us having changed first. I now wore a cropped running top and leggings, my hair up in a high ponytail. Griff had found a can of white spray paint and had drawn a makeshift field for us to play on. Mellie bounced up and down, simply excited to be hanging out with the adults like a big girl. We'd convinced her to leave Princess in the house so the stuffed unicorn wouldn't get dirty, but she'd put on a blue Cinderella dress and tiara for the occasion.

"Okay, team captains," Griff said to the group and tossed the football at Kolton. "I nominate Kol and Reid."

My brother caught the football, only to toss it right back. "It was your idea to play, Griff. I think you should be a team captain."

Griff caught the ball with a shrug, but I could tell he was pleased by my brother's comment. "Okay, then, let's pick teams. Reid, wanna choose first?"

"Sure," Reid said, looking relaxed and in his element. He crossed his arms and scanned the group, narrowing his hazel eyes as if in serious deliberation. They landed on me, and he smiled. But, with a swift wink, he looked away and said, "Melanie."

She squealed and clapped her hands, hurrying over to hug Reid's leg. At the surprised look on his face, I snickered under my breath. He had no idea that he'd just unleashed a monster.

It was Griff's turn to pick a teammate, and I waited for him to name Kolton. But when I glanced over at him, his eyes were on me.

Before I could prepare, he said loudly for all to hear, "I choose Vi."

CHAPTER 9

GRIFF

I was playing with fire.

I knew I needed to stop, but the problem was . . .

It was intoxicating.

Waking up with Vi in my arms had awoken something inside me, something I'd forced into hibernation the moment she'd announced she was dating Reid. Now that it was awake, all I could focus on was her.

She's forbidden, I tried to remind myself, but the words no longer held meaning.

I hadn't been the only one affected by what happened between us earlier this morning. Her body had responded to mine, going pliant as I'd intimately pressed her against me. Convinced that I was having a wet dream of her, I'd planned to rub her pussy against my throbbing cock until completion. Another few seconds, and I would have come in my pants.

But then she'd gasped, making me aware that it was real.

Real.

We'd actually been in bed together, our bodies close in a way they hadn't been in what felt like forever. And there was no mistaking the cloying scent that had followed.

She'd been aroused.

That simple fact had lit a match under me, and I'd spent the past hour paying way too much attention to her. Every little touch, every time our eyes made contact, fueled me onward. Even when she seemed flustered, I couldn't make myself back off. It only intoxicated me further, making me want to try *harder*.

She'd reacted to me, and I desperately wanted her to do it again.

So instead of doing the *smart* thing and picking Kolton first, I'd chosen her as my teammate. Kolton narrowed his eyes slightly as Vi moved to join me. I knew what he was thinking, and if I didn't knock it off soon, he would no doubt confront me.

Reid watched the exchange without comment, pausing only for a moment before saying, "I pick Kolton."

"Nora," I immediately said, and she grinned at me.

Reid chose Brielle next, leaving me with Jagger. The fact that he'd been picked last filled me with a small sense of satisfaction. It didn't usually bother me that Kolton had chosen him to be his second in command and me as his third, but I was feeling competitive today. That and way too juiced up. Jerking off in the shower earlier had barely done anything to cool the heat still crackling in my veins. Hopefully this game would help calm me down before I could cause any more damage.

But the three words Vi had murmured to me before falling asleep last night kept replaying in my mind.

"I have you."

Me.

She hadn't needed Reid yesterday. She'd needed *me*.

The words had filled me with way too much hope. We were close friends. We would *always* be close friends. But maybe, just maybe . . .

Realizing everyone was waiting for the game to start, I forced my mind back to the present and tossed the ball to Reid. "Away team gets the ball first. Plus, you guys have a really short player."

Aware of my teasing jab, Melanie popped her hands on her little waist with a huff. She looked so much like a young Vi—minus the princess dress and tiara—that I couldn't help but grin.

"Any rules?" Reid asked.

"No hybrid abilities," Brielle firmly said, and Reid nodded in agreement.

Bollocks, Whiskey grumbled.

"So I can't let Blue play?" Melanie whined, referring to her wolf familiar—who she named after her new favorite color and TV show character.

"No, Blue can't play," Jagger replied, staring at her sternly until she huffed and lowered her head in resignation.

"Okay, gather 'round, team," Reid said, and I did the same with mine.

Minutes later, the two teams were facing off with each other. Kolton hiked the ball to Reid, and everyone burst into action. As Nora beelined straight for her husband, Vi and I skirted around him, prepared to tackle Reid before he could throw the ball. I reached him first, lunging for his legs to trip him up. He fell backward but not before I saw him release the ball.

As we crashed to the ground in a tangle of limbs, Melanie screamed, "Go, Brie, go!"

I glanced back just in time to see Brielle take off with the football, but a few steps later, Jagger came out of nowhere and sidelined her. As she fell, he managed to grab hold of her and twist them around so that he hit the ground first. When they rolled to a stop, he immediately picked himself up and offered her his hand. She looked at it coolly, then accepted the help without a word.

Those two really needed to talk out their differences before they exploded. Then again, I had no room to judge, especially after what happened this morning.

Chuckling under my breath, I stood and offered Reid a hand. He readily accepted it, congenially patting my back as we parted. While the teams regrouped for another play, I couldn't help but watch him out of the corner of my eye. We hadn't hung out much since he and Vi had started dating, but he really was a decent male. Seeing how friendly he was toward me despite my past history with his girlfriend—and how close we still were—spoke volumes about his character.

Little did he know that I still dreamt about her . . . and allowed myself to envision her when I jerked off.

It was a betrayal, and I should feel guilty enough to stop. But I couldn't. Just like I couldn't stop my cock from twitching when Vi reached up to tighten her ponytail and her shirt rode up, revealing an enticing strip of flesh. Looking away before anyone could notice me ogling her, I crouched into position, ready to take Reid down again.

As the play started, I lunged for Reid, but he'd already passed off the ball behind him.

To *Mellie.*

"Vi!" I shouted, watching as the little rugrat cradled the football like one of her precious stuffed animals and slipped past all the chaos.

Vi skidded to a halt and reversed course, but Kolton shot by her to scoop Melanie up fireman style. The little girl squealed in delight, barely managing to hold on to the ball as he sprinted down the makeshift field.

"No fair!" Vi yelled, chasing after them only to throw up her hands in defeat. Jagger did the same, unwilling to tackle his alpha with Melanie bouncing on his shoulder like a sparkly sack of potatoes.

Reid and Brielle cheered their teammates on, sharing a high five when Kolton crossed into the endzone with his youngest sister.

"Cheaters," Vi grumbled, then shouted across the lawn to Reid, "I know this was *your* idea!"

He only laughed but didn't deny it.

"Guess we need to up our game," I said to him.

"Guess you do," he replied with a wide smirk.

I returned the smirk. "Game on, then. May the best man win."

I should have said *team*, but this game suddenly felt like a challenge. A challenge between him and me. A challenge to see who would come out on top.

Maybe I'd underestimated him. Maybe he preferred a more subtle approach when it came to proving himself.

Well, challenge accepted. I knew just how to win this battle.

As the ball was passed over to us, I drew my team in for a huddle and used hand gestures to communicate the play, not willing to risk being overheard. By the time we all got into position, I was buzzing with anticipation. Just like I knew he would, Reid set his sights on Vi, leaving Kolton paired against Jagger and Brielle with Nora. Mellie crouched in a defensive position and smiled at me impishly, letting me know they planned to sic the little urchin on me.

I stuck my tongue out at her, then got into position behind Jagger.

"Hike!" I barked, catching the ball as he snapped it back.

Kolton immediately charged, violently colliding with his second. Brielle and Nora did the same, albeit not so aggressively. Vi took off like a shot down the field, and Reid charged after her. Just as a little set of teeth latched on to my bare calf and chomped down, I wound back my arm and let the football soar.

As it flew through the air toward Vi, I pried the ankle-biter off my leg and sprinted forward. I was halfway down the field when Vi turned on a dime and jumped, gracefully catching the ball. But when she came back down, one of her legs buckled and she cried out, "My ankle!"

I ran faster.

About to tackle her, Reid skidded to a halt, worry etched on his face. As he reached down to help her, I put on a fresh burst of speed and plowed right into him.

He went flying. So did Vi. Right for the endzone.

"Go, Vi!" I bellowed, loudly whooping as she glided over the lawn like a gazelle.

When she crossed into the endzone with the ball, I hooted and hollered, running forward to celebrate with her. As I picked her up and swung her around, she threw back her head and laughed. At the carefree, lighthearted sound, my stomach swooped giddily. I laughed with her, holding her to me as we enjoyed our victory.

The play had been dirty, but so had theirs. I was pretty sure Melanie had taken a chunk out of my calf.

Somehow, Vi's legs ended up wrapped around my waist. As she beamed at me with her arms circling my neck, I felt a swift and sudden ache to kiss her. An ache so intense that the world melted away, ceasing to exist. All that remained was the need to feel my mouth pressed to hers.

I could barely breathe past the ache, could barely stand. Couldn't *think*. All I could concentrate on was her lips. It'd been so long since I'd kissed them, since I'd *tasted* them. Since I'd stroked her tongue with mine.

Our heads were inches apart, our mouths even closer. I could feel the warmth of her breath on my face, her scent dancing in the air around me.

One move. One small move, and our lips would touch.

All I had to do was lean forward. Just a little. Just enough to erase the agonizing inches separating us.

Vi's smile abruptly faded, warning me that I'd allowed my gaze to linger too long. I looked up, only to find her eyes now fixed on my own mouth.

A shaky breath escaped her, and I almost lost it. Almost lost all common sense and took what wasn't mine. As the air between us began to crackle with tension, my sense of hearing came back to me.

It was quiet. *Too* quiet.

Somehow forcing myself to look away, I glanced at the others and immediately knew I was in trouble. They were all staring at us, at the way Vi and I were wrapped around each other—in a way that *friends* weren't supposed to.

Especially Reid.

If it had only been a few seconds, we could have gotten away with it, but we'd been this way for too long. We'd stared at each other too hard.

Realizing our predicament at the same time, Vi swiftly unwound her legs and arms. I immediately set her down and let go, but it was too late.

Without a word, Reid turned away and left the field.

"Reid, wait!" Vi called and started after him.

"Vi, let him—" I began, reaching for her arm.

"Don't!" she snapped and jerked her arm out of reach. "Just don't."

She whirled and took off, but not before I saw the tears in her eyes.

I watched her go for a moment, then started after her.

"Griff," Kolton said, with such authority that I had no choice but to stop. Curling my hands into fists, I obeyed my alpha, albeit begrudgingly. "Everyone, back into the house. Griff and I need to talk."

I bristled at the words, but I'd known they were coming. It was my own fault for getting too close.

As the others silently filed toward the house, I picked up the football Vi had dropped. Turning it over and over in my hands, I waited for the others to pass out of hearing range. The second they were all inside the house and the front door closed, Kolton released a pent-up sigh and turned to me.

"What were you thinking?"

A wry smile tugged at my mouth. Cocking back my arm, I threw the football as hard as I could. It soared over the expansive front lawn and disappeared into the woods surrounding the property. "I wasn't."

Kolton grunted. "That's obvious. What's changed? You've been different the past few days."

With a shrug, I started walking in the direction I'd thrown the football. Kolton joined me as I replied, "She said she needed me. She hasn't needed me since . . . Well, you know when."

Kolton was silent for several beats, walking beside me in contemplation. Then, "I know my sister's gone to you for comfort ever since she was little. You two have always shared a close bond, one that I know you both still share. It's the only reason why I'm not mad right now. Over the past few days, she's needed comfort, and she naturally sought out that bond. It was instinct, a reaction from years of relying on you for help. But she's taken, Griff. She needs to seek comfort from *him* now, to rely on him when she needs help."

"I know," I quietly said, my voice strained.

"Reid is a good male," he went on, "but even an easygoing one will eventually snap if another male threatens to take what's his."

"I know," I repeated, then couldn't help but add, "It's been eight months, and he hasn't claimed her yet. They haven't even had *sex*."

Kolton uncomfortably cleared his throat, as if talking about his sister's sex life was his least favorite topic. "I'm aware, but that doesn't give you a right to have sleepovers in Vi's bedroom."

"It was an accident," I quickly defended myself, even though I understood his point.

"That may be, but she's obviously struggling to accept this new chapter in her life—one that is drawing her away from her family and everything she's known. In order for her to properly pursue this new chapter with Reid, she can't fall back into an old one. Namely . . ."

"Me," I bitterly finished, barely able to stop myself from punching a tree as we entered the woods. "Don't worry. What happened this morning won't happen again. The last thing I want to do is hurt her."

"I know," Kolton said, reaching out to clasp my shoulder. We fell into companionable silence after that, but his words plagued me for hours afterward.

A new chapter. Vi was pursuing a new chapter.

One that didn't include me.

CHAPTER 10

VIOLET

I watched the black town car disappear out of sight down the private drive, then reentered the house with a dejected sigh.

Reid knew everything now. I'd explained it all, sharing with him every detail I could think of. He deserved the truth about what had happened between me and Griff this morning, and I'd made sure to be totally honest.

Yes, I still had feelings for Griff, but we had a complicated past. We'd been sexual partners for *years*, and I couldn't just make my body forget that. Ever since my first heat at the age of fifteen, I'd gone to Griff for help. Twice a year for the past seven years, we would become locked together in heated passion until my raging pheromones faded. Outside of those times, though, we rarely had sex. Only when we *really* needed each other did we give in to our passions.

I'd explained all this to Reid because the physical intimacy Griff and I had shared didn't mean we'd ever been a mated couple. He'd never claimed me, and I'd never asked him to. We were just *friends*. Well, friends with benefits, but that was over now.

My body had just temporarily forgotten.

Reid had seemed to understand. He hadn't even been *mad*. More like resigned, as if he'd already known.

But when I'd insisted that Griff was my past and *he* was my future, Reid had left me with four words. Four little words that had shaken me to my core and made me question everything. Seeing my confliction, he hadn't stuck around much longer, and I was now alone to face the consequences of my choices.

Not quite ready to speak to Griff—or anyone else, for that matter—I shut myself in Kolton's office and got lost in work. Even when dinnertime rolled around, I didn't stop. Nora brought in a plate and gently hugged me before wordlessly leaving again. Other than that, no one disturbed me.

It was nearing bedtime when the office phone rang. Answering on autopilot, I replied, "Rivers' residence. Vi speaking."

"Vi? Oh, thank goodness you answered," Mrs. Bailey's frantic voice filled the speaker. "It's Desirae. I told her not to leave the house, but the need to shift was too strong. She took off into the woods a few minutes ago, and I'm so scared she's going to get hurt or worse. Please. You have to help me get her back."

"Kolton!" I shouted, jumping up from my chair.

Seconds later, my brother, Griff, and Jagger burst into the office, my shout clearly putting them on high alert. Ignoring the fluttery feeling I got when Griff looked me over as if to check for injuries, I quickly relayed Mrs. Bailey's message.

"Tell her we're on the way," Kolton said and strode from the office. Still holding the phone, I shot after him, elbowing past Griff and Jagger in the process.

"I'm going too," I told him, adding some dominance to my voice.

"Vi—"

"I can help. I *want* to help," I interrupted before he could shut me down.

"You were just injured—"

"It won't happen again. I'll be extra vigilant. I *need* this."

At that, he paused with his hand on the front doorknob.

Knowing he still wasn't convinced, I allowed myself to admit, "I need to feel like I'm still a part of Midnight Pack."

He turned to face me then, his expression softening. "You'll always be a part of Midnight Pack, Vi."

"Will I?"

Seeing my doubt, he exchanged looks with Jagger and Griff, then quietly sighed. "Fine. You can come, but you're to follow me at all times. That includes Sable."

"I promise," I breathed, rushing forward to hug him.

As I quickly assured Mrs. Bailey we were on the way, Nora joined us in the foyer. Kolton paused to draw her close and press a sound kiss to her lips, and I immediately thought of this morning's football game when I'd been wrapped around Griff like a koala bear. Heat had stirred in my belly when I'd caught him staring at my lips, the look in his eyes anything but platonic. And for one second, I'd allowed myself to return the look—and remember what it felt like to kiss him. Feeling that same heat stir in my belly now, I hurriedly looked away.

They were just residual feelings from the past. Once I took that next step with Reid and we became intimate, I was certain the feelings would fade away.

I would get over them.

I would get over *him*.

For the sake of my future with Reid, I had to.

"Stay safe. All of you," Nora said, dispelling my troubled thoughts. I could tell she wanted to come too, but her priority these days was protecting her two precious children. She was an amazing mother, and God help anyone who tried to come between her and her babies.

With a final kiss goodbye, Kolton turned from his mate and led the way out the door. I eagerly followed, not about to let him change his mind. It wasn't that I got a thrill from danger. I would just rather face it than let the ones I loved deal with it alone. Not knowing if they were hurt or worse was unbearable, so I'd much rather be a part of the action than get left behind.

"Did you make any headway on those fingerprints we pulled from the trap?" Kolton asked me as we left the porch and headed for the garage.

"Darin ran them through the database but hasn't found any matches yet," I replied, referring to our pack member that worked in the NYPD. "He'll have to contact the FBI to access Interpol's system, but do we really want their attention drawn to two werewolves?"

Kolton deliberated for a moment before saying, "We can hold off on that for now. No need to alert other countries to our search just yet. Did one of the males really look Russian to you?"

I shrugged. "In a cliche sort of way. He kind of has an accent, but I've only heard him say two words."

"I'd be surprised if Alpha Petrov was behind this. Even after I revealed my hybrid nature during the Alpha Meeting last year, she assured me of her intentions to remain an ally."

"But there are several Russian packs, and not all of them align with Midnight Pack," Jagger reminded us, following closely on my heels. "Any one of them could have sent those males to kidnap Vi and Desirae. We all know that countless packs around the globe covet Midnight Pack's wealth and power. The abductors could have come from anywhere."

I waited for Griff to chime in, but he was surprisingly quiet.

As we all piled into the truck and took off, I finally said, "Well, I for one hope we catch them in the act tonight. Then we can put this stupid mess to rest and go back to living our boring adult lives."

"Hear, hear," Jagger muttered with a snort.

The snort was what clued me in to his thoughts, which had most definitely jumped to this morning's fiasco. Yeah, maybe *boring* wasn't the right word. There was always some form of drama we had to sort through. Griff and I just happened to currently be at the top of the pile.

Refusing to acknowledge the snort, I focused on keeping my mind on the task before us. Desirae could be walking into a trap—literally—and we needed to find her before that happened. When we arrived at Mrs. Bailey's, we got right down to removing our clothes. The sooner we started the search, the better, and our best chance at finding Desirae was in wolf form.

I'd just tossed my clothes into the truck bed, about to follow after Kolton and Jagger, when Griff said, "Vi, hold up."

Kolton glanced over his shoulder and gave us both a stern look. "One minute."

As he and Jagger took off for the backyard, I watched them go, wishing I could follow. *Dreading* what Griff was about to say.

"Can we do this later?" I suggested, suddenly chickening out. "We really don't have time to—"

"We need to do this now," he quietly interrupted, and my stomach bottomed out.

"Fine. What happened between us shouldn't have happened, okay? End of story."

"I agree, but I can sense how guilty you still feel. You aren't to blame for what happened, Vi. It was all me. I'm sorry I fell asleep with you last night."

I stayed quiet for a moment, then blurted, "What about on the field?"

"What about it?"

"Seriously? You're going to make me *say* it? Fine. You wanted to kiss me."

Silence. Then, "I did."

At his confession, that same heat flushed through my insides.

"But I didn't," he went on, "because you're taken, and I know that."

A tremor shook my hands. "Do you?"

"I do. I just got caught up in the moment. It won't happen again, Vi. I'm sorry."

I shook my head, unwilling to let him take all the blame. "Griff—"

"Did you tell Reid?"

Sighing, I admitted, "Yes. I told him everything."

"And? What did he say?"

I ground my teeth together, then forced myself to say words that tasted like acid on my tongue. "He said that I needed distance from you. When I asked him how I could do that, he told me to move in with him."

Not waiting for his reaction, I took off after Kolton and Jagger. When it came time to shift, Sable barely showed any excitement. She was subdued, keeping her feelings hidden from me as she continued to process the words Reid had left me with.

"Move in with me."

A simple request, and yet it was the hardest decision I'd ever had to make.

Whiskey was equally subdued, and when he and Sable were fully in control, all they did was gently nuzzle each other. It was as if they were comforting one another, as if they knew this might be the last time they were together for a long while.

I almost called Sable out on her melancholy behavior but stopped myself short. They had a right to grieve. If I said yes to Reid, this chapter of my life would close. I would be leaving, possibly for good. My world would no longer revolve around the three boys I'd grown up with but around Reid. I would have to say goodbye to my pack and say hello to his. My responsibilities would no longer be to my family but to him.

The weight of that change hit me like a ton of bricks, and Sable quietly whined as she felt my pain.

Whiskey licked her muzzle, then took off after Kolton and Jagger's wolves. Sable followed suit, but her heart wasn't in the hunt this time. Still, she stayed vigilant, making sure to watch every step she took. We scoured the woods for *hours*, following every scent trail we could find.

When the sky started to lighten, announcing the start of a new day, Shadow finally turned and headed back the way we'd come. Exhausted, we arrived at Mrs. Bailey's just as the sun came up.

With heavy hearts, we shifted back into our human forms and prepared to deliver the bad news.

Desirae was missing.

CHAPTER 11

VIOLET

Over the next few days, we put all our effort into finding Desirae.

Practically all two hundred members of Midnight Pack were on the lookout for her and the two males who'd set the silver trap, convinced they were the ones who took her. We hadn't found evidence of a struggle or even their scents, but chances were, she'd been kidnapped by them.

As we waited for a ransom note or call detailing their demands, a call came in that was entirely unexpected.

"This can't be a coincidence," I told my brother the second he ended the call. "Another *hybrid* missing? That's three attempts in one week, which means they have to be connected."

"I agree," Kolton said, running a hand through his hair until a dark strand fell onto his forehead. "But that means your theory about this being a challenge is incorrect. The newest disappearance has nothing to do with our pack, and the only reason why the missing female's alpha contacted me is because he heard about how I tracked Nora down when she went missing—which he mistakenly thought I could do with *all* hybrids, not just my soulmate."

"Okay, so this isn't about your alpha position," I mused, wearing a path in his office rug as I paced. "Maybe this has nothing to do with Midnight Pack and everything to do with hybrids. But what do they *want* with them?"

I stopped pacing as a thought came to me, one that immediately filled me with dread.

"What if witches are behind this? What if they're trying to exorcise hybrid wolves again?"

Feeling sick to my stomach, I crossed my arms with a shiver.

"Let's not jump to conclusions," Kolton quietly said. "Everyone involved in that situation was taken care of, and we haven't seen a single witch in months."

I nodded, only feeling a little better. There were still two hybrids missing, though, and I'd almost been the third. Whatever the abductors were doing with them, it couldn't be good.

We received another call hours later, this time from a pack in Canada. Same story. A hybrid pack member had gone missing, and they were hoping that Kolton had information.

When we received a third call in less than twenty-fours, this time from a pack in Minnesota, we all came to the same conclusion.

They were targeting *female* hybrids specifically.

Four were missing now—that we knew about anyway. Kolton and I started making calls, and by the end of the week, nearly a dozen disappearances had been reported.

Female hybrids were missing everywhere. A few had escaped and shared stories similar to mine, but their would-be-captors had been different.

Whatever was happening was bigger than we'd thought. Our pack had only been one target, but it seemed like they planned on targeting *every* pack that had female hybrids.

On Saturday morning, Kolton announced his intention to hold an emergency Alpha Meeting. The goal was to unite in our efforts to track down the missing pack members, but there was risk in holding such a meeting. Community rules stated that all packs worldwide were to be invited, and if one of those packs was behind the disappearances, we'd be broadcasting our plans to them.

"It's worth the risk," Jagger commented after Kolton told us. "The missing females could be anywhere, and we need access to other pack territories if we're going to find them."

"Yeah, but the other packs weren't exactly willing to help us the last time we held an Alpha Meeting," I reminded them.

"Last time, hybrids were still in hiding," Kolton replied. "Last time, they had no *reason* to help us."

I raised an eyebrow. "And this time?"

"This time," Griff spoke up, "the entire werewolf community has been affected. They need our help just as much as we need theirs."

When we all agreed to move ahead with the meeting, I spent the entire morning and afternoon working on invitations. It was nearing evening when a text lit up my personal phone. I quickly checked it and froze.

We need to talk, was all it said.

Seeing that it had come from Reid, panic fluttered in my chest. I grabbed the phone and quickly responded, *Sure. What's up?*

In person, he immediately texted back.

The panic intensified until I thought my heart would burst. Cursing under my breath, I stood from the office chair and went in search of Kolton. Thoughts of what Reid wanted to talk about followed me the whole way, making my body tremble with nerves.

Was he tired of waiting for my reply? Did he need me to make a decision *now*?

I'd been so busy the past few days that I'd barely given a thought to his last words to me. Since then, we hadn't texted or called each other. It would have been too awkward.

He was waiting for me, as usual, and apparently wasn't willing to be patient this time.

I couldn't blame him, though. He'd been incredibly understanding about Sable's dislike of him and Griff's closeness to me. But the only way *we* were going to become closer was if I spent more time with him.

He'd been more than patient with me these past eight months, and it was time to tell him my decision.

I found my brother in the kitchen helping Mom cook dinner. Nora and Griff were in the kitchen too, each holding a baby. When I entered, Griff's head snapped up, and our eyes met. A second later, he looked away.

It had been like this between us ever since I'd told him what Reid had said. Other than to discuss the hybrid disappearances, we'd barely spoken to each other these past few days. I felt an ache in my chest every time he intentionally avoided me, but I understood why he was doing it. Still, I already missed our conversations and, dare I say it, his teasing.

Feeling that ache start to form again, I blurted while I still had the nerve, "I'm heading to Boston."

Everyone stopped what they were doing to gape at me, even Griff.

Before they could start arguing with me, I rushed to add, "Only for a day. You'll barely even notice I'm gone. Reid and I really need to talk in person."

Kolton opened his mouth, clearly about to tell me no. One look at Nora, though, and he slowly shut it. Setting down the knife he'd been chopping onions with, he instead said, "I'll let you go on two conditions."

"Name them."

"You take the jet."

"Done."

"And you let Griff go with you."

Now it was my turn to gape. "You're joking, right?"

"Deadly serious. It's too dangerous for you to travel by yourself right now. Griff goes, or you don't."

I threw a pleading look at Nora, but she just gave me a sympathetic smile and shook her head.

Great. Just great.

Kolton was calling my bluff. He thought I would back down rather than face an awkward as hell situation. They'd all noticed how tense things were between me and Griff ever since the football game. They also knew that Griff was the main reason why Reid had asked me to move in with him.

Well, the joke was on him, because I didn't break that easily.

"Fine," I said, lifting my chin. "But I want to leave within the hour. Reid has a game tomorrow."

Kolton's eyes widened a fraction, but he just nodded and withdrew the phone from his back pocket. "I can have that arranged. I'll tell Randy to expect you at the airfield in an hour. You can leave your Jeep overnight in the hangar."

"Thanks, Kolton," I replied, remaining stoic despite how shocked I was that he'd agreed. "I'll go pack an overnight bag. Meet you in the foyer in twenty minutes, Griff."

He nodded without comment, and I quickly left the kitchen before Kolton could change his mind. Twenty minutes later, Griff and I were in the foyer saying our goodbyes.

"Keep the tracking on for your phones and call immediately if you suspect you're being followed," Kolton said. He looked like he wanted to say more, but once again, he glanced at Nora—probably to have a quick telepathic conversation through their soulmate bond—and changed his mind.

Despite how protective he was feeling, I knew my brother

was trying his best to let me spread my wings. Yes, I was still his responsibility and hybrids were still going missing, but I had a life outside of the pack now.

Well, more or less, depending on how my upcoming conversation with Reid went.

Before leaving, I made sure to hug every single family member, even Jagger. If these disappearances had taught me anything, it was to remind me that everything could change in an instant. Nothing was more important to me than family, and I couldn't imagine being separated from them. Which made this trip to see Reid that much more terrifying.

He's a good male, I kept reminding myself. Whatever my decision about moving in with him was, I knew he wouldn't tell me to stay away from my family.

Well, maybe *Griff*, but that was different. Griff and I were . . . We were complicated.

Glancing his way, I saw him share a bro hug with Kolton, then nod at whatever my brother murmured in his ear. Probably something about keeping an eye on me without sabotaging my relationship with Reid any further. This relationship wasn't like my past ones. I didn't need to be protected from it.

Although, what happened between me and Griff earlier this week had nothing to do with *protecting* me.

Quickly looking away before I could start thinking about it again, I swept one more lingering glance over my family, then turned toward the door with my overnight bag. Griff joined me with his own bag, and we headed for the garage in silence. I had no idea what the sleeping arrangements would be once we got to Boston, but that was the least of my concerns at the moment.

I was essentially bringing my ex to my boyfriend's place, even though Griff and I had technically never dated. If that wasn't bad enough, I still hadn't made a decision about moving in with Reid.

I knew one thing for certain, though. This trip was going to suck.

Sure enough, the drive to the airfield was spent in awkward silence. Our contract pilot, Randy, was already there, busily inspecting the family jet before takeoff. I parked my Jeep inside the open hangar and grabbed my bag, sharing a few pleasantries with Randy before climbing into the plane. As I claimed a seat, Griff chose to remain outside until we were ready for takeoff. I couldn't tell if he was making sure we weren't followed or . . .

Trying to keep his distance from me.

When we were finally ready for takeoff, he chose the seat directly across the aisle from mine, sitting down without a word. Desperate to break the silence, I opened my mouth to say something lame, only to close it with an audible click. As the jet took off down the runway and lifted into the air, Griff slouched in his seat and shut his eyes.

A slow, torturous half hour ticked by.

I tried to speak into the deafening silence between us but failed miserably several times. Finally, I couldn't stand it any longer and snapped like a rubber band.

"Are you mad at me?" I blurted, knowing that Griff was still wide awake despite his relaxed position. "I'm sorry you got dragged along on this trip, but I *hate* when we're not speaking. It's agony. We're supposed to always be there for each other no matter what. We're friends, Griff. *Family.* You said that would never change, even if I—"

"Don't say yes," Griff quietly interrupted me with his eyes still closed.

I blinked at him in confusion. "Huh?"

Finally, he turned his head and opened his eyes to look at me. "Don't move in with him."

My mouth slowly fell open. He might as well have slapped me. *Punched* me. All the air left my lungs, and I couldn't breathe.

Before I could say anything, he faced forward again and closed his eyes.

The rest of the flight was spent in silence but for a very different reason this time. My brain was whirring, frantically trying to figure out why Griff had said that. I could have asked him, but I was too afraid of his answer.

No, not afraid. *Terrified.*

A town car was waiting for us when we arrived at the airport, and when I saw Reid leaning against its side, I wanted to curl up and die on the spot. I'd texted him earlier, warning him that Griff was coming with me, but I'd somehow thought the two males wouldn't see each other. Now, I realized how stupid that thought had been.

"Hey!" I brightly called anyway, approaching Reid to give him a hug. He pushed off the car to accept my embrace, but I noticed right away how stiff he was. When I pulled back to give him a quick kiss, I found his gaze locked on something behind me. I flicked a glance over my shoulder and spotted Griff only a few yards off, staring at Reid with equal intensity.

"Reid," he said, his face devoid of its usual smile.

"Griff," Reid replied back, his tone clipped.

My mouth dried.

Crap. Coming here like this had been a bad idea. A *really* bad idea.

I could practically *eat* the tension, it was that thick.

"Um, Griff can take a different car," I said, instinctively knowing that something had shifted between them. They were sizing each other up like opposing teams did before a football game, seeing each other not as friends but as competition.

It didn't help that I was wedged between them like the frickin' *ball.*

"No, I can't," Griff said, planting himself directly behind me. "We travel together, Kolton's orders."

I opened my mouth to object, only to close it when I saw him set his jaw like stone. He hardly ever pulled the rank card on me, but I could sense him doing it now. He was above me in the pack hierarchy, and if I pushed him, he would push right back.

I tried to swallow and failed, stuck between feeling annoyed and turned on. Realizing what I'd just admitted, I quickly looked away, only to discover that Reid was carefully watching me.

Okay, this was far worse than I imagined. I hadn't counted on them both acting so . . . so *male.* Any second now, I expected them to start fighting over me like I was a slab of meat.

Yeah, that wasn't going to happen.

"Fine," I said, throwing up my hands and stepping away from them both. "I've been around dominant males enough to know when they're about to go dickhead on me, and I'm not sticking around for the show. Sorry, Reid. We'll have to do this another time."

I turned and headed back the way I'd arrived, so frustrated that tears blurred my vision.

"Vi, wait," Griff called, his beseeching tone making me pause. He released a pent-up sigh, then quietly said, "I'll behave."

Surprised, I peered over my shoulder at him. "You'll let me speak with Reid alone without interference?"

He nodded.

"And you'll take a different car?"

His expression flattened. "You know I can't do that, Vi. Kolton would kill me."

"True," I said, and he smiled a little.

"He can come with us," Reid spoke up, surprising me further. I glanced at him next, then froze, not expecting him to look so sad. He smiled a little too, but it didn't reach his eyes.

Swallowing with difficulty, I faced them again and uttered a soft, "Thank you."

They nodded, and without a word, we all piled inside the town car. Griff sat in front beside the driver, leaving me and Reid in back. Knowing that the driver was human, I decided not to catch Reid up on the hybrid disappearances. Instead, we spent another trip in uncomfortable silence.

By the time we made it to Reid's apartment building, I was dying to speak with him, if only to finally clear the air. We'd never experienced this level of tension in our relationship before, even when we'd discovered just how averse my wolf familiar was to us dating. She'd been surprisingly quiet during the trip, though, which only amplified my agitated state.

I was sick to death of everyone being so *silent* lately.

The second we entered the lobby of Reid's apartment complex, I shared a look with Griff. A *hard* one. A pleading one. He studied my face for a long moment, then blew out a breath and said, "I'll wait here. Call if you need me."

Need.

The word felt weighted. Intentional.

Turning away before I could think about it too much, I joined Reid in the elevator. As we ascended, I expected him to relax now that Griff was no longer with us. Instead, he looked even *more* tense, a muscle in his jaw feathering as he stared daggers at the floor number panel.

"Reid," I began, unable to bear the silence any longer. "It's just us now. Speak to me."

I reached between us to capture his hand. When my fingers touched his, he went stiff as a board. My heart sank, and I let go.

"Reid," I tried again, suddenly uncertain how to make this better. There was probably only one thing that could. One *word*. An answer to the question he'd asked me. A response he'd patiently waited for and was still waiting for.

I opened my mouth to speak but nothing came out.

Seeing the look on my face, he shook his head with a light scoff. "That's what I thought."

Confused, I blinked up at him. "Huh?"

"You don't want to be with me."

My eyes widened in shock. "*What?* Reid, be reasonable here. I didn't even say anything."

"Exactly. You didn't *say* anything."

"Reid, I . . ."

Before I could say more, he leaned forward and pressed the emergency stop button, then turned to face me. "Look, Vi, I care about you. It's why I decided to tell you face-to-face that I can't drag this out any further. I want to be with you, I really do. You don't see me for my money and fame, and I'm so grateful for that. But the problem is, you don't see me at *all*."

"That's not—"

"Let me finish, Vi. I know your head wants to be with me, but your heart doesn't. I could see it the moment I asked you to move in with me. You're not ready."

"But—"

"And I don't think you'll *ever* be ready so long as Griff is in your life."

"Griff? This is about *Griff*? Let me explain—"

"There's nothing to explain," Reid gently, albeit firmly interrupted

104

me once more. "I saw all I needed to see at that game the other day. Today only confirms what I already knew. I've lost."

"*Lost?* But I'm not—"

"The way you talk to him, the way you laugh with him, the way your wolf readily accepts him. I can't compete with that."

"But that's not fair," I argued, growing desperate. "We've known each other since we were babies. We've *grown up* together. Griff is practically my brother."

Reid shook his head. "You don't look at him the way you would a brother."

I opened my mouth again, but words failed me.

"You keep saying your wolf is struggling to accept me, Vi, but I think it's because *you* are struggling to accept me."

"Reid, please don't do this. I just need a little more time."

"I'm sorry, Vi, but it's over. I'm competitive like all dominant males are, but I know when to admit defeat. I won't fight for someone that doesn't want to be fought for. It never really felt like you were mine anyway. It always felt like you were . . ."

The air rushed from my lungs, but I managed to whisper, "Like what?"

His expression softened, and he raised a hand toward my face. At the last second, he stopped and lowered his arm. Sighing, he quietly replied, "Like you were his."

My entire body froze, overcome with shock. I tried to deny his words, but no sound left my lips.

He tilted his mouth into a sad smile. Without a word, he reached back and restarted the elevator. When we landed on his floor and the elevator doors opened, he stepped out and faced me once more.

"Go home, Vi. It's where you belong," he said, the words filled with conviction. Finality.

Not waiting for my reply, he turned and walked away, leaving me alone to face the cold hard truth.

CHAPTER 12

GRIFF

"Let's go," she said, hurrying past me as I stood from the lobby chair.

"Vi, what—?"

She was out the door before I could finish the sentence, and I scrambled to catch up with her.

"Vi, wait."

"Taxi!" she belted out, holding up her hand like a seasoned New Yorker. When no one stopped for her, she began to book it down the sidewalk.

"Vi," I called again, trailing after her. "Vi, what happened?"

"Not now," she said, in a way that instantly filled me with worry.

I quickly ate up the distance between us and grabbed her arm. "Vi, stop."

"No!" she shouted, wrenching her arm free. "I said not now. Help me hail a cab or keep quiet."

The words would have stung, if it weren't for the pain I heard in her voice.

My protective instincts immediately went haywire, and I ground out, "I'm going to kill him."

"No, you're not," she snapped, whirling to face me. When I saw the tears brimming in her eyes, I stopped breathing. She whirled around again and took off down the sidewalk, saying loud enough for me to hear, "This is *my* fault, not his. My own *stupid* fault."

I opened my mouth to question her further, then wisely sealed it shut. She was on the verge of breaking down—or exploding. Whichever came first. And it was clear she didn't want that to happen in the middle of a city. The crowds had thinned, most humans now in their homes for the night, but Vi didn't cry in public. If I pressed her, she would only lash out in anger to keep the tears at bay.

As she continued down the sidewalk at a fast clip, her overnight bag tightly clenched in her fist, I trailed in her wake and kept an eye on our surroundings. I hadn't seen any Russian-looking dudes loitering around Reid's apartment building, but I remained vigilant all the same.

In Vi's current state, she probably wasn't paying much attention to anything. The need to hug her was a fierce ache that grew with each step she took, but I knew she wouldn't welcome my touch right now.

Something terrible had happened between her and Reid, and my mind raced with countless possible scenarios.

Bet she finally dumped the bleedin' blighter, Whiskey drawled in a British accent. *After all, you finally grew a pair and asked her not to move in with him.*

Not now, Whiskey, I shortly replied. *And can you stop with the accents for once?*

You know that it's my way of embracing the earthly plane's many cultures. No need to get snippy with me just because your girl didn't come running to you in a puddle of tears.

She's not my— I started but didn't finish. It was pointless arguing with him anyway. Even though I'd never claimed Vi, he'd considered her mine ever since I'd taken her virginity. To him, we were mates. It didn't matter that Vi only saw me as her friend or even that she dated other males. She would come to her senses, he always said, encouraging me to properly pursue her until she had no choice but to accept me.

I knew better, though. Vi couldn't be *coerced* into anything. Not since the betrothal her parents had set up for her had gone so horribly wrong.

Ever since then, the more someone pushed her, the more she retreated. If she knew *half* the thoughts I had about her, she'd run away so fast that I'd never be able to catch her again.

No, it was better this way. Better to be her friend, to be there when she needed me, to keep my true feelings buried so we didn't lose what we had.

Better for who? Whiskey butted into my thoughts again. *You're both horny and in desperate need of sex. It's been almost a year since you've tasted her supple flesh and plunged your dick inside her tight pussy. I don't know how you can even stand upright at this point.*

I tried to ignore his colorful words, but images flooded my mind before I could stop them. No, not images. *Memories.* Memories of me and Vi tangled together in heated passion. One memory in particular grabbed my attention—the last time we'd been intimate during Nora's pack initiation a year ago.

We'd just spent an entire night in wolf form romping through the forest. The whole time, Whiskey and Sable had heavily flirted with each other, and their sexual tension had slowly become ours. When it came time to shift back into our human forms, the tension had been too great to ignore. Right there in the middle of the grassy field, surrounded by our pack, I'd given in to my lust and kissed her.

It was the only time I'd ever done so without waiting for her approval.

Thankfully, she'd eagerly responded to the kiss instead of pushing me away. Beyond excited by her acceptance, the kisses had quickly turned into touching. My hands had feverishly roved over her bare skin, and she'd touched me back, lighting a fire inside so hot that I'd laid her down on the grass and covered her body with mine.

The second our skin had pressed together, I'd lost all control and began to rub against her. The friction sent pleasure cascading through me, and I'd planned to keep going until she orgasmed, which in turn would make me orgasm.

But then she'd stunned me by saying words I'd been longing to hear. Words she only said once or twice a year.

"I need you, Griff."

Just like that, I was inside her to the hilt, thrusting so frantically that we were both panting for release seconds later.

Remembering how good it had felt when we'd orgasmed together, I nearly fell to my knees.

See? This keeping silent thing isn't good for anyone, Whiskey grumbled. *If you don't bang your girl soon, you're going to combust.*

Shaking off the memory before it made me come in my pants, I refocused on the fierce brunette still hurrying down the sidewalk. She seemed to be lost in thought, unaware of the cab turning on to our street.

I raised a hand, and the taxi slowed.

"Vi," I said, but she was already stepping off the sidewalk and making for the cab.

The second we pulled away from the curb, she muttered under her breath, "I have to call Randy."

"I'll do it." I reached into my back pocket to pull out my phone. "Should I tell him we need to leave as soon as possible?"

She nodded, then looked out the window. I quickly relayed the message to our pilot, keeping an eye on Vi and our surroundings as we headed back to the airport. She didn't speak the entire way there, and I didn't press her for answers.

It was killing me, though. The not knowing. The possibilities.

What if she *had* broken up with Reid? Was I responsible for whatever had happened between them?

I'd tried so hard to give her space the past few days, to keep myself carefully in check after she'd told me what Reid had said. But the minute she'd announced her intentions to visit him, I'd started to unravel again.

"Don't say yes. Don't move in with him."

What the hell was *wrong* with me? I had *no* right to tell her that, but I hadn't been able to stop myself. The thought of letting her go for good had been too much, and I'd done what I swore I wouldn't do.

I'd tried to sabotage their relationship.

I felt awful, but I couldn't bring myself to apologize for the words I'd said. The second I'd uttered them, a great weight had lifted off me. I could breathe again. *Think* again.

My only regret was the part I'd played in causing Vi pain. She was staying strong like she always did, but I could sense how miserable she was. I almost reached across the seat to hold her hand. Almost. Not knowing if she wanted my comfort kept me from touching her, though.

Sex had definitely complicated our relationship despite my efforts not to let it. I would always be there for her. That would never change. But I couldn't help wanting more.

More than she was willing to give me.

Curling my hands into fists, I rested them on my thighs and allowed the silence between us to grow. It didn't matter what I wanted—not if *she* didn't want it. Still, I allowed myself to hope a little.

She was going home. That had to mean something.

Maybe, just maybe . . .

By the time we reached the airport, my hopeful thoughts were making it nearly impossible to keep quiet. Still, I made it all the way into the plane before finally breaking the silence. "Did you say no?"

From her spot across the aisle from me, she quietly snorted and replied, "He didn't give me the chance to." When she didn't elaborate, I opened my mouth again. "No more questions, Griff. Please. I just can't right now."

Hearing the quiver in her voice, the need to pull her into my arms was almost unbearable. Not knowing how else to comfort her, I respected her wishes and didn't question her further. As we taxied down the runway and took off, though, my mind kept throwing possibilities at me. For the next forty minutes, I thoroughly tortured myself with what-ifs, even entertaining Whiskey's suggestions.

We'd just passed over Mount Marcy when the jet suddenly shuddered. I looked out the window and quickly spotted the reason.

"Just a storm," I said aloud for Vi's benefit. "I'm sure Randy will—"

A clanking noise drew my attention out the window again, just as the engine burst into a ball of orange flames. I was out of my seat in a flash, racing for the cockpit.

"Randy!"

Before I could reach the front, the plane listed sharply to the right, violently throwing me sideways

"Griff!" Vi cried as my head cracked against a window. My supernatural healing immediately started to dull the pain and repair the damage, and I was up on my feet again seconds later.

Vi was suddenly there, latching on to my arm to help me upright, except that we were no longer upright. As the plane rapidly started to lose altitude, I grabbed Vi and tried to buckle her into a seat. Every time I tried, she batted my hands away and tried to force *me* into a seat.

"Violet!" I thundered, fear for her safety driving me to overpower her. I captured both her wrists in one hand, using the other to secure the buckle.

"No!" she shouted, fighting against my grip. The wind outside the cabin roared as we descended faster and faster, the plane spiraling out of control.

I prepared to make another run for the cockpit, but the second I released Vi, she grabbed my hand and sank her nails—no, *claws*—into my flesh.

"Don't leave me!" she cried, her voice filled with terror. For a brief moment, our eyes met. So many things passed between us in that split second. So many emotions and unspoken thoughts.

I opened my mouth to reassure her, but the world suddenly exploded around us. Vi screamed as a force violently tore my hand from hers, catapulting me into the air. I struck object after object, unable to control my speed. Pain splintered my vision, filling every corner of my body.

Metal shrieked. Wind snatched at my clothes and hair, ripping me farther and farther away from Vi.

Before I could find my way back to her, I hit the ground at breakneck speed, and the world went dark.

CHAPTER 13

VIOLET

Water pooled in my eyes.

Or maybe blood. I couldn't tell.

I reached up to wipe it away and immediately winced as pain shot up my arm. Lowering it, I lifted my other arm and rubbed at both eyes. When my vision was clear enough to see again, I focused on the red smear across the back of my hand.

Blood, then.

Reaching higher, I touched my forehead and pulled my fingers back to find more blood. The second I saw it, panic tightened my chest.

We'd crashed.

The plane had *crashed*.

As everything came rushing back to me, I glanced up and found a gaping hole in the cabin ceiling. Rain was slanting in, soaking me and everything inside the dark interior. While I waited for the ringing in my ears to fade, I continued to glance around, noting that I was still buckled in my seat. Only, my seat was angled backward now, leaving me in a reclined position.

Without thinking, I fumbled to undo the buckle with my injured arm. Agony flared up the length of it once more, stealing my breath away. Changing hands, I managed to unbuckle myself and sit up to better assess the situation. The front half of the plane still looked intact, but the back half was gone.

Like *gone*, gone.

I glanced around the broken cabin again, and my panic increased tenfold.

Alone. I was *alone*.

The only thing I could hear was my frantically beating heart. No others. Not Randy's. Not Griff's.

Remembering how Griff had been torn from me, my heart beat even faster. I struggled to stand and immediately doubled over in pain.

Some of your organs were damaged, Sable said. *Also, your arm is dislocated. You need to fix it before the bones heal wrong. Want me to take over?*

I shook my head, gasping out, "I need . . . to find Griff."

She started to protest, but I ignored her, forcing my battered body into motion. My injured arm hung uselessly at my side as I grabbed on to anything I could find and hoisted myself up the aisle. My instincts screamed at me to go the other way, to put all of my energy into finding Griff, but I had to check on our pilot first.

"Randy," I wheezed.

No response.

With only a few yards to go, I gritted my teeth and pulled my body the rest of the way up. When the cockpit door wouldn't budge, I used my good shoulder to force it open, barely managing to swallow a pained cry as the move jarred my injuries.

Squeezing past the busted door, I immediately spotted the pilot still in his seat. He was blankly staring up at the ceiling—with a shard of glass from the shattered windshield protruding from his left eye.

Bile rose up my throat. I turned and retched into a corner, then paused to stare at the dark blood I'd just vomited.

You need to stop moving and let your body heal, Vi, Sable spoke again, her worry clear.

I stubbornly shook my head again and stumbled from the cockpit. There was nothing I could do for Randy, but . . .

"I need . . ." I started, only to double over and cough up more blood. Switching to mindspeak, I finished, *to find Griff.*

And I need to find Whiskey, but you're in no condition to—

She stopped as I lost my footing and practically slid down the slippery aisle. When I tumbled out of the plane and hit the ground, I couldn't suppress a cry of pain this time.

See? You're not as tough as you think you are, young lady. Take a second to—

She growled her annoyance as I continued to ignore her and lumbered to my feet once more. Pausing only a brief moment to scan my surroundings, I took off at an awkward gait. The trees and rain were thick, making it hard to get anywhere fast, but the desperation clawing at my chest drove me onward.

I needed to find Griff. I needed to find Griff.

Nothing else mattered right now.

The front half of the jet had plowed through the thick forest before crashing against the base of Mount Marcy. The back half, on the other hand, was nowhere to be seen.

"Griff!" I called out as loudly as I could, and my body rewarded me by succumbing to another coughing fit.

Pausing only a second to spit out more blood, I kept going, frantically searching for any sign of him. I didn't know how much time passed, but I kept going and going, pushing my body to its breaking point.

Finally, it gave out on me.

As I crashed to the hard-packed earth, I cried out in despair. The wail rose into the night, transforming into a mournful howl.

Exhausted, I lowered my head, moments away from bursting into tears. That's when I heard it. Over the wind and rain, a familiar voice answered my cry.

The voice was faint. Weak. But it filled me with so much relief that adrenaline surged through me, and I was on my feet a second later.

"Griff!" I shouted for the umpteenth time, and this time, he answered back.

I started to run, cradling my dislocated arm against my stomach so it wouldn't flop around. I probably looked like a zombie on crack, but I didn't care. All I cared about was getting to Griff.

"Griff!" I shouted again, following the sound of his voice every time he answered.

Half a mile later, my night vision spotted something bright up ahead. A patch of blond spiky hair. *Griff's* hair.

A sob tore from my raw throat, and I scrambled forward as fast as I could to reach him. He was lying beside the opposite bank of a stream, and I quickly splashed across. Still crying, I staggered up the bank and promptly threw myself beside him.

"I was so worried," I got out between sobs, trying to hug him. When my dislocated arm wouldn't let me, I sobbed harder. "I thought . . . I thought . . . I thought you were *dead.*"

He allowed me to cry for a moment, then reached up to feather a hand over my injured arm. "You're hurt."

"It's . . . It's dislocated. I'll recover."

It was then that I finally noticed how still he was. Glancing down, I immediately saw the *tree* sticking out of his chest.

"Oh, my God, Griff!" I wailed, reaching for it, only to quickly yank my hand away.

It was more of a stump, actually, with jagged ends that had

impaled him all the way through. The tree's roots were still in the ground, and the trunk was thick enough that I couldn't wrap both hands all the way around it.

Seeing it protruding from his body filled me with fresh panic, and I started to hyperventilate.

"Guess I got a splinter on the way down," he weakly said between my gasping breaths.

"This isn't the time for *jokes*, Griffin!" I cried, barely able to see his face through the rain and my tears. His complexion was too pale, his pupils too large, and his breaths were way too shallow.

I forced myself to stop crying, to stop *breathing* so I could listen to his heart.

Too slow, just as I feared.

"It punctured my heart a little but not much," he lightly said despite the excruciating pain he must be in. "I could try shifting."

"No!" I yelled at the same time Sable did. "The tree could tear into your heart more if you do that."

"But—"

"*No*, Griff. I won't lose you to a *tree*. Just give me a second to think."

Rocking back on my heels, I forced my gaze to the tree sticking out of his chest again. Nausea roiled in my gut, but I somehow managed not to throw up. "Okay," I said, inhaling a shuddering breath. "Okay, I can figure this out. M-maybe I can perform a sleeping spell. I'm a little rusty, but—"

"I want to stay awake for this," he firmly said.

"Okay, fine. Maybe I can—"

"You have to pull me off of it, Vi."

I stared at him like he'd gone insane. Then violently shook my head. "I can't do that."

"It's the only way."

"I can't, Griff. I *can't*. What if I damage your heart even more, and—" A whimper left me before I could contain it.

"Remember when I was ten and fell into that old well on Mr. Scavinski's property?" he asked. "Kol and Jag were too far away, but you heard my cries for help. I couldn't climb out, so you threw a rope down and pulled me out all by yourself."

I nodded, sniffling. "You were so embarrassed. You told me not to tell Kolton and Jagger about it. I never did."

"Because you're dependable and strong. I need help again, Vi. I need *you*. I know you can do this."

I shook my head again, feeling anything but strong. "Reid broke up with me," I blurted, suddenly needing him to know just how incapable I really was. "Randy's dead. *Dead*. And you . . . You're hurt. Like *really* hurt. This is all my fault. I keep screwing up and hurting the people I care about, and I can't . . . I can't hurt you even more. I can't do it, Griffin. I'm so sorry."

I started crying again. Sobbing. Sounding more and more hysterical by the second.

Pain contorted Griff's face as he watched me fall apart. Lifting a hand, he whispered, "Come here."

I immediately curled forward, allowing him to slide his hand behind my neck and guide my head down to his. My wet hair fell against his cheeks like a dark curtain as he pressed our foreheads together and said, "I'm fine. I'm right here. I know you're afraid, but I won't leave you."

"Y-you don't . . . You don't know that," I cried, punctuating the words with a hiccup.

"Yes, I do. Nothing can take me away from you, including this little toothpick in my chest."

"That's not . . . That's not funny."

"It kind of is. Although, saying I got impaled by wood might be funnier."

"Griffin Hayes," I tried to growl, but his name came out as a pathetic whine.

"Violet Jane," he replied, amusement in his voice despite the awful situation. "Just breathe. That's all you have to do right now. Breathe."

I let my eyes flutter shut, using his calming presence to soothe my panic.

As my thundering heartbeats began to slow and my breathing evened, he hummed his approval. "Good girl."

I sank into his warmth and allowed my nose to lightly brush his. His hold on my neck suddenly tightened, drawing me even closer. As his breath fanned across my mouth, I tensed and opened my eyes. His eyes lifted as well, and the message in them was clear.

"Griff," I started, whether to warn him or encourage him, I wasn't sure. Before I could decide, he drew my head down even lower and feathered his lips over mine. Tiny darts of electricity danced over my sensitive skin, and I sucked in a quiet gasp.

Startled by the unexpected kiss, I held still, my eyes wide like saucers. He pulled back a little to study my expression, then firmed his grip on my neck and brought our mouths together again. *Hard.* This time, the kiss streaked through me like bolts of lightning.

A breathy moan escaped me, and he kissed me again, so deeply that all I could feel and taste was him. My pain and fear melted away, and I was suddenly kissing him back with a desperation that stole the air from my lungs. The moment I did, a violent tremor shook him, his fingers spasming on my neck. He groaned, the sound equal parts pleasure and pain.

I broke the kiss with a cry of dismay. "I'm so sorry. Did I hurt you?"

He peeled his eyes open to blink up at me. "Yes, but you can hurt me like that any time."

A smile crept onto his face, and I scowled, smacking his shoulder. "Seriously, Griff?"

He grunted but waved away my worried look. "Worth it. You're feeling better already."

My scowl deepened. "You kissed me to make *me* feel better?"

"It worked, didn't it? You're back to your usual bossy self."

"*Bossy*? I'm not—"

When he chuckled, I rolled my eyes and changed the subject.

"Let's get this over with before I start freaking out again." I reached for him, only to pull back with a sharp hiss.

He immediately sobered, taking in the way I cradled my injured arm against my chest. "That needs to be popped back into place first."

I nodded with a grimace.

Sure, listen to him*, not me*, Sable grumbled.

"It's already started to heal wrong," I told him, stiffening when he slid his hand to my injured shoulder joint.

"I'll be quick," he said, bringing his other hand up to brace me.

My heart started hammering in my chest again, and I squeezed my eyes shut. "Okay, just do it before I chicken out. No counting or—" *Crack*. "AAHH! Mother of—"

I swore colorfully as Griff jerked the bone back into place. Seconds later, though, the pain began to fade.

"Need another kiss?" Griff asked as I slowly rotated my shoulder.

"Shut up," I muttered, even as my lips warmed at the thought of being pressed to his again. Quickly shaking off the thought, I gave him a stern look. "Okay, your turn. Sable and I will do all the work, so don't even think about trying to be all manly and help out."

"Wouldn't dream of it. My life is in your hands. Literally."

I pursed my lips at his blasé attitude but didn't comment. Calling on my wolf familiar's aid, I waited for the partial shift in my arms and legs to finish before reaching for Griff again. When I carefully slid my furry arms beneath him, he obediently kept still.

"Put your arm around my neck," I quietly instructed, suddenly feeling the weight of what I was about to do. If I pulled him off the tree at the wrong angle . . .

Griff wrapped his arm around me, and the close contact instantly soothed some of my panic.

"I'm gonna need a kiss after this," he lightly said, but I didn't miss the strain in his voice. He was starting to panic too.

Knowing there was no way to shelter him from the pain to come, I replied, "Make it through this alive, and you can have all the kisses you want."

"Promise?"

At the change in his tone, I let my eyes meet his. The usual chocolate brown was now a bright yellow, and I swallowed hard at the sight. Firming my grip on him, I nodded.

"Cross my heart," I promised, then gritted my teeth and pulled.

CHAPTER 14

GRIFF

Fire. Everything was *fire*.

I thought for sure I would pass out from the pain, but I felt every agonizing second as Vi pulled me off the jagged tree stump.

A muffled scream escaped my clenched teeth, my body trembling from the effort of holding still. The entire time, Whiskey kept howling inside my head. Not from the fiery pain, but from the fact that I'd kissed Vi. He was ecstatic, and a little pain wasn't going to rain on his parade.

Truthfully, I was equally elated. Not wanting to spook her, I'd played off the kiss as a simple way to calm her down, but that hadn't been the real reason why I'd kissed her. I'd expected her to push me away, especially after everything that had happened between us this week—not to mention Reid breaking up with her. Instead, she'd done something I'd been entirely unprepared for.

She'd kissed me back.

Not softly either. *Feverishly*. Like she'd been missing me as much as I'd been missing her.

By thunder, yer back in the game, laddy! Whiskey crowed like a pirate. *Aye, yer little wench is thirsty for ya, that's for bloody sure. She practically sucked yer bleedin' face off.*

Despite the derogatory comment, I couldn't help but laugh. The movement sent fresh pain ripping through me, but I only laughed harder.

"Idiot. Would you stop laughing?" Vi growled, and I tried my best to stop. A second later, I burst out laughing again. "Griffin Hayes O'Neal, I swear I'm going to kill you after this!"

Hearing the fear in her voice did the trick, and my laughter quickly faded.

Moments later, she pulled me free of the stump and helped me stand. When I listed sideways, she kept her arms around me and held me upright.

"Easy. You lost a lot of blood," she said, nearly my height in her half-shifted state. I gratefully leaned against her, not the least bit embarrassed by her help. She was a capable alpha female, and any male intimidated by that was simply weak.

As we stood together by the stream, thoroughly soaked by the falling rain, I folded my arms around her and buried my face in the crook of her neck. We didn't move for several long moments, allowing our bodies to heal from the devastating plane crash.

Finally, she started to shrink in my arms, reverting back to her human form. When the transformation was complete, she pulled back, and I reluctantly let her go.

Through the rain and gloom, I watched her eyes flit up to my face, then down to my chest. Pursing her lips, she murmured, "Let me see."

"It's fine, Vi. Already healing," I said, but I didn't stop her from grasping the hem of my ruined shirt and lifting it. She hiked the material all the way up to my collarbone, gasping softly when she caught sight of my bare chest. At her reaction, I couldn't resist drawling, "I mean, I know my pecs are awesome, but you've seen them hundreds of times."

"Shut up, Griff," she tightly replied, reaching up to gently prod at my skin. I flinched at the contact, and her eyes immediately flew up to mine. "Did I hurt you?"

I shook my head, silently watching as she resumed her poking and prodding. For a brief second, I glimpsed the gnarly half-healed hole in my chest, then firmly returned my gaze to Vi.

"What's the prognosis, Doc?" I asked her, grimacing when I felt my sternum snap back into place.

She stopped poking to glance up at me again. "You'll live. Your breathing and heart rate have returned to normal. You're still bleeding a bit, though, so you'll want to take it easy until the wound is fully closed."

A grin tugged at my mouth.

Seeing it, she rolled her eyes and huffed out, "What now?"

"You're just cute when you play caretaker."

"Really, Griff? Do you take *anything* seriously? You almost *died.* I nearly lost you, and . . . and how did this even happen? That jet was in mint condition. Randy always took such good care of her, and—" Her hand suddenly flew to her mouth. "Oh, God. *Randy.* I can't believe he's dead. We'd probably be dead too if we were human. I can't . . . I just can't . . ."

As she teetered on the edge of another meltdown, I pulled her into my arms again, hugging her fiercely. She trembled against me, her body shaking with silent sobs. I held her close for several moments, offering my comfort as well as seeking my own.

When she no longer trembled, I murmured against her damp hair, "I'm sorry. This is no laughing matter. Jokes just help me cope."

A shuddering sigh left her. "I know. I was just really scared."

"Me too," I whispered, tightening my hold even more.

She let me hold her for another minute, then sniffed back tears and pulled away. "Do you have your phone? I think I lost mine."

I felt in my back jeans pockets but came up empty. "Guess we should head back to the crash site and have a look around."

She shivered but nodded in agreement.

We walked in silence, each lost in our own thoughts. Whiskey kept heckling me to kiss her again, but now wasn't the time. She was clearly traumatized by all that had happened, and it would be selfish of me to pursue her right now. Instead, I continued to offer her my comfort and support, sticking close to her side the entire way back.

When we reached the crash site, I released a low whistle. "Well, that explains why I ended up so far away."

"Yeah," she said, looking everywhere but at the broken plane. "I didn't see our stuff inside, so I'm gonna look around out here. Holler if you find anything."

She took off before I could say anything, her gait stiff and decidedly nervous. Knowing she needed some space to process, I forced myself not to follow her and veered toward the jet. The rain continued to beat on my head, harder than it had a few minutes ago. A flash of lightning lit up the crash site, followed closely by a rumble of thunder.

We were in for a very wet night. The ground had already grown saturated, and it was only then that I finally noticed my feet were bare.

Guess Vi was right about the flip-flops, I thought wryly, carefully avoiding a shard of glass. No need to impale myself a second time.

A few minutes later, I was standing in the cockpit, looking down at Randy's body. Hesitating, I finally moved to check his pockets for a phone. Relieved when I found one, I pulled it out only to sigh in disappointment when it wouldn't turn on. Everything was too wet. Even if we did find our own phones, they were probably in the same condition due to the rain. I checked the radio, but it too was fried.

With the realization that help probably wasn't coming anytime soon, I started to unbuckle the pilot. He deserved a proper burial, not to be picked apart by wild animals.

I was just about to hoist him over my shoulder when a noise above the rain caught my attention. It was faint, but there was no mistaking the sound. Voices. *Several* of them.

Whiskey immediately rose up, growling quietly. Heeding his warning, I left the pilot in his seat and silently slipped from the cockpit. As fast as I could without making noise, I made my way out of the plane, pausing every few seconds to listen.

There were at least four of them. Maybe five. All male by the sound of it.

A part of me wanted to call out to see if they were friendly, but a bigger part cautioned me not to. We were in the middle of nowhere, miles from any form of civilization. And I'd been replaying Vi's words from earlier about the jet. It *had* been in mint condition. The engine shouldn't have gone out like that.

I suspected foul play, and these males could be involved.

Problem was, I was in no shape to confront them at the moment. My chest wasn't fully healed yet, and there was no way I would put Vi in danger without knowing what we were up against.

But as I landed on solid ground, a voice from behind me said, "Found my bag. My phone was inside, but it's not—"

I lunged for Vi, quickly silencing her with a hand over her mouth. She instinctively tried to pull away, but I pressed her tightly to me and softly hissed in her ear, "Listen."

She stilled.

A few seconds later, pounding footsteps reached our ears.

"Run," I said. In a flash, I grabbed her hand and took off. Thankfully, she didn't argue, keeping pace with me as I led us away from the crashing footfalls. Less than a mile later, a sharp *crack* rended the air and something smacked into the tree beside me.

"Move!" I roared at Vi, not bothering to keep quiet anymore.

"What's happening?" she cried, now running beside me at full tilt.

Another crack cleaved the air, and I veered sideways just in time to avoid being shot in the back.

Yup. Definitely not friendly.

"We're being hunted," I grimly told her.

She threw me a wide-eyed look, letting me know that she was thinking the same thing. Her abductors had come back for her, and they'd brought a few friends this time. Plus weapons no doubt loaded with silver ammunition designed to bring down werewolves.

We definitely weren't prepared to fight them right now, and I could tell by Vi's expression that she felt the same.

So, at the same time, we called on our wolves for aid. They immediately rose to the surface but knew we didn't have time for a full shift. A few bone cracks later, and we were running at twice the speed, our shifted legs swiftly carrying us out of shooting range.

Still, we didn't slow. Didn't stop. We ran and ran, plunging deep into the forest without direction, our only thought on escaping our pursuers.

We ran for hours, until our still-healing bodies started to give out. Until we were thoroughly lost. Until we could no longer hear the males hunting us.

Even then, I continued to run, encouraging an exhausted Vi onward. Because I knew, just *knew* they wouldn't stop hunting us.

If they were willing to orchestrate a plane crash, they had no intention of going home empty-handed—wherever home was for them. What was worse, I was pretty sure they weren't after me. I was just inconveniently in the way, and they probably wanted nothing more than to shoot me dead.

They wanted *Vi*, and that fact gave me the energy to keep going. No way was I letting them take her. No way was I letting them even *touch* her.

If they tried, they'd find out just how feral a hybrid werewolf male protecting his female could become.

CHAPTER 15

VIOLET

I was in pretty good shape, but the energy needed to heal my internal injuries had taken its toll on me.

Still, I was tenacious, and seeing Griff run for hours without faltering kept me going. It was sometime after midnight, the rain still beating on our heads and saturating our torn clothing, when my trembling legs finally gave out. I hit the sodden ground hard, further ripping my jeans and bruising my tired body.

Griff was immediately there to help me up, bearing most of my weight as I struggled to stand. One look at my face, and he said, "That's it. You need a few hours of rest."

"I can keep going," I panted, tugging free only to stumble again.

Griff caught me before I could fall. "You're dead on your feet, Vi. Even Sable can't keep going."

Sable softly whined in agreement, her energy linked to mine. She was beat and definitely needed a break.

"Fine," I got out, still trying to catch my breath. "One hour."

"Two," Griff countered, his jaw set like stone. "If they catch up to us, you'll need energy to fight them."

Knowing he was right, I didn't argue back. If we covered our tracks well enough, we should be able to buy ourselves a couple hours of uninterrupted rest. With that in mind, I started searching for a stream or other body of water that could help hide our scent. Griff followed suit, and a few minutes later, we found a stream deep enough to mask our trail. We traveled another mile or so upriver, planting false trails as we went, then began the painstaking process of seeking shelter.

My eyelids would barely stay open by the time Griff spotted a shallow cave just large enough to fit the two of us.

"It's a tight fit," he said, grabbing some nearby brush to camouflage the entrance, "but it'll keep us dry."

Dry. I'd almost forgotten what that felt like.

Minutes into our mad dash to escape, I'd decided to drop my bag. There hadn't been anything important inside, but I regretted the decision now, simply for the fact that I *really* wanted to change out of this filthy outfit.

We'd shifted our legs back to our human ones, and both of our jeans were in tatters from the transformation. As Griff continued to collect foliage to hide our temporary bed, I started to unbutton my jeans. Hearing me struggle to remove the wet fabric, Griff whipped his head up to look at me.

"There's no way I can sleep with this wet clothing on," I explained, even though it was pretty obvious what I was doing. Still, I became hyper-aware of my half-naked state as Griff watched me undress.

Pretending not to care, I finished pulling off my pants, then shimmied out of my top. My shoes hadn't survived the lengthy shift, unfortunately. I left my dark purple underwear on but felt entirely naked when I peeked up at Griff and found him still watching me.

Swallowing hard, I waved at him and said, "Your turn."

He slowly blinked at me as if coming out of a trance. "Huh?"

"I'm not letting you sleep beside me with those clothes on. Off. Now."

At the command, his eyes flashed bright yellow, and my breath caught.

Despite her exhaustion, Sable perked up in interest. *You just turned him on. Both of them. They've always enjoyed being bossed around by their females.*

Too flustered to contradict her words, I ducked into the cave to lay out my clothing in one corner. By the time I straightened and turned back around, Griff was already undressed. My eyes immediately dropped below his waist. Only for a split second, but long enough to see that he'd left on his boxer briefs, and . . .

His dick was rock hard.

I jerked my gaze back up but not quickly enough. When our eyes met, Griff's irises were liquid gold again.

Sable snickered, making the situation ten times worse.

For goodness sake, get a grip, I grumbled to myself. *He's a virile male in his prime. Looking at himself in the* mirror *makes him hard. We're just friends.* Friends.

You aren't with Reid anymore, Sable said, clearly listening to my private thoughts. *It's okay if you want to have sex with Griff again.*

No, it's not okay, I all but yelled at her, desperately trying not to think of the kiss Griff and I had shared earlier. *Stop interfering, Sable. I'm confused enough as it is.*

But if you would just—

Not letting her finish, I practically yanked Griff's clothing from his hands and crouched to lay them next to mine. Unsure what to do next, I straightened and gestured at the cave. "Um, maybe you should go in first. There's more room at the back."

"Sure," was all he said, then bent down and crawled inside.

Inhaling a calming breath, I crawled in after him.

Right away, I realized how cramped the space was. In order to keep dry, I'd have to be pressed up against him from head to toe.

Cozy, Sable purred.

Pursing my lips, I rolled over and scooted backward until my spine brushed his chest and torso. Realizing my legs were still getting wet from the rain, I bit back a frustrated sigh.

"Here," Griff said and slid an arm around my middle to pull me tighter against him. As I felt his erection press into my backside, I tried not to stiffen. He maneuvered his other arm beneath my head to act as a pillow, which drew me that much closer to him. His warm breath feathered over the shell of my ear as he rumbled, "Is this okay?"

Fighting back a shiver, I simply nodded and closed my eyes.

After a few minutes, his warmth and scent filled the cramped space. I waited for my body to relax like it always did when he touched me, but the longer we were pressed together, the more my body buzzed with energy. I was still exhausted, but this was the kind of energy that didn't care how tired you were. It was persistent. *Demanding.*

And entirely inappropriate.

Proving just how much it didn't care, an unmistakable scent permeated the air. I silently cursed and squeezed my thighs shut, but the damage had already been done.

Griff stirred behind me, and my eyes popped back open.

"Can't sleep?" he asked, a husky edge to his voice.

Ah, crap. He could definitely smell it.

"No," I replied, cursing my stupid body for betraying me this way.

He was silent for a long while, so long that I didn't think he would respond. What could he say anyway? It's not like he was going to—

"Do you need my help?"

Oh, hell no. He did *not* just ask that.

No, no, no, no, NO.

At the same time, Sable loudly howled, *Yes, yes yes! She definitely needs your help! Oh, I've been longing for this. It's finally happening.*

My girl is going to get some!

A scream built in my head, one that threatened to explode from me. Sable's eagerness brought to mind Reid's final words to me, which only served to arouse me more.

"It always felt like you were his."

His.

Griff's.

But I wasn't his. I'd ended things between us last year for a reason.

Before I could remind myself of that reason, Griff added, "This doesn't have to affect our friendship. I just want to help you sleep."

Oh, God. I practically melted at his words, remembering all too well that he'd said something similar after he'd taken my virginity seven years ago.

"We're family. That will never change."

He just wanted to help me. Help. And I desperately. *Desperately.* Needed it.

At the thought of him touching me in that way, a way I hadn't felt in so long, my mind emptied. Common sense fled me, and I nodded.

The second I did, a sound vibrated his chest. A growl. At how possessive it sounded, more arousal spiked through me. His arm around my middle lifted, and he flattened his hand over my stomach. As he splayed his fingers wide to span the entire length, my stomach went crazy with butterflies.

A breath stuttered out of me, and I curled my hands into fists.

Encouraged by my reaction, he slid his hand lower, making the butterflies flip and twirl until I thought I would be sick.

Friends. Childhood friends, I reminded myself as his fingers slipped inside my panties. *Good friends. Really good friends. But we were just—*

My lips parted in a silent moan as one of his fingers slid between my folds and found my aching clit. He pressed down, and I saw stars, my eyes rolling shut as bliss lit up my core. He started to rub my clit in tight circles, working it in a way that had me arching against him with a breathy gasp. His arm under my head bent and crossed over my chest, allowing him to slide a hand inside my bra and cup my breast.

I gasped again, placing my hand over his as he kneaded the sensitive flesh and coaxed the nipple to harden. When it peaked, he rolled it between his fingers and squeezed, making me see more stars.

"Griff," I whimpered and reached down with my other hand to guide his movements, urging him to go faster.

"I know how to pleasure you, Violet Jane," he breathed against my neck, nuzzling the spot that met my shoulder. "Let me do it."

I quivered in his arms, wholly turned on by his gentle dominance, not to mention his confidence. He *did* know how to pleasure me. That wasn't arrogance speaking. He'd always been an extremely attentive male, especially when it came to my pleasure, as if learning how to make my body sing was a passion project of his.

He slid his finger farther down and found my arousal, thoroughly coating the tip before pulling back up to rub my clit some more. At the added wetness, euphoria rushed through me, and I jerked against him with a groan. The action drove my backside against his erection, and he emitted a groan of his own, briefly pausing to press me hard against him.

The pressure of his entire hand against my core nearly made me come, and I stiffened all over. Sensing how close I was, Griff started to rub me again, this time at the pace I'd been hoping for. Struggling to breathe, I gripped both of his hands and trembled through the pleasurable onslaught, trying my best to keep silent. As I felt my orgasm begin to build, though, tiny breathless whimpers escaped my lips.

Griff rocked against me, his own breaths growing ragged. I felt his cock swell and knew that my pleasure was fueling his as it always had in the past. I didn't even have to touch him—my pleasure alone got him off. More than pleased that his body still responded to mine in this way, I shuddered through the pleasure a few seconds more, then let it consume me.

Biting my lip to muffle my scream, I came against his fingers, losing myself to the sea of ecstasy. As I did, he jerked against me with a guttural groan, spilling his release inside his briefs. I rode the high for several long blissful moments, allowing Griff to keep his hands where they were. He cradled me to him, his ragged breaths keeping time with mine.

When we finally came down, I was nothing but contentment in his arms. Sable purred within me, relaxed and calm in a way she hadn't been in a long time. Feeling a sense of peace settle over me, I easily drifted off to sleep.

CHAPTER 16

VIOLET

Griff and I stayed tucked away in our little cave longer than planned, loath to leave our warm cocoon. But when the rain stopped and the sky lightened to a slate gray, we forced our bodies into motion once more.

As we dressed, neither of us spoke about what had happened between us. We were both thinking about it, though. I could tell by the way Griff kept looking at me. Not directly, but when he thought I wouldn't notice. I knew he wanted to talk about it, but I had nothing to say. Nothing good, anyway.

I'd slipped up. End of story.

Yeah, it had felt good. *More* than good. Truthfully, I'd desperately missed being intimate with him. He always managed to make each moment feel like the first time, pouring every single ounce of his attention into *me*. That kind of attention was addicting. It made a girl feel desired. Special.

But now that I was thinking more clearly, I realized what a mistake it had been, and I had every intention of pretending it never happened. Only, as we took off again in a northeasterly direction, shifting our legs once more to cover ground faster, Griff made it clear he wasn't ready to let it go.

"Last night can be whatever you want it to be, Vi," he said. "You needed comfort, and I gave it to you. Just know that I'm here for you whenever you need me. That will never change."

Sudden guilt pierced my chest, and I forced myself to say, "Thanks, but that won't be happening again."

He didn't respond, and the guilt intensified, making it hard to breathe. I'd really screwed up this time, but it was better to tell him now than let him think I was open to being intimate again. That chapter was closed. *Closed.* It had to be, for both our sakes.

If only I hadn't forgotten that last night. If only I hadn't been *weak*.

Oh, Vi, Sable mournfully sighed.

Don't start, I firmly told her, and she thankfully lapsed into silence.

I expected Griff to do the same. He'd never been one to pressure me into speaking when it was clear I didn't want to. So he startled me again by saying, "Why did Reid break up with you?"

Heat flushed up my neck. It was on the tip of my tongue to say that it wasn't any of his business, but I'd already hurt him enough. The least I could do was give him an honest answer. Well, *half* of one anyway.

"He said I didn't want to be with him. My heart didn't, at least."

Griff mulled over my response before replying, "Was he right?"

I almost said no, but that would be a lie. Hopping over a felled tree, I answered, "Yes."

I cared about Reid, I really did. Any female would be lucky to be with him, but . . . but he'd been right. I'd never completely invested my heart in our relationship. I'd wanted to, yet something had held me back.

I flicked a glance at Griff to find him already watching me. Genuine empathy shone in his eyes as he said, "I'm sorry it didn't work out."

A lump formed in my throat, and I quickly looked away before he could see my tears. "I'm sorry, too."

Not about Reid.

About him and me. *Us.* About the relationship I'd ended before it had even begun. The relationship that should have always remained friendship and nothing more. And I was sorry for jeopardizing that again, for putting him into an unfair position. For treating him once more like a *security* blanket.

"Griff, I—" I started, feeling brave enough to finally tell him that. To repair the damage I had caused our friendship over the past several years. Before I could, he jerked up a hand and came to a dead stop. My heart immediately leapt into my throat, and I froze, throwing out my senses for any sign of our pursuers. When I couldn't hear anything, I whispered, "What is it?"

Griff inhaled deeply, then threw me a devilish grin and whispered back, "Breakfast."

When he started to strip, my eyes flew wide. "What are you doing?"

"Come on. It'll be faster this way."

As he removed his shirt and pants, I continued to protest. "But the carcass. Our pursuers will smell it."

"We'll bury it after. Our clothes too."

He tugged off his boxer briefs, and I quickly looked away. "Come on, Vi. We need food if we're going to keep running. We're still hours from civilization, and we have no idea how close our pursuers are. I say we give our wolves control for a while."

"And what will we wear when we shift back?"

"Guess we'll have to travel in the nude until we can find new clothes."

At the slight amusement in his tone, I threw him a glare. "I'm sure you'll enjoy that very much, but we don't have any money. If we make it back to civilization, we'll be walking around butt naked. Any humans that see us will think we're insane and call the cops."

"Sounds like a future problem," he said with a shrug. "We'll figure it out as we go."

With that, he dropped to all fours and started to shift.

Over the sound of breaking bones, Sable whined, *Give me control, Vi. I promise to be good. I won't let Whiskey mate with me, even if he tries.*

With a groan, I finally gave in, quickly stripping before dropping to all fours. The second I relinquished control to Sable, she gleefully surged to the surface and initiated the change. A minute later, she shook off the transformation with an excited yip and bounded toward Whiskey. As they took a few moments to nuzzle and lick each other, I grumbled, *You promised to behave.*

Killjoy, she grumbled back, giving him one final lick before getting down to business. She and Whiskey used their sharp claws to dig a hole in the damp earth, then buried our shredded clothing in it.

Good riddance. I never wanted to see that gaping tree-sized hole in Griff's shirt ever again.

When they finished, a loud growl rumbled through Sable's empty stomach. She whined softly, and Whiskey licked her cheek sympathetically. Then they took off into the trees, their strides in sync as they ran side by side. Not long after, they picked up the scent Griff had smelled earlier. Like a switch being flipped, they went into hunting mode, following the trail swiftly and with barely a sound. As the scent intensified, they split up, hunting their prey from opposite directions.

The move was like a choreographed dance, one they'd practiced countless times over the years. They'd always worked beautifully together, and I took a moment to silently appreciate the connection they shared. I knew they both wished that Griff and I would become mates so that *they* could become mates, but I couldn't forget my reason for denying them that bond.

It might seem cruel. It *was* cruel. But the alternative was so much worse.

At least they were still together. Not as mates, but this way, they didn't have to worry about being separated. About *losing* each other.

And neither would Griff and I.

Moments later, Whiskey let out an ear-piercing howl. Sable shivered with anticipation, barely controlling her excitement. A crashing sound through the trees alerted her to their prey, the howl's intent working as planned. The deer bounded to the left, frantically trying to escape Whiskey. In doing so, it headed directly for Sable. Putting on a fresh burst of speed, she lunged for the deer, opening her jaws wide.

The buck bleated in terror as Sable's teeth sank deeply into his side. Blood exploded in her mouth, and I tasted it right along with her. He tried to kick her off him, but Whiskey was there a second later, jumping onto his back. The two wolves easily brought the deer down, killing him within seconds.

Ravenous hunger burned in Sable's gut, and she immediately began to feast on her prize. Whiskey did too, but when Sable growled at him softly, he stopped eating to look at her.

Knowing what she was up to, I internally rolled my eyes. *Let him eat, Sabs.*

But we always do this, she said, staring him down while she fed.

Exactly. But you promised me you would be good.

I am.

This is foreplay. *You're trying to rev him up.*

I didn't promise I wouldn't make him horny.

Let him eat, Sable, I growled, done with her nonsense.

With a disgruntled huff, she lowered her eyes, giving Whiskey permission to feed. He seemed confused, but after a moment, he went back to eating. In no time, the two hungry wolves demolished the deer, then dug a hole to bury the remains in.

Tell me again why hybrid wolves can't portal? I muttered, impatiently waiting for them to slake their thirst at a nearby stream. It was still morning, and there hadn't been any sign of our pursuers yet, but I wasn't looking forward to the dangerous journey ahead.

Neither Griff nor I had told Kolton we were heading home early, but he'd probably discovered something had gone wrong by now. Knowing him, he was already searching for us, and that worried me. Our pursuers meant business, and if their weapons really were silver, even a powerful alpha could be killed. The sooner we found a phone, the better. Problem was, we were *literally* in the middle of nowhere. Even if we stumbled upon a random hunting cabin, there was no reception out here.

The ether won't accept us, Sable answered my question, raising her head to lick her lips clean. *The Universe demands balance, and allowing a spirit tied to the earthly plane—namely, one that's wholly contained in a single body—to traverse the celestial plane upsets that balance. It's why only witches and warlocks can portal. Their mortal bodies house only a small fraction of a spirit, so the ether doesn't see them as a threat.*

Still seems like discrimination to me, I replied with a huff.

She laughed quietly. *On the contrary. It keeps us immortals in check. Our limited ability to use magic on Earth keeps most spirits on the celestial plane instead of here. If we had access to our full power in these physical forms, it would incite Armageddon, and life as we know it on Earth would perish.*

Jeez, okay already, I muttered. *Guess I should be grateful your kind isn't trying to take over the world through our bodies.*

I wouldn't say that, she joked, her laughter turning dark.

You scare me sometimes, I said, not even a little amused.

Hey, I might be a she demon in another life, but that doesn't automatically make me evil. I chose you as my earthly host, and although some find that unethical, I would never take over your mind in order to control you.

I know, I gently said, realizing I'd struck a nerve. A nerve I was sensitive about as well. *You're not even remotely like Zuriel, and he's gone now. He can't hurt us or our family ever again. Neither can Arrow, now that he's free of him. Besides, Zuriel was an angel. I think demons are way cooler.*

Love flared through our bond. *Thank you, Vi. I think you're pretty cool too. A bit stubborn at times, especially about your feelings for—*

Okay, okay, stop while you're ahead. Now get your furry butt going so I can sleep in a real *bed tonight.*

The cave was warm and cozy, though, and that orgasm was amazing. You haven't felt that relaxed since—

La-la-la, not listening! I yelled, drowning her out.

With a snort, she turned from the stream. Whiskey immediately did the same, and they took off once more. With their bellies full, they easily covered lots of ground. We'd been knocked off course last night and had traveled west instead of north, but at the pace our wolves were going now, we should reach Lake Placid in a couple hours.

Around noon, the sun finally broke through the heavy clouds like a little ray of hope. We were almost there. We were going to make it. Sable and Whiskey surged forward, energized by the thought of almost being home. Sable pulled ahead, her eagerness making her fly over the forest floor at breakneck speed. I saw the sun catch on something shiny up ahead a second too late.

Before I could warn her, a sharp *whoosh* cleaved the air, and a huge net swallowed her whole.

CHAPTER 17

GRIFF

Whiskey was *livid*.

The net that had snatched up Sable and left her dangling several feet off the ground was coated in silver. When she cried out in pain, he started to shift. Not into my human form, but into his true form. His *demonic* form.

His hind legs lengthened, transforming into a shape that allowed him to stand upright. Muscles rippled over his already muscular body, beefing up his chest and biceps. His paws became monstrous hands tipped in long deadly claws, and I felt his canines descend even more. His coat was still a tawny hue, but I knew his eyes were now flashing a deep blood red.

I allowed the shift without question, his anger and desperation fueling my own. They'd set a trap for us. They knew we'd go this way. Knew we'd return *home*. And we'd walked right into it.

Whiskey tipped back his massive head and belted out an unearthly roar. Sable answered it with several pitiful whimpers, helplessly thrashing in the net. I could see now that it wasn't made out of rope but some kind of metal. Probably steel. The rattling sound drove Whiskey into a frenzy, and all nine feet of muscular demon wolf lunged for the trap. As he latched on to it, the contraption holding the net up bent and snapped under his weight, and Sable fell.

He caught her before she could hit the ground, then set her down to claw at the silver-coated links. Burning flesh and fur permeated the air, but Whiskey ignored the pain, his sole focus on saving his female. Sable tried to help, but it was clear that the close contact with silver was already weakening her.

Afraid that the hunters were nearby, ready to shoot Whiskey before he could free Sable from the net, I urged him to go faster. He redoubled his efforts, breaking link after link until a gap formed, large enough to pull Sable from the trap. She whined as he dragged her out, several patches of her beautiful dark coat burned away by the silver. When he set her down, she struggled and failed to stand.

He immediately picked her up in his massive arms, cradling her to him tenderly. "Shift, beloved," he said in his deep, gravelly voice. "Let me carry you."

With one last whine, she lifted her head to lick his muzzle, then relinquished control to Vi. The second Vi's petite frame took Sable's place, I finally allowed myself to breathe. I looked down at her through Whiskey's eyes, taking in the angry red burns on her flesh. They were already healing but not fast enough.

Taking control of Whiskey, I carefully maneuvered Vi's body so I could gently touch her cheek with one of his large fingers. Her lips tipped up in a faint smile, and she weakly lifted a hand to pat him on the snout.

"Sable and I will be fine, Whisk. Now get us out of here before those hunters arrive."

"Your wish is my command, fair lady," he gallantly replied, making her smile grow.

Before taking off, he licked her palm with his big tongue, and a sudden possessiveness tightened my chest.

A gravelly laugh that sounded like a distant rockslide rumbled from him. *Easy there, chap. I'm only licking her as a friend. Then again, she seems to* like *male friends licking her, so maybe you should be worried.*

Watch it, I tightly growled at him.

With another laugh, he surged into motion, loping through the forest on his powerful hind legs with Vi held securely against him. Now that the immediate danger was over, I could sense that the contact with silver had taken a toll on him as well. Although he could easily take on a handful of unshifted werewolves in his current state, I couldn't discount their weapons or Vi and Sable's condition.

Go west, I reluctantly told him. *We can't head for home like this. The hunters could be lying in wait for us.*

He huffed in annoyance but didn't argue with me. The females' safety came first. One glance at Vi, and we found her fast asleep. Good. She'd heal quicker that way.

Whiskey loped through the woods for hours without slowing. He probably would have continued on for several more if I asked him to, but I didn't want to completely undo all the progress we'd made. With a little rest and some food, we should be well enough to face the hunters and their weapons and traps. It was the only way we were going to get home again.

As the sun started to fade into the trees, I urged Whiskey to search for shelter. We were approaching a small lake when he suddenly slowed, his gaze shooting to the far side. At the sight of a log-cabin style house, I said, *Let's go check it out.*

Whiskey wasn't so eager, nervously pacing beside the lake until Vi stirred awake in his arms.

"What's wrong?" she groggily asked, rubbing at her eyes before opening them to look around. When she spotted the house, she immediately perked up. "Oh, thank God. They could have a landline."

As she wiggled in his arms, Whiskey reluctantly set her down. She took off at once, running along the lake's edge toward the house in all her naked glory. Whiskey charged after her, and I couldn't help but chuckle a little at how overprotective he was acting.

You would be too, but you're too busy staring at her pretty backside, he grumbled.

True. I was enjoying the view. But the nap had done wonders for her, and my worry lessened the longer I watched her gracefully move. Besides, I couldn't hear any sounds coming from the house. No one was home.

Feeling the need to run beside her, I said to Whiskey, *Give me back control.*

Now it was his turn to chuckle. *Feeling frisky, mate?*

When it came to Vi? Always. But he already knew that.

Confident that I had my eye on her, he let the change sweep over us. We paused only briefly while our bones shifted into place like a jigsaw puzzle; then I took off in human form, quickly catching up with Vi. When I pulled even with her, her gaze dipped to my wagging cock.

"Like what you see?" I couldn't help but tease, smirking when her eyes jerked up to mine.

With a scowl, she shoved me, hard enough that I lost my balance and tumbled into the lake. As I submerged beneath the water, Whiskey howled with laughter.

She got you good, my man. Looks like you're not the only one feeling frisky.

I popped back up a moment later, opening my eyes to see a grinning Vi. The sight took my breath away, and I accepted her hand with a good-natured laugh. As she pulled me onto solid ground, I shook my head like a dog, spraying her with water.

She yelped and tried to shove me again, but I snaked an arm around her waist and swung her around, pretending like I was about to throw her in. Kicking her feet, she shrieked and demanded I let her down, all while holding back laughter.

I set her down, my arm still around her as I grinned like a fiend. "Say 'Uncle.'"

She mock-glared at me, her hands on my chest while I kept her firmly in place. "We're not kids anymore, Griff. Aren't we a little old for this game?"

"You're never too old for a game of Uncle," I purred, tightening my hold on her. "Say it, or the Tickle Monster's gonna get you."

Her eyes widened. "Don't you dare. I need to pee."

I barked a laugh. "All you have to do is say it. One little word, and I'll set you free."

Instead of submitting, she started to thrash against me like a feral animal. I grinned even wider and crushed her to me, using my free hand to tickle her side. She screamed like she was being tortured, but I didn't let up, relentlessly tickling her until she had no choice but to laugh. She laughed and laughed, her body going limp against me. Still, she wouldn't surrender, so I continued to tickle her.

"I have to . . ." she gasped out between giggles. "I have to *pee!*"

"Say the word, Vi, and this will all be over," I crooned, barely avoiding her attempt to knee me in the balls. "Naughty girl. For that, you get *The Claw.*"

"No!" she wailed, weakly squirming as I lengthened my nails into claws and ran them over her stomach. She choked on more laughter, struggling to breathe. But after only a moment of enduring the torture, she burst out, "Uncle!"

The second I stopped tickling her, she shoved at my chest. *Hard.* I released her, and she stumbled back.

"What's wrong?" I asked, confused, but she turned and took off without explanation. Not before I caught a whiff of something familiar, though. Something alluring and wholly intoxicating. Something she *clearly* didn't want me to smell.

Her arousal.

"Vi, wait. It's okay," I said, going after her.

"No, it's not," she tossed over her shoulder, picking up speed until she was almost jogging.

"Why not?" I dared to press, matching her pace. "Because you only see me as your brother's best friend?"

There. I finally said it. I held my breath, anticipating and dreading her answer. Hoping. Preparing. Imagining all the different things she could say.

"What? No. Well, sort of, but it's more complicated than that. You know it is."

"I don't think I do. We're two consenting, unclaimed adults who are sexually attracted to each other. What's the harm in exploring that?"

She stopped dead, and I halted in my tracks as well.

"The harm?" she quietly said, slowly turning to face me. "It harms *everything*. My future. Yours. Sable's and Whiskey's. We're supposed to be moving on. *You're* supposed to be moving on. We can't cross that line again. Our friendship is too important, and giving in to these *feelings* will only jeopardize what we have."

"But what if I don't *want* to move on? What if I have everything I need right here?"

At that, she sucked in a gasp. I waited for her to say something, and it was hands down the most excruciating thing I'd ever endured.

After what felt like an eternity, she shook her head and said, "You don't mean that. I remember how upset you were when I told Nora you helped me during my heat. And when your brother mentioned it at the Alpha Meeting last year, I had to stop you from attacking him.

I know you never wanted that to happen between us, so you can stop trying to protect my feelings, Griff. I set you *free*. You're not obligated to help me in that way anymore. I'm a big girl and can take care of my own needs, including my heat. How do you think I survived this past year?"

The ache in my chest grew with each word she uttered, making it harder and harder to breathe. Wrong. She was so wrong. About *everything*. I opened my mouth to tell her so, to set the record straight about all the terrible things she believed were true. But the last thing she said struck me the hardest, and I found myself demanding, "What do you mean 'including my heat'? What did you do, Vi?"

She suddenly looked like a deer caught in the headlights. She started to look away, but I stepped forward and grabbed her chin, forcing her gaze back to mine.

"What. Did. You. Do?" I slowly enunciated, making sure she felt every last ounce of my dominant energy.

Her bottom lip quivered, but I didn't let up, continuing to stare at her intensely. She fought it. Fought *me*. But in the end, she broke. Her face crumpled, and she replied through trembling lips, "I went to the bunker."

My heart stopped beating. "When?" I asked, gentling my voice.

"Th-three months ago. I didn't know what else to do. Reid and I weren't having sex, and I've only ever been with you. But I couldn't . . . I couldn't ask you to help me, and . . . I got through it, though. It was painful, but no other males found me and I didn't die."

When she released a shaky laugh as if to play off the undoubtedly hellish experience, my heart broke.

"Oh, Vi," I hoarsely whispered. "I'm so sorry. I didn't know."

She laughed again, pulling her chin out of my grip so she could wipe away a tear. "You weren't supposed to know, Griff. We're *friends*, and that's the way it needs to stay."

And we were back to that. *Friends.* Only this time, I didn't feel like accepting it.

I opened my mouth, prepared to challenge her. To press. To *push.* We'd been suffering long enough, caught in a limbo of unspoken feelings and secret pining. *Mutual* pining. Her words were saying one thing, but her body was saying something entirely different. This misery had to end. I needed to tell her. Needed to voice the words I should have uttered *years* ago. Before another excruciating second could pass, I needed the female before me to know how I really felt.

"Vi, I—"

"We should go," she abruptly said, cutting me off. An almost desperate look crossed her face, and she quickly turned, resuming her jog toward the house.

With a frustrated sigh, I moved to follow her.

She thinks you don't want her, Whiskey quietly said. *She thinks you're ashamed to be with her, like Arrow was.*

His words nearly brought me to my knees. I placed a hand over my chest, half expecting the hole to have reopened.

How could she think that? How could she *believe* that? After all we'd been through together, how could she not see how I felt about her?

I opened my mouth again, but shockingly, it was Whiskey who stayed my tongue this time. *Not right now, lad. She's a proud female— one that's feeling raw and exposed at the moment. Give her time to compose herself.*

I forced my mouth shut again, knowing he was right. I wouldn't wait long, though. It was time she knew the truth, whether she was ready to hear it or not. I couldn't let her go another day believing those lies.

It no longer mattered if she felt the same way. No longer mattered if she rejected me for good this time.

For her, I would strip myself bare. For her, I would risk *everything*.

CHAPTER 18

VIOLET

My heart wouldn't stop racing. I hadn't meant to tell Griff that much.

Especially about taking care of my last heat at the bunker. *Alone.*

He no doubt pitied me but was too nice to say so. And that was the problem. He was too *nice.* Too nice to push me away. Too nice to make me deal with the harsh realities of life on my own. He'd always been there for me no matter what, just like he'd promised me seven years ago.

Only I realized now how selfish I'd been to accept that promise. To accept his help and comfort over and over again without thinking about how *he* felt. Without asking if he even *wanted* to be with me in that way.

Deep down, though, I'd always wondered. Always assumed he'd chosen to pursue me out of pity. Because he was too *nice.* Because he was my brother's best friend. It was almost like he'd *expected* to help me with my heat when the time came. Jagger certainly wasn't going to do it, and Mason . . .

Well, Griff's older brother had tried to pursue me, but I'd known he'd only done so to get closer to Kolton. To rise in the pack ranks. And to piss off his brother, of course.

It had been easy to reject him. But Griff, on the other hand . . .

He'd always been my greatest source of comfort. My *security* blanket.

Rejecting him was next to impossible, and ending things between us last year had nearly broken me. I'd needed to do it, though. Needed to do it before something terrible happened.

He was nice. Probably the nicest male I'd ever known. But it wasn't fair of me to take advantage of that. To *exploit* it. Eventually, he would have grown to resent me, so I'd left before he could leave me. Before the damage became irreparable.

Letting him go so he could find a female worthy of being his mate had been the most selfless thing I'd ever done. I thought for sure we could both move on yet still remain good friends. As long as he was in my life, I could survive it if he pursued another female.

But as he followed me toward the empty house, it hurt. It still hurt to be this close to him. To keep rejecting him, especially after he'd confessed words I couldn't get out of my head. Confusing words that didn't make any sense.

I couldn't possibly be everything he needed. He deserved so much more than what I'd been willing to give him. He was only saying that to spare my feelings. It was obvious that our wolves were head-over-heels for each other. Whiskey was probably struggling to accept other females in Griff's life the same way Sable struggled to accept other males. Their feelings often bled into ours, making it hard to differentiate them.

The attraction Griff felt toward me had no doubt originated from those feelings. Even more, he probably never would have offered to help with my heat if it wasn't for Whiskey and Sable's connection. But it was clear he didn't fully see that; otherwise, he wouldn't have started to pursue me again.

Reid had been right. I needed space from Griff. We were making the same mistakes all over again, and I was terrified of the consequences should it continue. But this past chaotic week had forced us back together, and I couldn't seem to distance myself from him no matter how hard I tried.

It didn't help that we were currently traipsing through the woods naked, running on adrenaline highs, and heading toward an empty house together.

Yeah, I was screwed. So screwed.

Still, I ignored him and my racing heart as best I could, focusing on finding a way inside the cabin without breaking anything. The door was locked, of course, and so were all the windows on the first floor. Griff easily hoisted himself up to a second-floor balcony in back, then checked the french doors. As they swung open, he looked over the railing at me with a victorious grin.

I grinned back before I could stop myself. He was just so . . . so *Griff*. Always finding ways to help. Always brightening even the most bleak situation with his wit and contagious smiles. I definitely wouldn't have gotten this far without him.

As he disappeared inside the house, a thought formed. I tried to shake it off, but it persisted. Touching my arm, I turned the idea over for a moment longer, then headed around to the front of the house. Griff greeted me at the door, still grinning as he opened it wide for me to enter.

"Any sign of a phone?" I asked, stepping into the foyer.

"No. I think this is a vacation home. The human scents are faint like no one's been inside for weeks, and the fridge is empty."

Running a hand through my tangled hair, I sighed in disappointment. "Well, keep looking. We'll reimburse the owners for our stay after we get home. I'm going to take a shower, but holler if the hunters arrive. I have a bone to pick with them."

Cracking another smile, he nodded and moved aside so I could brush past. I almost stopped and told him of my idea, then chickened out and hurried toward the stairs. A hot shower was just what I needed to clear my head. It was getting harder and harder to think straight around him.

After a blissfully long shower, though, I still couldn't get the idea out of my head. I stayed upstairs long enough to blow-dry my hair and slip into a white terry cloth robe, then went in search of Griff. I found him standing at the wide windows in the living room that overlooked the lake.

Still naked.

His back was turned to me, and I allowed my gaze to take him in. Even after two decades of seeing him in various stages of undress, I never failed to appreciate how perfectly sculpted his body was. A sudden urge to caress his skin with my fingertips shivered through me, and I bit back a frustrated curse.

"Take your time," Griff lightly teased, still facing the windows. "I always enjoy being admired. Why do you think I walk around naked so often?"

"Jagger used to tell me you have a skin condition that doesn't allow you to wear clothing for long periods of time without breaking into hives."

Griff barked a laugh. "He's always been jealous of my cavalier nature. And the fact that my dick is bigger than his."

I snorted. "Sure you wanna stick with that story? I've seen both of your dicks."

"Why, Violet Jane," he said, turning toward me with mock surprise. "Are you trying to make me jealous? 'Cause it's working."

I rolled my eyes, fighting back a smile. Remembering my idea, I quickly sobered and, before I could chicken out again, blurted, "I want you to bind us."

The mock surprise on his face immediately transformed into *real* surprise. "Bind? With *this?*"

When he lifted his right arm to point at the dark snake tattoo wrapped around his forearm, I nodded.

"Why?" he asked, furrowing his brow.

I nervously bit my lip before admitting, "Because those hunters obviously want to kidnap me and are going to great lengths to do so. If they're successful—"

"They won't be."

"If they *are* and we get separated, I want to ensure we're able to find each other again."

His frown deepened. "You don't think we're going to make it back home?"

"I didn't say that, but . . . several hybrid females have been taken already. These hunters are skilled, and I want to be prepared, just in case."

He studied me for a long moment, then said, "The binding spell is dangerous. It's infused with dark magic and can be unpredictable. You saw what happened to Nora when Kolton performed it on her."

"Because she tried to *break* it. The pain only flared up when she attempted to back out of their deal. If you perform the ritual with me, I can guarantee I won't try to break it. Not willingly anyway."

His lips thinned. When he didn't respond, I prepared to put up a fight. But he surprised me a moment later by saying, "Okay."

I blinked at him. "Okay?"

"Yes. It's a good idea. Just in case."

I nodded in agreement. "Just in case."

"With one condition."

I raised an eyebrow. "Name it."

"We seal the deal with that kiss you promised me."

I stopped breathing.

Seeing the shocked look on my face, he took a step forward. "Just one kiss, Vi. One little kiss. Seems like a small price to pay for my snake."

I knew he meant the tattoo, but my eyes darted below his waist all the same. Curse my stupid eyeballs. When they looked back up at Griff's face again, his lips were curling into a knowing smirk.

"Shut up," I said before he could say whatever teasing remark was in his brain. He didn't say a word, but his smirk grew. Forcing my gaze to remain on his and not that wicked mouth, I blew out a sigh and muttered, "Fine. You have a deal."

The second I agreed, his chocolate eyes turned molten. Great. He definitely wasn't planning on this being a quick peck. At the realization, my body eagerly warmed, making my skin feel way too hot in the robe.

Traitor, I hissed at my overactive libido.

But my fear of being separated from Griff kept me from backing out of the deal. It was a kiss. One kiss. It wasn't like he asked me to have sex with him.

I could handle a kiss. One last kiss between friends, right?

As I felt a drop of sweat slither down my spine, Griff gestured for me to sit on the living room couch. I stiffly perched on a cushion, watching him slowly approach me. Expecting him to sit beside me, he startled me by kneeling on the rug at my feet. Our eyes were level now, and something about the position felt intimate. He wasn't even touching me, but I almost couldn't stand the sudden tension sparking between us.

Not knowing what to do next, I waited for his direction. He searched my face for a moment, as if to make sure I was truly okay with this. I stared back, silently assuring him I was. With a small nod, he held out his hand to me and said, "Violet Jane Rivers, do you wish to bind yourself to me?"

Ah, hell. That almost sounded like a marriage proposal. Why did I think this would be a good idea?

Too late to back out now.

Swallowing hard, I forced my fist to unclench and placed my trembling hand in his. "I do," I whispered.

His eyes flared brightly, and he gripped my hand tightly, murmuring a single word in Latin: *"Conecto."*

An electrical charge immediately zapped my palm, making me jump. Griff held fast to my hand, using his free one to push up the sleeve of my robe. I glanced down just as the snake tattoo that he, Kolton, and Jagger had all gotten several years ago started to move. Fascinated by the magic that allowed a tattoo to come alive, I watched the snake slither off Griff's skin and onto mine. It wrapped around my forearm once, twice, three times, the black head coming to rest near my elbow.

"Cool," I said, admiring the snake's detailed skin. Griff let go of my hand, only to trace a finger down the snake's body like he was petting it. Except that he was petting my *arm*, and the skin pebbled pleasantly at his touch. To cover up my body's reaction, I glanced up at him and teased, "Miss your snake already?"

He cracked a small smile, continuing to stroke my arm. "It looks good on you."

As he slowly met my gaze, I tried to swallow and failed. His irises were still bright, and there was no mistaking the message in them. It was time to hold up my end of the deal.

"What now?" I quietly asked, knowing all too well what was next.

Still, he humored me by answering, "We kiss."

As my heart started to race, his finger on my arm stilled.

Watching me closely, he added, "But only if you want to as badly as I do."

Oh, God. Why? Why did he have to say stuff like *that?*

Barely able to breathe, I managed to whisper, "Griff?"

"Hmm?"

"Shut up and kiss me already."

His nostrils flared, and his eyes glowed even brighter. I knew from experience that Whiskey was riding him hard right now, encouraging him to kiss me. But I suddenly didn't care. Even if Griff only wanted to kiss me because his wolf familiar wanted him to, the need to feel his lips on mine one last time was all I could think about.

So when he leaned forward, lifting his hand to grip my nape, I held perfectly still. And when he brought our heads slowly together, watching me the entire time, I didn't look away. I didn't flinch. Didn't protest. Didn't do anything but allow it to happen.

He obviously wanted to take his time, though. Each movement was calculated, as if his intention was to milk the experience for all it was worth.

One kiss? Fine. He was going to make it a kiss worth remembering. A kiss that left a mark similar to the one now on my arm. A brand. A *claim*, so to speak. Not a claim between mates, but a claim nonetheless.

He wanted to kiss me so I would never forget. Forget *what*, I didn't know. Forget him? Impossible. He'd crawled inside me and imprinted on my soul a long time ago. This kiss wasn't going to change anything.

Or so I thought.

The first sweep of his lips over mine, I knew I was done for. The charge that had been building between us burst, and I sucked in a sharp gasp. He paused to soak up my reaction, his mouth scant centimeters from mine. The tension started to build again, the electrical charge crackling in the breath of space between us. I fisted the robe in my lap, forcing myself to draw air. Air that was laced with his spicy clove and cinnamon scent. Air that we were *sharing*. Every breath that left him entered me, and every breath I expelled entered him.

Holy hell, what was this? We'd never done this before. Never shared breath as if feeding each other oxygen. It was intimate. *Erotic*. And every breath I accepted from him warmed my insides and left me trembling for more.

"Griff," I softly whimpered, needing more so badly that I felt sick.

He inhaled my whimper, watching me tremble for another moment before brushing another kiss over my mouth. The electrical charge burst again. Only this time, it zipped through my insides, heading straight for my clit. When it struck, I stiffened all over with another strangled gasp, shocked when my core fluttered with a small orgasm.

A kiss. A *kiss* did that.

Griff released a low growl, and I knew he'd just scented my arousal. "Open your legs for me, Violet," he said in a guttural tone, then wedged his body between them when I complied. "Now open your mouth," he continued, with such authority that my core fluttered again.

The second I obeyed him, he grabbed one of my hips and plunged his tongue into my mouth. As it firmly stroked mine, the world exploded around me. His scent and taste ensnared my senses, and I arched against him with a low moan, letting my eyes roll shut. His hold on me tightened, drawing our mouths and bodies closer together. My hands raised to grip his neck and hair, and my legs lifted to securely lock behind his waist. The move pried open my robe, and I remembered too late that I was naked underneath. That *he* was naked.

His hot arousal pressed against my throbbing core, and I

breathlessly cried out into his mouth. He went feral at the sound, feverishly thrusting his tongue against mine. His hand on my hip pulled me closer still, making the deep dorsal vein in his shaft rub my clit. When the friction grew wet with my arousal, it was his turn to moan into my mouth.

I full-body shuddered, completely turned on by the sound. We kissed and rocked against each other for several long moments, long enough that I was about to lie back on the couch. About to encourage him on top of me. About to *beg* him to slide that glorious dick inside me. I was ravenous for him. *Obsessed.* Had it always been this good between us?

Yes. *Hell,* yes.

I'd just forced myself to forget. To move on.

But why? Why would I want to forget and move on from *this*?

Nothing compared to this. He was the only male I'd ever been intimate with, but I knew, just *knew* that no other male could compare. I'd been kissed by a handful of other males before, and the kisses had been nice. But Griff brought me to life. He set me on fire and made me *sing*. He—

He abruptly broke the kiss and pulled back, breathing heavily. When he stopped rocking too, I peeled open my eyes with a disappointed whimper.

"Why did you stop?" I asked, my mind a haze of lust and confusion.

"Because the deal was a *kiss*, not sex," he replied, his own eyes clouded with desire. "I just wanted you to know."

"Know what?"

"That I want you. That I've never been ashamed to be with you. You aren't an obligation to me, Vi. Never have been, never will be."

"Griff . . ."

"No, it's *my* turn to speak now, Vi, and you're going to listen," he said, giving my head a little shake. "I love you."

I lost the ability to breathe. "I . . . I love you too, Griff. We're family."

"No, Vi. Not like that." Tugging one of my hands free, he pressed it firmly to his thundering heart. "You feel that? It beats for you. *Only* you. Have you ever wondered why I've never pursued other females since being with you? Because you're all I see. You're the first thing I think about when I wake up and the only thing I dream about when I fall asleep. I've been wrapped around your little finger for as long as I can remember, and there's no disentangling myself from you. You're the one for me, the *only* one. And even if you continue to see me as only a friend, I needed you to know how I truly felt."

I stared at him, my eyes wide as I tried to comprehend all that he'd just said.

When I didn't say anything, he pressed a soft kiss to my forehead and whispered, "No matter what, I'll be here for you. Never forget that."

With one final kiss, he let go of me and stood, then silently left the room.

CHAPTER 19

VIOLET

I was scarfing down the second bag of Doritos I'd found in the kitchen when Sable's voice finally invaded my thoughts.

Girl, he just handed you the moon. Why are you stuffing your face with junk food right now instead of swooning?

I shoved another Dorito into my mouth without answering. Honestly, I *should* be swooning. I'd never heard Griff say something so beautiful before. Each word had been open. Raw. *Genuine.* I couldn't stop replaying them in my head. Couldn't stop weaving them into the tapestry of our past.

Yes, I'd always wondered why he hadn't pursued other females, even while he was helping me with my heat. I'd never had a claim on him, and he could have dated whenever he wanted. And yet he hadn't.

I'd assumed his promise to me, his feelings of *obligation* toward me, had stopped him from moving on with his life. Not because he *loved* me. The kind of love that terrified the hell out of me.

He said that he wanted me. That he *saw* me. But for how long?

Sighing, I set down the Dorito bag and turned toward the stairs. He'd gone up to take a shower, and I could still hear the water running. We'd only been here for about half an hour, but I already felt the itch to keep moving. We were so close to home and yet so far away. The others were undoubtedly frantic with worry by now.

I pulled up my robe sleeve to study the snake tattoo again. I didn't regret the decision to bind myself to Griff, even if doing so made things that much more complicated between us. With this tattoo on my arm, he could find me anywhere. It was like a tracking device, one that sent signals directly to his brain. If those hunters *did* manage to separate us, I could hold on to hope that Griff would find his way back to me.

But, for the first time ever, I wondered if he would even *want* to. If he'd wash his hands of me and walk out of my life forever if . . . if I pushed him away again.

Burying the awful thought before it could finish forming, I straightened my spine and headed for the stairs. He'd just poured his heart out to me, and I'd left him hanging. The very least I could do was talk to him. About what, I wasn't entirely sure. I knew he wanted me to say the words back, to be open and honest like he'd been with me. But . . . but I wasn't ready.

Wasn't ready to bare my soul and let him see what a terrible mistake he'd made. I wasn't strong enough for that yet. Probably never would be.

My heart felt heavy as I trudged up the stairs and walked down the hall to the bathroom he occupied. I raised my hand to knock, then rolled my eyes and reached for the handle.

This was *Griff*. I might be drowning in self doubt and fear, but he was still the nice guy I'd grown up with. Still the fun-loving goofball that got under my skin yet made me laugh like no other.

Twisting the handle, I opened the door and stepped inside. As I did, he looked up from washing his hair, and our eyes met. All the words he'd spoken downstairs suddenly came rushing back at me, and I almost looked away. Pursing my lips, I pushed past my cowardice and moved to hop onto the counter. He silently watched me, continuing to rinse the shampoo from his blond hair. We'd been in this position countless times over the years, casually chatting while one of us took a shower or bath.

It had never been awkward before. Until now.

And I hated it. Hated that I was the reason. Me and my stupid baggage.

"How long have you felt this way?" I asked him before I could chicken out. "About . . . about me."

"A long time. Way before your betrothal to Arrow," he replied. "I was devastated when your parents made the announcement, but what could I do? You were only fifteen, and I couldn't offer you what Arrow could. My feelings didn't matter."

"Of course they matter," I protested, hating that he'd endured these feelings alone all these years, even while I'd dated Reid. No wonder he hadn't wanted me to move in with him. "Is that why you scared off all the guys I tried to date in high school?"

Griff cracked a small smile. "Yes, but also because they were dicks. None of them deserved you."

I opened my mouth, then thought better of it and quietly said, "What about Reid? Did *he* deserve me?"

Griff searched my face through the glass before replying, "Not if you didn't want to be with him."

Hmm. Guess I couldn't argue with that one.

Tilting my head, I decided to ask, "Why didn't you tell me sooner?"

"I didn't think you were ready to hear it. I tried to at the Alpha Meeting last year, but before I could get the words out, you ended things between us."

I froze, dredging up the painful memory to replay it in my mind. His brother, Mason, had just finished calling him my little heat whore, and I'd quickly stepped in before Griff could punch him. Recalling how furious Griff had been, I replied, "After I saw how upset you were by what Mace said, I thought *you* were going to end things between us. I thought . . . I thought you were embarrassed to be with me, so I decided to let you go so you wouldn't have to. So you could finally be free to pursue your own mate."

Crap. I hadn't meant to tell him all that. I immediately felt naked, even with the fluffy robe on.

As his expression fell, I wanted nothing more than to scurry away with my tail between my legs. Pitiful. I was *pitiful*.

Before I could, though, he said in a hoarse voice, "Did you ever think, just once, that I *was* pursuing my mate?"

My breath caught.

He lowered his arms, his hands forming fists at his sides as he continued, "It bothered me every time your heat was mentioned because I didn't want anyone to think I was with you only for the sex. I didn't want *you* to think that. I've always wanted us to become more. But months turned into years and that never happened."

"I didn't . . . I-I didn't think you wanted more," I whispered, so quietly that I doubted he could hear it over the rushing water.

But he did, staring at me with such deep intensity that I shivered. "Well, I *do* want more. I want it so badly that I can barely think straight most days. I'm envisioning all the ways I want more with you right now, current danger be damned."

Good God, I didn't know how to handle this side of Griff. I could get lost in it so easily. Even more terrifying, I *wanted* to get lost in it. I wanted to *submit* to it. Not as an omega would, but as an alpha female would to her mate because . . . because she felt *safe*.

And that was dangerous. So very dangerous.

I'd never been one to hide from danger, but that's all I seemed to be doing lately. I realized how cruel it was to leave Griff hanging again, but I'd rather face the *hunters* than continue down this nerve-racking path a second longer.

I wasn't ready. I wasn't ready for this all to blow up in my face.

"We should go," I abruptly said, jumping off the counter. "If we don't leave soon, the hunters could catch up to us."

As I hurried toward the door, Griff stopped me with one word. "Stay."

I froze, quietly cursing under my breath. "Griff, I—"

"*Stay*, Vi. Stay and let me prove just how much I want more with you. Please. We can leave right after."

I squeezed my eyes shut, barely able to stand under the weight of his words. After all that he'd done for me, after all that he'd *said*, how could I possibly deny him? I'd almost lost him in that plane crash, and it made me realize even more how much I needed him in my life. The thought of rejecting him now when he was being so vulnerable with me was more than I could bear.

I could feel Sable urging me to stay, could sense how much she wanted this for me. What's more, my body felt the same way, all but chanting, *Stay, stay, stay*.

God, I wanted him. I couldn't deny that. Griff had a way of anchoring me in the present so that for a blissful moment in time, I completely forgot about the past. Being with him made me feel *whole* again. Like the girl I'd been before my family broke apart and left me to pick up the pieces.

I desperately wanted to be that girl again. To experience the carefree confidence Griff made me feel when I was with him.

He said he wanted me. Said he *loved* me.

I was safe with him. Safe with my blond-haired, puppy-eyed security blanket.

For now.

But now might be all we had *left*. I knew all too well how quickly everything could change and fall apart.

One last time. One last passionate moment with the male who made me feel like the girl I used to be.

Without a word, I untied my robe, letting it fall to the floor before turning around. Our eyes met and held for a long moment; then I moved to join him.

CHAPTER 20

GRIFF

She came. She came to *me*.

She'd never come to me like this before. I'd always been the one to go to her. When she needed me, I was there. She asked, and I gave. That's how our relationship had worked for years.

But I'd finally dared to push, dared to pursue her, dared to express my own needs.

I'd asked her, and . . . and she'd come.

As she approached, my dick started to harden. It couldn't be helped, but she didn't seem to mind. In fact, her eyes dipped below my waist as if she knew the effect she had on me. And when her gaze lingered, my cock stiffened even more, proudly saluting the air. She continued to eye it, and I half expected it to start wagging like a golden retriever's tail.

"Keep staring at me like that, and I'm going to come," I gruffly told her.

A little smirk tilted her lips. "Wouldn't be the first time."

At the playful way she said it, I had the sudden urge to howl, roll on the floor, and show her my belly.

Whiskey, get out of my thoughts, I growled at my familiar.

But you used to like it when I helped guide your movements, he huffed in disappointment. *I know Vi definitely liked it.*

This moment is for me and her only. She's struggling to accept what I told her, so I need to handle this carefully.

He huffed again, but I knew he understood. Vi hadn't said she loved me back. Hell, she hadn't even said she *wanted* me.

But she was here. She'd stayed, and that said more than any words could. I wasn't just a friend to her. She had feelings for me. Just how deep they were, I didn't know, but I was willing to find out slowly. To move forward at the pace she wanted, no matter how excruciating that may be.

She was my future, and we had all the time in the world to explore our feelings.

Even so, I could barely contain my excitement when she stopped before the shower door and our eyes met again. I didn't move a muscle. Didn't even blink. The only sound was the steady rush of water from the showerhead.

The decision was hers to leave or stay. If she left, I would be heartbroken, but I didn't want her to stay if she didn't want to. I openly conveyed that message with my eyes, hoping she could see it. Hoping she knew the choice was hers and hers alone. No matter how I felt, I would never force myself on her. She could walk away from this forever, and I would respect that decision.

But I ached for her to stay. Ached for her to open the shower door and join me. I longed for it so deeply that I couldn't breathe. My heart started to thunder, and I grew lightheaded as I continued to wait, hoping with all of my heart that she would—

She lifted a hand and opened the glass door, and I nearly dropped to my knees in relief. Still, I didn't move, watching her slowly step inside and shut the door behind her. But as vulnerability flashed in her eyes, I eased forward, raising my hand to tuck a lock of hair behind her ear.

"If at any time you don't want this, just say the word," I gently said, letting my hand linger on her face.

Her swallow was audible, and she nervously nodded.

"Hey," I soothingly said, reaching up to cup her other cheek. "It's *me*, Violet. You have nothing to be nervous about."

She huffed an embarrassed laugh. "I know. It's just . . . It's different this time. And I haven't . . . I haven't done it in so long."

I gave her a small smile. "Me neither. I might have even forgotten how to do it."

Just like I'd hoped, she scoffed at the joke. "Yeah, right. You probably have a sex doll in your closet."

My brows rose. "Now there's an idea. Why didn't I think of that?"

She poked my chest. "Don't pretend innocence with me, Griffin O'Neal. I've caught you jerking off more than once, you know. One time with a sock and another time with that stuffed teddy bear Mellie got you for Christmas two years ago."

"*Teddy bear?*" I incredulously said, choking back laughter. "I was *cuddling* with it, not humping it."

"Cuddling it with your *dick*, you mean. Your naked dick."

"You know I always sleep in the nude."

"Yeah, and now I know why."

I burst out laughing, still cradling her face in my hands. Feeling the tension drain out of her, I dropped my forehead to hers and said, "God, you're so adorable when you flirt with me."

"Flirt? This isn't flirting. I'm just calling you out on your bull—"

I captured her lips with my own, effectively silencing her. The pressure was firm yet gentle, giving her the opportunity to pull away if she wanted to. When she didn't, I kissed her again, tipping her face up to deepen it. Her hands came up to grip my arms, and when I felt them tremble, I began to tremble as well.

She wasn't nervous anymore. She was turned on. *Excited*. And that excitement fueled my own.

I caressed her mouth with mine, each sweep slowly prying her lips apart. When they were opened enough, I slipped my tongue inside and found hers. She sighed into my mouth, and I dug my fingers into her hair, all of my focus on tasting and inhaling her dark chocolate scent. A moan of pleasure rolled up my throat, and her knees buckled at the sound. I caught her before she could fall, slowly backing her against the slick tiles.

Dragging my mouth from hers, I breathed against her lips, "Do you feel that?"

Her chest rose and fell sharply, pushing against mine. "Feel what?"

I took one of her hands and slid it over my pounding chest. "This." I brought her hand lower, my stomach flexing as her nails scraped over my abs. "And this." Opening my eyes to meet hers, I tugged her hand even lower and firmly wrapped it around my swollen cock. "And this."

Desire sparked in her violet eyes, making them glow, and I nearly came right then and there.

"Every part of me is yours," I said, my voice deeper, rougher than before. "Every inch belongs to you and only you. Touch it. I want you to. I'm *begging* you to."

Her lashes fluttered, and her hold on my shaft tightened. Pleasure shot down the length, settling into my balls, and I expelled a harsh breath.

"That's it," I said, struggling to speak. "Touch me. I'm yours."

"What if," she whispered, her hold suddenly loosening, then falling away completely.

Panic beat at my chest. Had she changed her mind? Was she going to leave?

"Yes?" I managed to get out, barely able to breathe.

"What if . . ." she repeated, then lifted up on tiptoe to breathe in my ear, "What if I want to *lick* you instead?"

At her words, my legs nearly gave out.

My heart was all but pounding out of my chest now, and breathing was practically impossible. She was wrecking me, and I loved it. Loved the way she submitted to me one minute, only to dominate me the next. I'd always thought her alpha side was sexy, especially in the bedroom. She wanted control, and I gladly gave it to her without resistance.

"Lick me, suck me, blow me. Whatever you want. Take what's yours, Vi."

She made a soft humming noise, clearly pleased by my words. Her tongue darted out and flicked the shell of my ear, and it was all I could do to hold still. *She* was in charge now, not me.

"What a good boy," she crooned, reaching up to pat my cheek. When I turned my head and kissed her palm, she patted my cheek again. *Hard.* And lightly growled, "Behave."

A crooked smile crept over my face, and she paused to peck my lips. My smile immediately turned into a frown. "That's it?"

"You said whatever I want," she replied with a shrug. "Behave, and I'll give you more."

Obediently holding still—and fighting back a smile—I let her have her way with me. Satisfied that I wasn't going to interrupt her again, she pressed another kiss to my mouth.

Better. *Much* better.

I tried to pull her face closer to mine and kiss her back, but she grabbed my wrist and, in a flash, reversed our positions. As my back slammed against the tiles, she tightly gripped my jaw and forced my mouth open, then thrust her tongue inside. The dominant move made me wild with excitement, and I violently shuddered as she thoroughly licked the inside of my mouth.

She'd been rough with me before, especially during her heat, but it felt different this time. It almost felt like she was marking me. *Claiming* me. And the possibility of that happening filled me with euphoria.

I tried to touch her, but she grabbed both wrists and pressed them against the tiles. This was *her* moment, and she was making that perfectly clear. Her tongue left my mouth, and I immediately mourned its loss. A second later, though, she pressed an open-mouthed kiss to my jaw, then my neck. I tipped my head back to give her better access, and she instantly took advantage, sucking on my neck hard enough to leave a bruise.

Realizing how close she was to the claim spot between my neck and shoulder, I inhaled sharply between my teeth, my instincts going haywire. Every molecule of my being wanted her to nuzzle that spot, to bite it. *Hard.* Hard enough to draw blood. The harder she bit, the harder she claimed me as hers.

What I wouldn't give to have her scent buried beneath my skin, to proudly wear it like a badge of honor.

But after another moment, she moved on from my neck to kiss and lick my collarbone, then my chest. I thoroughly enjoyed it, but I couldn't help feeling a little disappointed. Or a lot.

Slowly, I reminded myself, looking down as she flicked her tongue over one of my nipples. She wasn't ready to claim me, and that was okay. She was ready for *this,* so I set aside my need to be claimed and focused on what she was doing to me.

"Don't forget the other one," I dared to speak as she sucked on my hardened nipple. "It's lonely." She bit down on the nipple as payback, and I choked out a groan. "That's it, baby. The rougher, the better."

She released the nipple to look up at me. "Griff?"

"Yeah?"

Sticking her tongue out, she slowly licked a path up my chest and throat. As I felt her hands join in, sliding up the length of my stomach to rest on my pecs, I bit back another groan. Standing face to face with me again, she caressed her lips over mine, then whispered, "Shut up."

I grinned, just as she dropped to her knees and, in one fell swoop, swallowed my dick whole. The swift and unexpected move punched the air from my lungs. Not giving me time to catch my breath, she sucked on me hard, so hard that her cheeks hollowed out.

Her name burst from my lips as pleasure shot to every corner of my body. She looked up and met my eyes as I slowly unraveled, wholly lost to the feeling of her lips and tongue milking my pleasure. She'd done this to me a few times before, but *I* was usually the one between her thighs.

Seeing her down there with her mouth on my cock sent my body into overdrive, and I was fighting back a release only seconds later.

"Vi," I groaned, the sound almost a plea. My legs trembled as she continued to milk me, making my balls tighten. I was so turned on that a single touch from her would shove me over the edge. But I didn't want to orgasm right now. Not yet. Not like this. I had a greater desire, and I silently conveyed that message, hoping she would understand.

Seeing it, she stopped sucking on me, then slowly released my dick with a wet pop. The greedy appendage twitched in disappointment, painfully swollen to the max, but I ignored it and reached down to help Vi to her feet. The second she stood, I switched off the shower and swept her into my arms.

"Griff, what—?" she started, but the words died as I exited the shower and strode with purpose to the nearest bedroom. Seeing where I was headed, she protested, "I'm wet."

"I bet you are. After frantically sucking my dick like your favorite lollipop, you're probably soaked."

A noise that sounded a lot like a giggle escaped her. Vi *never* giggled. Pleased, my swollen dick twitched again. Reaching the king-sized bed, I laid her on the heather gray comforter.

"Yes, I'm practically *dripping*," she sassily replied, looking up at me through her dark lashes. "Or maybe you're just full of yourself."

"Guess I should check, then," I purred, sitting on the bed beside her. When I reached between her slightly parted thighs and found her wetness, she sucked in a quiet gasp. "Mmm," I rumbled, watching her face as I slowly dipped a finger inside her entrance. "You're definitely dripping. And tight. Tighter than I remember."

"It's *been* awhile, doofus," she said, then gasped again when I added a second finger, sliding them both in as far as they would go.

"Guess I should help you prepare, then," I replied, satisfied when her body quivered. "My dick has grown since the last time it was inside you."

"Has not. You're so full of your—" Her words ended in a breathless cry as I curled my fingers inside her. Her slick walls spasmed and tightened around my fingers, and the sensation made me impossibly hard, my cock aching to be there instead.

"You'll soon be full of me too," I gruffly said. I started pumping my fingers in her deliciously warm pussy, and she arched off the bed with a moan. The sight made my balls tighten again, her pleasure becoming mine. If I continued pleasuring her for much longer, I was probably going to make a mess all over the gray comforter.

I'd always been able to get off while watching her come undone by my touch. It was stimulating, *thrilling* to see how she reacted to me. Every moan, every gasp for breath, every quiver and cry sent me into a euphoric state.

As I started to drown in her pleasure, overwhelmed by how good it felt to be filling her trembling body with utmost bliss, I prepared to orgasm right along with her. It hadn't been my goal to end the moment like this, but I couldn't hold it back any longer.

She was *breathtaking*, taking my fingers like such a good girl, and all I could think about was falling over the edge with her.

But she suddenly gasped out, "I need you, Griff."

Just like that, she set my world on fire. I was ablaze with desire and excitement, eagerly responding to her words. She was my match, and I was her flame, burning hotter and hotter by the second.

I immediately slid my fingers free to crawl on top of her, my arms and legs slightly shaking as I looked down at her bright eyes. They were filled with desire, desire for *me*, and the sight took my breath away. I lifted one of my hands and gently stroked her cheek, marveling at the way she leaned into my touch.

So responsive. So *ready* for me. My heart could barely take it, swelling so big that I thought it would burst from my chest.

"I've been intimate with you many times before," I told her, my voice hushed and almost reverent as I continued to stroke her cheek, "but I want this time to be different. This time, I want to make *love* to you." Her breath caught. "With your permission, of course," I softly added, hoping she could see that love shining through my eyes.

She stared at me for a long moment, and I struggled to hold still, to keep breathing. After what felt like an eternity, she finally nodded and whispered a word. One little word that made me feel like the luckiest man on earth.

"Yes."

CHAPTER 21

VIOLET

I knew he was as desperate for this as I was. Desperate to feel our bodies become one. To experience the euphoria that connection gave us both.

He was trembling, and so was I, the sexual tension between us about to snap.

Love. He wanted to make *love* to me.

I could see in his eyes how much he wanted me to believe that.

He loved me. He loved me. He *loved* me.

And for a moment. One blissful moment. I allowed myself to actually believe that I was the love of his life. That I was *his* in mind, body, and soul.

It felt incredible. It was everything I wanted and more. And as he slowly lowered himself on top of me, I clung to that love with all of my might. I clung to *him*, to my childhood friend, to my comfort and safety, to the male who'd always been there for me.

His touches turned sweet, gentle, caressing me like I was the most precious thing in the world to him. Like he *cherished* me above all others. I could barely stand how good it felt, how perfect, each touch acting as a balm to heal my wounds. Not just the physical ones I'd endured this past week, but the emotional ones I'd been wearing for years like invisible scars.

When it finally came time for us to become one, he slid into me slowly. Reverently. Filling me up so completely that tears blurred my vision. He wiped them away as they fell, softly kissing my cheeks. He became the beautifully attentive male that stole my breath away, responding to every little thing I did. When I gasped at the first thrust, he made sure I wasn't in pain. When I reached for him, he lowered his head to let me kiss him. When I started to unravel, he unraveled with me, our ragged breaths in perfect sync.

We were like yin and yang, an equal balance of give and take. In that moment, it felt like we were meant for each other. *Made* for each other. Like the Universe itself had ordained our union.

It was the most beautiful thing I'd ever experienced, but I knew it would have to end. Even so, I stayed locked in the beautiful moment for as long as time would let me. For as long as *he* would let me.

Griff's body was hot and slick against mine, his movements frantic, his pounding heart deafening as the end neared. Still, I knew he wouldn't come until I did, no matter how desperate he was for it. And he was definitely desperate. The veins in his neck were distended, and his eyes were wild with need. They silently begged me to let him come, all while he gripped my hands tightly in his and drove into me over and over like a man possessed.

Finally, I couldn't hold back the wall of tension a second longer. It snapped like a rubber band, sending wave after wave of ecstasy crashing through me. As I cried out in bliss, Griff dropped his forehead to mine and thrust one more time. My walls squeezed his shaft in a vise, milking his release from him, and he cried out right along with me. As the pleasure swept us away, I held on to the moment for dear life.

Held on to *him*.

But I wouldn't be able to forever. Reality would catch up to us soon enough, and he would see. He would *finally* see.

That loving me wouldn't last.

Sable's incessant voice in my head startled me from a deep, dreamless sleep. I started to grumble at her, only to stop when I inhaled smoke.

Fire! Fire! Get up! she frantically shouted.

I pried my eyes open, disorientated when I didn't recognize the room. It was dark, and my night vision was struggling to pick out details for some reason. I inhaled another lungful of smoke and immediately started coughing.

Griff stirred against me with a sleepy groan, then abruptly bolted upright on the bed.

"Vi." He reached for me, dragging me off the bed with him as I continued to cough.

"What . . . happened?" I gasped out, finally realizing that smoke was filling the room.

"The hunters found us," Griff replied grimly. "They're trying to smoke us out."

Or burn us alive, Sable whimpered, clearly terrified.

I could hear the crackling flames below us on the first floor, which reminded me of the time our family estate had burned down with us still inside. Terror gripped me as well, and it became even harder to breathe.

"Look at me, Violet," Griff said, grabbing my face with both hands as he sensed my panic. I looked up at him with wide eyes, my heart thundering uncontrollably. "We're going to be okay. Say it."

I opened my mouth, but nothing came out.

"*Say* it," he ordered, his voice filled with so much authority that some of my panic eased.

"We're going . . . We're going to be okay."

"Good girl." He pressed his mouth to mine in a brief, albeit searing kiss. "They might outnumber us, but we can overpower them. It's time we fight back."

Fresh panic squeezed my chest. "They could separate us."

"They won't. I'll kill them if they try." He said it with so much conviction that I couldn't help but believe him. I soaked up his confidence like oxygen, willing my racing heart to slow so I could better focus.

"We should shift," I suggested, trying and failing to hear anything over the raging fire below. "We'll be faster and stronger that way."

Griff nodded in agreement. "Into our wolves' true forms."

"Okay. But we stick *together*."

"I won't leave your side, I promise," he said, then pulled me in for one final kiss and breathed against my lips, "I love you."

"And I love you," I automatically replied, then froze, realizing what I'd just done.

He pulled back to look at me, and his expression nearly broke my heart.

Joy. Pure, unadulterated *joy* lit up his entire face.

I hadn't meant to say the words. They'd just slipped out. But there was no undoing them now. If we both survived whatever fresh hell the hunters had in store for us, I'd have to face the consequences of what I'd just done. But for now, I kept silent. Griff was absolutely thrilled, and I wasn't about to take that away from him—not when it could help him get through the danger about to swallow us whole.

Taking a step back, I allowed the shift to overtake me. He followed suit, and less than a minute later, Sable and Whiskey were standing where we'd been, their heads practically touching the ceiling.

"The balcony?" Whiskey rumbled to my familiar, the fierce glow of his red eyes cutting through the smoke.

"They'll be expecting that," she replied, her voice an octave lower than mine. "Follow me."

"I'll follow you anywhere, beloved," he said, and for once, I didn't comment when she approached him to nuzzle and lick his mouth. It could be the last time they did so on this plane if one or both of us didn't make it out of this alive. They deserved a moment to say goodbye, in case the worst happened.

The sweet moment came and went all too soon, though, and Sable turned toward the closed bedroom door. Toward the *fire*. I could feel her fear, but that didn't stop my brave familiar from facing it anyway. Pausing only for a second, she launched herself at the door and smashed it down with a single blow.

Whiskey was hot on her heels as she burst into the hallway. A wall of fire greeted them, and she cringed away from the intense heat.

"This way!" she shouted, hugging the right side of the wall. As they neared the end of the hallway, both of them took a running leap and bypassed the stairs completely. Two resounding thuds announced their arrival on the first floor; then they were off like a shot, loping full tilt toward the front door.

Smoke filled Sable's lungs, the fire licking at her fur as she raced past, but she plowed on anyway, determined to get us both to safety. Whiskey pulled ahead at the last second, using his shoulder to ram the door down. It exploded outward in a shower of sparks, fire and smoke chasing after the two wolves as they burst out into the night.

Fresh air bit at Sable's nostrils, and she coughed to make room in her lungs for it. Before she could take a moment to reorientate herself, a sharp *bang* lit up the night. Whiskey yanked her sideways just as something whizzed by her ear, clipping the edge. Pain flared from the spot, and she yelped.

At the sound, Whiskey's eyes went scarily bright. With the glow of the flames striking his face, he looked like a bonafide fire demon from hell. Whirling toward where the shot had been fired from, he bellowed a terrifying roar, then charged like a freight train.

Sable followed his lead, zeroing in on the hunter that had almost shot her. I immediately recognized him as the werewolf who'd thrown a bag over my head and tried to inject me with something. Sable recognized him too, and she released a howl of fury. The male raised his gun again and pointed it at Whiskey, and Sable went feral. Pushing off the ground, she launched herself at him like a missile.

The sight was terrifying enough to make any man pee his pants, human or supernatural. The male startled, and his shot went wide. A second later, Sable was on top of him. He screamed as she sank her razor sharp claws into him and knocked the gun from his hands. He immediately put up a fight, but even though he was a dominant male, his strength was no match for my demon wolf. She immobilized him within seconds, leaving him to face a seething Whiskey.

Griff's familiar towered over the male, staring down at him with a creepy as hell grin.

The male began to tremble in Sable's arms, but he glared up at Whiskey and said, "You can't stop us. We're going to take her, and when we do—"

Whiskey grabbed the male's head and ripped it off in one swift move. As blood sprayed over his chest, he tossed the head aside and growled, "One down, four to go."

Another shot fired, and he ducked, but not fast enough. He grunted as the slug hit him in the back. Sable dropped the decapitated body with a cry. Before she could help Whiskey, more shots fired. The bullets pelted into the earth and trees surrounding them, one slicing into Sable's arm as it whizzed past. The burn was painful enough that I instantly knew the bullets were silver.

Whiskey roared again, shielding her from the chaotic volley as best he could, but the shots came from *everywhere*.

We were surrounded.

If enough silver hit us, Whiskey and Sable's superior strength would weaken. The hunters would overpower us. *Separate* us. And the thought of them killing Griff to get to me terrified me so much that my fight instincts switched off.

We have to run! I screamed at Sable.

She froze, torn between obeying and seeking vengeance on the hunters. I tried to wrestle control from her, but that only made her lose focus. She barked in pain as another bullet clipped her, and Whiskey officially lost it. Throwing his head back, he bellowed at the night sky, then charged at the nearest hunter.

No! I wailed, watching in horror as another hunter shot at Whiskey and hit him in the side. He stumbled, and that was all it took. Bullets rained on him, hitting him over and over and over, dragging him to the ground.

Sable cried out and moved toward him, but one of the hunters shot at her feet, warning her back. She looked up at the male, and my insides turned to ice. It was the Russian-looking hitman, the werewolf who'd followed me from the football stadium. Sable bared her dagger-like fangs at him, and he pointed his gun higher, directly at her heart.

Stand down, I ordered her, sensing how close she was to charging him. She wouldn't make it. A silver bullet to the heart was almost always fatal.

Realizing she'd lost the fight, Sable tipped back her dark head and released a mournful howl. Almost immediately, a howl answered her back. Then another.

Sudden hope surged through us both. We *recognized* those howls. The hunters froze with indecision, and I watched with glee as their faces paled. Above the sound of crackling flames, a new noise could be heard, growing louder and louder by the second.

Something *huge* was crashing through the trees. Make that *two* huge somethings.

The hunters listened for a moment more; then Hitman lowered his weapon and bellowed, "Retreat!"

Too late.

A dark demon wolf and a pitch black one burst from the woods and collided with two hunters. Screams sounded and shots misfired, but the hunters met a grisly end within seconds. Seeing her chance, Sable lunged for Hitman. Before she could reach him, the only other surviving hunter stepped into her path, his gun trained on the new arrivals.

With a savage snarl, she swept a clawed hand out and tore his arm clean off. As the gun fell harmlessly to the ground, along with the severed appendage, the male let out a bloodcurdling scream. Sable clamped her jaws around his neck and silenced him a second later, shaking him like a ragdoll several times before letting go. He crumpled to the ground, unconscious but still alive.

She opened her maw again to finish him, but I quickly stopped her. *Don't. We should keep him alive for questioning.*

She growled her disappointment but didn't argue with me. Lifting her head, she sought out Hitman again, but he was nowhere to be seen.

"Coward!" she roared, raising her nose to track his scent. The sound of breaking bones distracted her, and she turned to see Whiskey halfway through the shift.

Give me back control, I immediately demanded, all thoughts of tracking down Hitman disappearing the moment I caught sight of Griff.

But, Sable started with a whine, bloodlust still pumping hotly through her veins.

Now, Sable! I barked, panic gripping me when I saw bloody bullet holes in Griff's tanned skin.

She relinquished control without another word, allowing the shift to overtake us. Seconds later, I was scrambling toward a trembling Griff on the ground.

"Let me see. Let me see!" I said in a high-pitched voice, reaching out to help him into a sitting position. Moments later, I felt two more bodies crowd in close, but I already knew who they were. Without looking up, I told them in a shaky voice, "Sable left one alive. We could use him for questioning."

"I'll get him, Boss," Jagger said to my brother before taking off again.

Kolton crouched by my side and lifted a hand to help me with Griff, but I snapped, "Don't *touch* him."

Kolton's hand froze midair. "Vi," he quietly, *softly* said, as if speaking to an unhinged person. And I *felt* unhinged, the need to protect Griff a feral thing inside me. "He's been shot with silver bullets. They have to come out."

"I'll do it. I'll take them out."

My brother was silent for a moment, then said, "You don't want to do that, Vi."

"Yes, I *do!*" I shot back, turning my head to glare at him. He studied my face, his own expression impassive. Whatever he saw made him slowly nod and sit back on his heels.

"He's all yours," Kolton said, his voice remaining calm despite how I'd spoken to him. "I'm here if you need me to take over."

"I won't," I firmly replied, returning my focus to Griff. He was awake, but I could tell by the grimace on his face that he was in excruciating pain. Gentling my voice, I said to him, "Let me put you under."

He barked a laugh, then sucked in a pained hiss through his teeth. "Not a chance. If you're going to play doctor on me, I want to watch."

"Griff, this isn't funny."

"I know," he groaned, trying to shift into a more comfortable position. "This pain might actually be worse than the tree. But at least none of the bullets are rubbing against my heart."

"Tree?" Kolton couldn't help but question.

"We have a lot to tell you," I said, searching Griff's back until I found the first bullet that had hit him. When I saw that his skin had already started to heal over it, nausea stirred in my gut.

"Apparently," Kolton muttered. "Mind explaining why you're wearing Griff's tattoo?"

Oh crap. I glanced down at the snake on my arm, then at my brother's face. He didn't look mad, per se, but he definitely looked troubled.

"It was in case we got separated," Griff answered for me, his voice sounding weaker by the second.

Kolton looked between us, then bluntly asked, "And the sex?"

Ah *hell*, he did not just go there.

"That's none of your business, Kolton," I said, giving him a warning look to back off.

"It is when my best friend promised me that something like this wouldn't happen. It is when he *knows* my little sister goes to him for comfort, and he chose to take advantage of that."

My jaw dropped. "That's not—"

"I love her, Kol," Griff interjected, his voice firm, even as his breaths came in short spurts. "Vi is no longer dating Reid, and I finally told her how I feel. If you still think I overstepped, I take full responsibility for my actions and will face whatever punishment you believe I deserve. But Vi is innocent in all this. She did nothing wrong."

I opened my mouth but quickly shut it again, knowing that now wasn't the right time to undo all that I'd done. Griff was in enough pain already.

Kolton slowly blinked at us both, looking a bit shell-shocked. He opened his mouth only to close it, not willing to stir the pot further for the time being.

Refocusing on the rapidly-healing wound on Griff's back, I said, "One last chance, Griff. This'll be a lot easier for us both if you're asleep."

"Sorry, but you're just gonna have to endure my screams," he wheezed, swaying enough that he'd probably pass out on his own if the bullets remained in him much longer. But I couldn't wait that long, couldn't stand seeing him in pain for one more second.

"Okay. I'll be as quick as I can," I reassured, more to myself than him. In a situation like this, there was nothing we could do but dig the bullets out. And the fastest way to do that was with our claws. Pursing my lips, I willed my claws to emerge and gripped his shoulder to hold him steady. "Don't move, or this will hurt worse."

"I won't—" he started, then hissed out a curse when I sank my claws into his flesh. I tensed when he tensed, his added pain almost more than I could bear. But I had to do this for him. *Needed* to. Because if even one more person caused him pain right now, I was going to lose it.

"It's out. It's out," I said a few moments later, quickly dropping the bullet onto the ground as it started to eat at my own flesh.

A great sigh shuddered from Griff. "Much better. I think there's one or two more, though."

"More like six," Jagger muttered above me. I glanced up to see that he'd thrown the unconscious one-armed hunter over his shoulder, fireman style. "Sure you don't want me or Kolton to—"

"No," I interrupted him, my tone brooking no argument. He lifted an eyebrow at me but didn't argue. Resuming my work, I focused on the bullet in Griff's side next. By the time I pulled the final bullet out, I was breathing almost as heavily as Griff.

The second the bullet hit the ground, Griff turned and drew me into his arms. A relieved whimper left me, and I fiercely hugged him back.

"They didn't separate us. We're safe now," he murmured against my hair, soaking up my comfort as I soaked up his. A sharp cracking noise from the house drew our attention, and we both turned our heads just as the second story fell, crushing the floor below it with a loud *boom*.

"Poor house," I sighed, grateful that we weren't still in it.

"Well, that brings back memories," Jagger murmured as we all watched it slowly burn to ash.

"How did you guys find us?" I asked, resting my head on Griff's shoulder.

"When I couldn't reach either of you or Randy, I tracked the jet and found out you'd left early," Kolton answered. "But when it didn't arrive, I alerted the pack to begin a ground search. A few hours ago, Buck and several other pack males were scouring the area just south of Lake Placid when they came across a silver-coated trap with your scents on it. Jagger and I followed your trail from there in wolf form. I'm assuming the males we just killed had something to do with the plane crash?"

"Yeah," I replied, then quietly added, "Randy didn't make it."

Kolton sighed. "I know. Another pack member found him earlier today. He was a great pilot and family friend. Buck went to collect his body, but we'll have to tell his family what happened. Well, some of it anyway."

"I'll do it," I offered.

Kolton glanced down at me. "Vi, you've been through enough already."

"*Please*, Kolton. Let me do it. I . . . I feel responsible."

He frowned, but it was Griff who said, "You're not to blame for this, Vi. You couldn't have known those bastards would orchestrate a plane crash just to get to you."

When I didn't respond, Kolton's frown deepened. Not ready for a lecture, I forced myself to leave Griff's warm embrace and pushed to my feet. "We should get going in case someone saw the fire and called the police. There are three other bodies we need to take care of before they arrive."

"Wait, where's the fifth?" Griff asked, turning his head to look around.

Wincing, I muttered, "He got away."

Griff swore under his breath.

"At least we have him," Jagger said, jerking a thumb at the unconscious male over his shoulder. "I'm sure he'll sing like a bluebird after a few hours of torture."

I snorted and corrected, "Like a canary."

He shrugged. "Whatever. After what he put you two through, he'll sing however I want him to sing."

At the menacing tone to his voice, I didn't doubt him for a second.

"We'll clean up the area and stash the bodies in the woods; then I'll go and get the truck," Kolton said, stepping toward the two males he and Jagger had killed. I moved to help him, but he waved me away. "Griff still needs you. Jagger and I will take care of the cleanup and bodies."

I turned to Griff again, and sure enough, he was struggling to stand. I quickly moved to help him, slipping beneath one of his arms so I could bear some of his weight.

"Good thing I'm not full of myself, or I probably wouldn't let you help me," he teased.

Instead of elbowing him like I normally would, I just rolled my eyes. "Be a good boy, or I'll carry you like a baby instead."

He chuckled, then quietly groaned, "I might actually need to be carried like a baby."

"Suck it up," I said with another eye roll, but I let him lean on me even more.

By the time we cleared the site and stashed the bodies deep in the woods, even *I* was struggling to stand. The adrenaline from the fire and fight was finally wearing off, and when Kolton returned with the truck an hour later, I couldn't wait to pass out in the backseat.

And that's exactly what I did, but not before draping a blanket over Griff and helping him inside. He had plans of his own, though, ones that didn't involve us sitting on opposite sides. Without a word, he leaned over and wrapped me in the blanket as well. When I was snug against him, he laid us down on the seat with me pressed tightly to his chest.

At the sound of his steadily beating heart, any resistance I had fled. My body melted against his and his against mine.

Safe. We were finally *safe*. That's all that mattered right now.

Within seconds, we were both fast asleep.

CHAPTER 22

VIOLET

"Nora's going to kill me when she finds out I let you be here for this," Kolton muttered, his gaze glued to the video monitor as the captive hunter slowly regained consciousness.

"No, she won't. She knows how stubborn I am," I replied. When Kolton softly snorted in agreement, I bumped his shoulder with mine. "Hey, I have a right to be here. This dude wants to kidnap me, and I want to know why. At least I didn't insist on leading the interrogation."

"Only because you know you couldn't make him talk," Griff said from my other side. I almost shoulder-bumped him too, then decided against it. Not because he was still healing, but because I'd woken up an hour ago still wrapped tightly in his arms and had never wanted to leave.

But we were safe now. The danger had passed for the time being, which meant that I needed to face reality again. The longer I didn't, the harder this would be.

And so I simply replied, "You're right. I would end up killing him the moment he could speak again."

"Me too," Griff said, glancing away from the monitor to look at me. It took all of my willpower not to meet his gaze, to share a moment of understanding with him, a moment he clearly wished to share with me.

Feeling like crap for intentionally avoiding him, I dug my nails into my palms, hard enough to break the skin.

It's for the best, it's for the best, I silently chanted, until he finally looked away.

Breathing a bit easier, I refocused on the video that showed us what was happening inside the cavernous underground room. Kolton had decided to interrogate the male at the bunker our father had acquired decades ago. The space was sometimes used to contain feral werewolves, allowing them a safe environment to calm down before they hurt anyone—or themselves.

Kolton himself had been held here not too long ago, and the shadows of that terrible time still clung to the place. So did the memory of my own time here a few months ago. I'd *chosen* to come here, though. Chosen to bear the pain of my heat alone by going somewhere no one would think to find me.

I could still hear the haunting echoes of my agonized screams. I'd writhed on the floor for hours until I'd finally passed out from exhaustion.

Knowing I'd probably have to endure that again in a few more months, dread shivered up my spine.

Griff looked at me again as if he knew where my thoughts had strayed, and my tension returned. I never should have told him about my time at the bunker. I doubted I would be able to slip away like last time now that he knew.

I silently cursed myself for my stupidity. Not just about that, but about the countless other stupid things I'd done this past week. The last twenty-four hours had been the worst, though.

Did *everyone* in my family know that Griff was my go-to for comfort? If they didn't, they would soon enough. Even though I'd showered in the bunker's communal bathroom and was now fully-clothed, I still smelled like sex. Like *Griff*.

Less than a day after being dumped, I'd fallen into bed with another male.

Not sure what that said about me, but it definitely wasn't anything good.

A groan from inside the locked room saved me from further reflection, and all three of us drew closer to the video screen. Only Jagger was inside to interrogate the one-armed hunter, a decision we'd come to unanimously. Midnight Pack's second in command had a way of drawing words out of people without uttering a single one himself. His eerie silence alone was torture enough sometimes, although I doubted the hunter would be so easily cowed.

Jagger had planted himself in a metal chair across from the hunter, deathly quiet and equally as still. Groaning again, the hunter lifted his head just enough to notice that his arm was missing. He bit out a curse and struggled against his bonds for a moment, then spotted Jagger and stiffened. Even as his eyes widened in fear, he managed to rasp, "Don't bother. I won't talk."

Jagger didn't say a word. The male cleared his throat and rotated his neck, clearly still in pain from the way Sable had treated him like a chew toy. Several minutes ticked by. The hunter coughed on occasion, his throat no doubt bone dry. Half an hour came and went, and he started to squirm under Jagger's silent stare.

"Fifty bucks says he breaks in an hour," Griff said under his breath, even though the walls were too thick for the hunter to hear him.

"One hundred says he breaks in the next ten minutes," Kolton wagered back.

I scoffed at them both. "Two hundred says Jagger has to torture him for at least three hours." Both males turned to me with incredulous looks, and I shrugged. "Jagger's good, but these hunters aren't betas."

"Yeah, but they're not hybrids either," Griff pointed out. "If Jag lets Onyx take over, I bet the male wets himself and spews everything he knows without a finger being laid on him."

"Onyx isn't *that* scary," I grumbled.

Griff chuckled. "Sounds like someone is jealous."

"Hey, Sable is *fierce*. She's terrified plenty of people."

I felt her preen at that, obviously pleased by the compliment.

"Yeah, but do they *wet* themselves?"

Cheeky boy, Sable huffed.

Annoyed, I shoved Griff's shoulder. He stumbled sideways with a laugh.

"Careful. I still have boo-boos."

"*Boo-boos?*" I repeated, throwing him a flat look. "Are you forever going to talk like you're five?"

"If it gets a rise out of you, yes."

"A rise? Seriously, Griff. You're such a child."

"Ah c'mon. You love it when I tease you."

I opened my mouth, but at the mention of the word *love*, all of my witty comebacks flew out the window. Trying and failing to regain my mojo, I huffed out a sigh and muttered, "Let's just focus on the interrogation. Two hundred still says this'll take hours."

We lapsed into silence after that, but I could feel both males side-eyeing me. Great. They could sense that something was up with me. The days ahead were going to be painful, that was for sure.

"Water," the hunter abruptly croaked, drawing our gazes back to the screen.

Jagger was silent for another few minutes, then finally said, "Tell me why you're abducting females, and I'll give you all the water you want."

The hunter's laugh quickly turned into a hacking cough. "You think I'll break"—cough cough—"that easily?"

"I think you'll break the easy way or the hard way. Which one it will be is up to you."

"Ooh, now we're gettin' somewhere," Griff said, rubbing his hands together.

"I could still win," Kolton commented.

"Not a chance. Jag wants to play with him a little first."

My brother grunted but didn't argue. It was clear that Jagger was taking his time with the dirtbag.

Tired but not willing to miss a second of the interrogation, I hid a yawn by glancing up at Kolton and murmuring, "Thanks for finding us. We wouldn't have survived much longer if you and Jagger hadn't arrived when you did."

He looked at me, then at Griff, saying, "We feared the worst when we learned of the plane crash. Thank you for keeping each other safe. I don't know what I would have done if something had happened to either of you."

At the vulnerable look in his eyes, I turned and wrapped my arms around him. He blew out a sigh and hugged me back, then reached around me to drag Griff into the embrace. Griff readily locked his arms around us both, sandwiching me tightly between their hard bodies. Any tension I'd been holding on to instantly drained from me.

Wedged between two of the strongest hybrid werewolves in existence, I couldn't get much safer than this. And maybe that's why I kept my mouth shut and shoved down my growing guilt, clinging to the comforting moment instead.

I would face reality tomorrow. But right now, I needed this. I needed one more moment to feel like the innocent little girl I used to be, surrounded by her boys.

Several more minutes passed by, and it became clear that the hunter wasn't going to take the easy way. He was practically hacking up a lung but refused to accept Jagger's deal. Without a word, Jagger rose from his chair and approached the bound male. The hunter stiffened all over, his eyes going wide again.

"What are—" Cough cough. "What are you doing?" he wheezed, craning his neck around as Jagger stopped behind his chair and began to untie his remaining arm.

"Setting your arm free so I can more easily remove it," Jagger bluntly replied.

"Oh, *snap*," Griff exclaimed, choking out a laugh.

Yes, do it, Sable morbidly encouraged. *Finish what I started.*

"Wait," the hunter said, his voice filling with terror as Jagger's words sank in. "You're seriously going to leave me *armless?*"

Jagger ignored him, his movements calm and unhurried. *Unfeeling.*

"Wait, *wait!*" the hunter cried, fruitlessly beginning to struggle.

"He's breaking. He's *breaking*," Griff whisper-yelled.

"I-I'll tell you why we're taking the females. Just don't rip my arm off."

Jagger paused, then resumed untying the arm.

"Hey! I said I would tell you!"

The binding fell away, and Jagger firmly gripped the arm, placing his other hand on the hunter's shoulder to hold him steady. "Speak quickly, or the arm comes off," was all he said, then gave the limb a sharp tug as if to test how strong it was. Or weak.

"Okay, okay!" the hunter shouted, the whites of his eyes clearly visible. "We need the females for breeding."

My breath caught.

Jagger was silent for a lengthy beat, then jerked on the arm again, hard enough to make the hunter cry out. "Tell me more."

"W-we're outcasts. Packless rogue males. Too dominant for another pack alpha to accept us, so we formed our own pack. But we don't have females."

"So you're *stealing* them?" Jagger growled, finally showing a shred of emotion.

"Yes. How else are we supposed to get them? The pack won't grow and thrive without females."

Jagger pulled his lip back in a silent snarl. "There's more you're not telling me. You're targeting *hybrid* females specifically and going to great lengths to do so. Why?"

The hunter suddenly clamped his jaw shut. Jagger yanked on the arm again, this time with brutal force. The hunter's mouth popped back open again as he released a bloodcurdling scream.

"*Tell* me," Jagger barked, his eyes flashing dangerously bright.

"I . . . I can't." Cough cough cough. "They'll kill me!"

"Then give me names. Who's your leader? How many of you are there? Where are the females being kept?"

"I . . ."

"Tell me!" Jagger thundered, then jerked on the arm so hard that it popped out of the socket.

The hunter screamed, and I reached up to rub at my own shoulder, phantom pain flaring in the joint. Griff noticed and moved closer to wrap an arm around me. When I felt him tremble with barely-suppressed anger, I leaned into him, accepting his comfort as well as giving my own.

"They'll kill me, they'll kill me," the hunter continued to sob.

"Sounds like I no longer have use for you or your arm," Jagger muttered. As he tightened his grip on the hunter's arm, I braced myself, prepared to watch the limb get severed.

"No, wait. *Wait!*" the hunter cried. "I-I can tell you a little more. We're only taking *unclaimed* hybrid females, so your alpha female and the rest are safe. We only want the dark brunette one, your alpha's sister. If you give her to us, we'll leave Midnight Pack territory. We'll—"

"Boss," Jagger abruptly called. "I can't do this anymore."

"I'm going to kill him," Griff seethed beside me, trembling almost violently now. His hold on me had tightened, just short of becoming painful. "I'll tear his arm and legs off. Then his *dick*. Then I'll tear off his head but not before cramming his puny cock down his *throat*."

I nearly choked on my spit. I'd never heard Griff talk like this before, each word laced with pure hatred.

I should have eaten him, Sable growled, equally furious.

That's disgusting, I told her. *I don't care how evil he is. We're not carnivores.*

Kolton pressed the speaker button and said in a deathly soft voice, "Knock him out, Jag."

Faster than I could blink, Jagger punched the hunter, so hard that his head violently snapped to the side. As the hunter slumped forward unconscious, Jagger stormed toward the exit. On his way, he knocked aside the metal chair he'd vacated, and it soared through the air, crashing against the far wall with a loud *bang*.

Kolton moved to unlock the thick door, and when Jagger emerged from the room, his eyes went straight to me. He stared for a moment, then strode forward with purpose. As he approached, Griff's hold on me tightened even more.

"Hand her over, Griff," Jagger demanded.

A possessive growl rumbled from Griff, making me blink in surprise.

"I'm not *taking* her from you, idiot," Jagger growled back. "I just want to hold her. I *need* to."

Something about the words resonated with Griff, and with a begrudging sigh, he loosened his grip on me. The second he did, Jagger pulled me into his arms, hugging me so fiercely that I released a tiny squeak.

"Not a word of this to the others," he gruffly said.

A small smile trembled on my lips. "Promise."

He held me a moment longer, then abruptly let go. When he did, another pair of arms swooped in and took his place. Recognizing them as my brother's, I squeezed my eyes shut and hugged him back.

"We won't let them take you," he said and pressed a kiss to my hair.

"I know," I whispered, feeling tears sting my eyelids.

When he finally pulled back, Griff took me into his arms again. I didn't complain, more than happy to soak up their attention. It kept me from freaking out over what the hunter had said.

They wanted to breed me. *Breed* me. What the actual hell?

CHAPTER 23

VIOLET

"I still can't believe they're kidnapping females to breed them. That's so twisted."

I softly snorted at Brielle's comment, then looked up when my mom came bustling into my bedroom with a glass of milk and a plate of freshly baked cookies.

"Here you go, honey," she said, handing them to me. "Do you need anything else? I could make you a sandwich too. You must be starving."

"Thanks, but I'm okay, Mom," I replied with a small smile. "These cookies smell delicious."

She returned my smile, but it wobbled a little. "Okay. I'm just down the hall if you change your mind."

As she leaned over the bed to kiss my cheek, I soaked up her scent and warmth once more. It helped anchor me to the present, to the reality that I was finally *home*.

"Love you, sweetie," she whispered, sniffling a little. "I'm so glad you're safe."

"I love you too, Mom," I replied, but my tears had long since dried up. We'd arrived back before dawn, but Nora, Brielle, and my mom had all been up to welcome us home. The second I'd felt their loving arms around me, I'd burst into tears. I'd cried and cried until I couldn't cry anymore and then had spent the next hour snuggled between Nora and Brielle on my bed.

I'd told them everything, including the breakup with Reid, the hunters' reasons for kidnapping females, and what had happened between me and Griff. They were still digesting all the shocking news, but Nora had seemed less shocked about the profession-of-love part. She'd even bitten her lip to hide a smile. I was too tired to question her about it, though.

Kolton and Jagger had promptly left again with the one-armed hunter. We didn't have anywhere to keep him long term, and since he could still be used for questioning, Kolton had decided to contact the Supernatural Containment Agency.

They had the right facilities to keep him imprisoned and full-time staff to pressure him into revealing more information. Bill Andrews, the warlock Sheriff from Maine who'd helped us imprison Arrow and several witch elders last year, had agreed to meet them halfway and transport the hunter to one of the SCA's high-security prisons.

He would stay in touch with any new information he learned about the hunters and even assured us that their field operatives would start searching for the missing hybrid females right away.

It was a relief knowing that they would help, but the world was a vast place. The hunters could be keeping the females *anywhere*.

Poor Desirae. She must be so frightened right now.

Bone-deep exhaustion suddenly swept over me, and I nearly dropped the plate of cookies.

"Okay, time for Vi to get some sleep," Nora said, taking the plate and glass of milk from me and setting them on the nightstand. "We can talk more after she's rested."

I gave her a sleepy smile, barely able to keep my eyes open as she, Brielle, and my mom tucked me in.

Before leaving, Nora leaned down to give me one last hug and whispered in my ear, "I'm so happy for you and Griff. He absolutely adores you."

Sudden emotion clogged my throat, robbing me of speech. Thankfully, she didn't wait for a reply, sweeping from the room to quietly shut the door. As silence settled over the familiar space, I closed my eyes and waited for sleep to drag me under. I was exhausted, so exhausted that I couldn't think or see straight. Falling asleep should be *easy*.

But several minutes ticked by, and sleep wouldn't claim me.

I was too . . . too *alone*.

My body needed physical contact, needed *warmth* from another. Needed the comfort of their scent and presence.

There was only one person who could give me all of that, one person who could put my fears to rest with a single touch.

Do it, Sable softly whined. *I miss Whiskey too.*

I locked my limbs in place, desperately trying not to give in. It wasn't *fair* to him. Seeking Griff out now would only send the wrong message. This was my chance to fix things, not make them *worse*.

But as time crawled by, my need for him overrode common sense, and I shoved my blankets aside. On autopilot, I stumbled from bed and crossed the room, pausing at the door to listen before opening it and slipping into the hall. I could hear faint sounds down below, probably Mom getting the kitchen ready for breakfast, but no one was in sight.

Soundlessly shutting the door behind me, I stole down the hallway like a guilty thief, hugging the rectangle-shaped banister until I neared the bedroom directly across from mine. I paused a moment more to make sure no one was watching, then silently opened the door and slipped inside.

Right away, I noticed that the door to the attached bathroom was closed. The sink faucet was running, and I could hear Griff brushing his teeth. I almost left then. Almost sneaked out with my tail between my legs, Griff none the wiser for my slip. But something on his king-sized bed caught my eye, and I couldn't help but smile.

Tucked between his pillows was the replacement teddy bear Melanie had gifted him this past Christmas. Teddy the Second, she'd named him, after the first one had been lost in the house fire.

I took a moment to inspect the rest of his room, realizing I hadn't been in here since we'd rebuilt. The walls were slate blue, and the black, silver, and gray decor was decidedly masculine. There was a TV mounted on the wall and a weight bench in one corner, but nothing about the space screamed *Griff*. He used to have nerdy sci-fi posters on his walls and little action figures. Silly stuff that I used to tease him about yet stick in his Christmas stocking every year. They were all gone now, casualties of the fire that had destroyed our home.

I'd have to rectify that. His room needed a makeover pronto.

Curiosity lured me to his walk-in closet next, and I quickly poked my head inside. Nope. No sex doll. Unless he kept it under the bed.

A familiar-looking bag on one of the shelves drew my eye, and I picked it up with a gasp.

"Yeah, you weren't supposed to find that," a voice from behind me drawled.

I whirled to discover a shirtless Griff in the closet doorway, a sheepish grin on his face. Thank heavens he was wearing *pants*, although they were the gray sweatpants that hugged his dick, making it really hard to focus. Still, I shook the lingerie bag in my hands and hissed, "Griffin Hayes O'Neal, I looked *everywhere* for these. Why are they in your closet?"

Leaning against the doorframe, he rubbed the nape of his neck before admitting, "I couldn't stand the thought of Reid seeing you in them. Especially the purple one."

My mouth fell open. "You . . . You were jealous?"

"Ah c'mon, Vi. You bought that lingerie while thinking of another male. You wanted him to look at you, to lust after you, to have *sex* with you. Of course I was jealous. The thought of him eyeing you in that getup made me crazy."

I blinked at him stupidly, unable to stop my stomach from fluttering. "Oh. Well, um . . ." I cleared my suddenly dry throat and tried again. "You could have just tossed it."

A small laugh left him. "That would be a waste of perfectly good underwear. Just because I don't want Reid to see them on you doesn't mean *I* don't want to see them."

This time, my stomach swooped with full-blown butterflies. It was strange hearing him be so honest with me about how he felt—but not a bad strange. It felt nice. *Really* nice. I could become addicted to this feeling. *Deliriously* addicted.

I tried to think of a witty comeback, but my brain was suddenly empty of all thought.

When I just stood there gaping like an idiot, he studied me a moment before asking, "Why are you in here, anyway? Did you need me?"

"Uh, no. N-not for *that*," I quickly stammered, feeling heat creep up my neck. "I just . . . I couldn't sleep and thought . . . I thought that maybe . . ."

"You could sleep with me?" he gently finished for me, his understanding expression doing funny things to my insides.

Biting my lip so I couldn't stammer some more, I simply nodded.

He stared at me for another beat, then pushed off the frame and approached. As he did, the closet suddenly felt too small. A swallow got stuck in my throat, but I didn't retreat, even when he took the bag from me and placed it back on the shelf. Even when he stepped closer to trail his fingers down the snake tattoo on my arm. Even when he slowly linked our fingers together and pressed his warm palm to mine.

Without a word, he turned and tugged me after him, guiding me straight to his bed. When he pulled back the comforter and sheets, my heart decided to betray me. It started to race, and Griff paused to glance at me.

I tried to look casual, unfazed, but failed miserably. In actuality, I probably looked like a petrified rabbit about to be eaten.

Confusion flitted across Griff's face. He opened his mouth to question me, then must have thought better of it. With a quiet sigh, he simply said, "We'll just sleep. If you want more, all you have to do is ask."

I nodded again, feeling my heart rate begin to slow. Sleep. I could handle that. It was the *other* stuff I couldn't handle.

As we both settled onto the bed, Griff picked up a remote on his nightstand and turned off the light. The room plunged into darkness, his blackout curtains sealing out the early morning sun. After a moment, though, my night vision kicked in, and I could clearly see him beside me on the bed.

He was on his back, staring up at the ceiling as if he was . . . waiting.

Waiting for *me*. For direction.

My heart rate picked up again, and I froze in place, uncertain what to do.

I shouldn't be here, shouldn't be here, shouldn't be here, I chanted to myself, and yet I couldn't make myself leave.

"What's wrong?"

I startled at the sound of his voice like a jittery deer. "W-what? Nothing's wrong."

"C'mon, Vi. I *know* you. You're jumpy, hesitant, and your heart is beating like a drum. You're terrified, and this isn't the first time you've acted this way. It's almost like . . ."

When he paused, I whispered, "Like what?"

He turned his head to look at me, his mouth set in a grim line. "Like you don't know what you want."

"I *do* know what I want," I automatically replied before I could stop myself.

And I did. Oh God, I did. I *truly* did.

"Then tell me. Tell me what you want, Vi, because I'm starting to think that you don't want—"

"I want you to hold me," I blurted before he could finish.

He stared at me in silence for a long moment, then rolled onto his side and pulled me to him. When I was tucked securely against his chest, he quietly rumbled, "Is this good?"

I nodded, my heart slowing again as his warmth seeped into me. He brushed a lock of hair off my cheek, then gently ran his fingers through the silky tresses, making me want to purr like a cat.

A purring sound filled my mind, and I internally rolled my eyes at Sable.

Contentment settled over me, and my eyes drifted shut, but after several minutes, I was still wide awake.

Griff continued to stroke my hair, but when I didn't fall asleep, he murmured, "Tell me what you want."

I stiffened, my eyes snapping back open.

"Tell me what you want, Vi," he repeated, the words a gentle nudge, a *push*. He knew I needed something more, and he wasn't waiting for me to ask this time.

"I want you to kiss me," I said, then nearly gasped, shocked by how readily I'd answered.

He'd pushed, and I'd willingly let him. I'd almost *welcomed* it. Oh God, what was happening to me?

Without a word, he placed his fingers beneath my chin and tipped my face up, then pressed his lips to mine. At how intoxicatingly warm and soft they felt, I immediately melted. He stretched his hand along my jaw and kissed me more fully, making my toes curl beneath the sheets. All on their own, my hands slid to his back and pulled our bodies closer. Closer. Not close enough. I tangled my legs with his, but it still wasn't close enough.

"Tell me what you want, Vi," Griff breathed against my lips

"Touch," I whimpered back. "I want you to touch me."

His body reacted to the words by shuddering against mine. A breathy moan escaped me as he pulled me impossibly close, close enough that I felt how hard I'd just made him. Slipping a hand beneath my night shirt, he slid his hot palm all the way up my spine. His other hand did the same but to my front, sliding up my stomach and between my breasts.

Frantic butterflies erupted in my belly as he broke the kiss to tug my shirt over my head, leaving my upper half bare. Then he rolled onto his back again so that I was sitting on top of him, straddling his waist. The sheets slid off of me, revealing my nakedness, but I didn't care.

I *wanted* him to see me. I wanted him to *look* at me. To want me. To lust after me. And that's exactly what he did.

As he took in my bare breasts, his eyes went molten.

"Gorgeous," he said in a hushed whisper. "You've always been so incredibly beautiful."

My bottom lip quivered, and I leaned down to kiss him. He dug his fingers into my hair and kissed me back, his mouth hot and needy against mine. The kiss turned passionate, our tongues seeking each other out as the need for more trembled through us both. My thighs tightened around his waist, and he gripped one to guide me onto his erection. As I felt it pulse through our clothing, I moaned into his mouth, my own core growing wet in response.

Sliding his hand to my butt, he gripped it hard and rocked against me. Pleasure unfurled in my center, and I arched back with a gasp. Griff lifted his head and kissed my exposed throat, continuing to grind himself against me. I placed my hands on his chest to steady myself, quivering with growing desire. His kisses trailed downward, making my breath come in short spurts. Still rocking against me, he lifted up even more so he could reach my breasts, kissing them both lightly until my nipples hardened.

When they did, he took one into his mouth. I arched back even more, completely lost to the moment. All I cared about was how it felt to be with him. Nothing else mattered. Any reasons I had for not wanting this to happen again fled my mind, because the only thing I wanted was *this*. It felt so achingly good to have him kissing and touching me. He knew just how to please me, and I was helpless to resist it.

As he continued to lick and suck on my nipples, leaving me a panting, quivering mess, his hand left my backside and slid between my spread thighs. The first touch of his fingers against my ultra sensitive clit nearly made me come. He wasn't even touching my bare skin, choosing to rub me slowly through my pajama shorts and underwear.

"Griff!" I gasped out, grabbing on to his shoulders as my body bent backward even more. I quivered uncontrollably against him, pressing my knees into the mattress while he pleasured my nipples and clit in tandem. His free hand went to my spine, securing me in place so I wouldn't topple over backward.

"Is this what you want, baby?" he murmured against my skin.

"Yes. *Yes*," I breathlessly cried.

My body was happily thrumming, basking in the incredible high his tongue and skilled fingers were giving me. Nothing compared to this. Being with him in this way was pure magic, and I never wanted it to end. I clung to him for dear life and panted through each wave of pleasure, refusing to come down.

This was what I wanted, and I had to have it. Had to have *him*.

I held on for several minutes, every inch of my body blissfully alive. *Don't come, don't come, don't come*, I told myself, desperate for the incredible sensations Griff was making me feel. But when he abruptly slid his fingers into my underwear and touched my swollen clit, I lost it.

Euphoria exploded through me, punching the air from my lungs. I opened my mouth in a silent scream, my body stiffening as the orgasm consumed my entire being. As I shot sky high, he stiffened as well. With a deep groan, he jerked once, letting me know that he'd just come in his pants. The realization tipped me over the edge again, and I came against his fingers a second time.

Overwhelmed by the pleasure flooding my system, I went limp against him. He caught me, lowering my boneless body to the mattress while I continued to spasm from pleasurable aftershocks. With one hand still in my underwear to prolong the orgasm, he lifted his other to sweep the hair off my face.

Still trembling and spasming, I opened my eyes to see him already looking at me. The contentment, the *happiness* on his face—it was almost more than I could bear.

"I love pleasuring you," he said in an awed voice. "Watching you come is one of my favorite things ever."

A breathy laugh left me. "And what is your favorite thing?"

"You," he automatically replied, his smile so devastating that I couldn't breathe. "*You* are my favorite thing, Violet Jane Rivers."

CHAPTER 24

GRIFF

"Sure you're up for this?" Kolton asked me as we watched the first guests start to arrive. Jagger was directing cars into parking spots along the private drive, and the females and children were still inside, so it was just Kolton and me on the wide porch.

"Not really," I openly admitted, "but this Alpha Meeting needs to happen. I'm glad you didn't postpone or cancel it."

"It's definitely casual compared to the last one," Kolton said, clearly still uncertain about his decision to host the meeting at the Rivers family estate.

Alpha Meetings were usually few and far between, but it was an opportunity for the hosts to display their influence, power, and wealth. The estate alone was worth hundreds of millions, but he and Nora had decided against decorating for the occasion. We weren't even offering food or beverages to our esteemed guests.

After what had just happened to me and Vi, it didn't seem appropriate.

"I had to wear a suit and tie at the last meeting," I responded to Kolton's comment. "This meeting is much more my style."

He grunted at that, sweeping a glance over my business casual attire. I was wearing dark gray pants and a white collared shirt with sleeves rolled up to the elbow. His apparel was similar to mine, and so was Jagger's. "At least you're wearing shoes."

I barked a laugh. "They pinch my feet, but Vi would kill me if she caught me wearing flip-flops to this shindig."

His gaze went to my right arm, to the spot where my snake tattoo should be. "How is she?"

Even though Vi was his sister, it didn't feel strange to hear him ask me that question. They'd always been close, but she and I were closer, even as kids. If she needed to confide in someone, she usually went to me. Problem was, she had a tendency to bottle up her feelings and put up a brave front instead of talking things out. After the morning we'd just had together in my bed, though, I'd hoped to wake up and coax some of those feelings out of her. But she'd sneaked out of my room before I had a chance to.

With a quiet sigh, I answered Kolton, "Staying strong as always, but I'm worried. After visiting Randy's family this afternoon to tell them the bad news, she went right back to work as if nothing had happened. She's been through a lot lately, and I don't think she's taken the time to process any of it yet, including . . . including us."

Kolton was silent for a long beat, then replied, "Although I was surprised that you two were intimate so soon after Reid broke up with her, I understand why. You've loved her for years and have always been there for her. After you started helping with her heat, I'd hoped you two would become a mated pair."

I blinked, relieved to hear him say that. "Me too. I assumed she wasn't interested in me that way, only to find out that she thought *I* wasn't. She even thought I was ashamed to be helping her. That's why she ended things between us last year, so I could move on and find a true mate."

"Oh, Vi," Kolton said, shaking his head. "I think she's still holding on to what Arrow did to her. That, and she still blames herself for what happened afterward."

I stared out at the cars quickly filling the private drive, the evening sky darkening by the minute. As if on cue, the tall lamps circling the roundabout and lining the narrow road flickered on, lighting up the growing dusk.

"I think you're right," I replied, then decided to take the plunge and say, "But after what that hunter said, all I can think about is claiming her. If they're only kidnapping unclaimed hybrid females, then maybe they'll leave her alone if I mark her."

I held my breath, half-expecting my best friend to be angry at me for having such a thought. Vi was his little sister, and I was talking about *biting* her. Sex was one thing, but leaving my mark and scent on her was a whole other level.

But, to my surprise, all Kolton said was, "Claiming her is a smart idea. But are you sure she wants that?"

I blew out a pent-up breath, rubbing at the back of my neck before replying, "I don't know. She seems to want me one minute, then pulls away the next. She even said she loved me. But after we slept together this morning—"

"Watch it," Kolton rumbled in warning.

"After we slept for hours without touching each other," I amended with a smirk, "she bolted."

Kolton hummed softly in thought but didn't say anything.

"The last thing I want to do is force her into something she doesn't want," I continued, even as my heart broke a little at the thought of her not wanting me.

"I know that feeling all too well," Kolton wryly replied, reaching up to clap me on the shoulder. "Sounds like you're doing a better job at being patient than I was with Nora, though."

I snorted, remembering how determined he'd been to marry his soulmate before she was ready. At least Vi hadn't hit me over the head with a serving tray. Yet.

"I'll talk to Nora and see if she can get Vi to open up," he added, giving my shoulder a squeeze before letting go. "Vi went several years without close female connections, but she's getting better at confiding in them. There are just some things she can't talk to us males about."

Before I could reply, noises from inside the house interrupted our conversation. Knowing that Vi and Nora were about to join us, we dropped the subject for the time being. Mrs. Rivers and Brielle would be watching the children during the meeting, so they were staying inside. Kolton had almost decided against holding the meeting here so close to the children, but going anywhere else could leave them vulnerable. Even after learning that the hunters were packless rogues and wouldn't be at the meeting, they were still a threat. Besides Vi, we still had one other unclaimed hybrid female in the family that needed our protection.

Melanie.

She was only seven, but I wouldn't put anything past those sick bastards.

Until we dealt with the rogue males and found the missing females, we weren't taking any chances. Hosting an Alpha Meeting was all the risk we could afford. But knowing that I'd have to see my *brother* tonight was testing the limits of my control. He had a way of getting under my skin like no one else could, and I was already on edge from everything that had happened this past week.

Only a year older than me, Mason had always resented my close friendship with the Rivers family, not to mention my hybrid abilities. Our entire lives, he'd tried to cut me down in order to rise up in the pack ranks. When that hadn't worked, he'd gone after Vi. Even though I'd wanted to pursue her slowly at the time, I hadn't been able to stomach the thought of him being intimate with her.

So, I'd pursued her as well, and she'd chosen me to help with her heat.

Mason had given up after that, deciding to leave Midnight Pack and branch off on his own. He was now the alpha of Moon Bay Pack, his territory just north of here in the Montreal, Canada area. It was small, but he'd gotten what he had always wanted.

To be number one.

I'd only spoken to him once since he'd left the pack, and recalling that conversation left a bitter taste in my mouth. If he decided to poke at me in a similar manner tonight, I doubted I would be able to keep my cool.

My thoughts were suddenly distracted by the front door opening. I turned just as Nora exited the house, and she smiled when I gave her an appreciative look. She was wearing a white cocktail dress, one with a high neckline and semi-transparent sleeves. As she gracefully moved across the porch, her flowy skirt swishing against her thighs, I glanced over at Kolton to find him practically drooling.

"Save it for the afterparty, man," I joked, but he didn't even hear me. When his wife was near enough, he drew her into a possessive hold, sliding one hand beneath her skirt to grip her thigh. She chuckled softly, and he swooped his head down to capture her lips. Unmindful of the growing audience out on the lawn, he kissed her like a starving man, brazenly lifting her leg to grind himself against her.

Used to their public displays of passion, I just shook my head. It was entirely real, but the PDA served as a message as well, one that clearly said Midnight Pack's alphas were still in love and wholly united. They were a power couple, and to challenge that was to risk your life.

Noticing movement in my peripheral, I turned and saw Vi standing in the doorway. She was dressed in a flowy short cocktail dress as well, but it was a deep purple color, sleeveless, and plunged at the neckline. Her cleavage was on full display, and a swallow got stuck in my throat as I recalled burying my face in that very spot this morning, right after I'd come in my pants.

Feeling my cock start to harden, I brought my eyes back to her face. She looked breathtaking, her bangs perfectly in place and the rest of her dark tresses loosely curled. Her makeup was flawless, highlighting her already gorgeous features. But her eyes—they weren't on me. They were locked on her brother and Nora, and I watched as the color slowly drained from her face.

Concerned, I stepped toward her, and her gaze immediately flew to mine. Her violet eyes were wide, and the look in them was unmistakable.

She was terrified.

The need to comfort her was instantaneous, and I reached out to take her hand. Before I could, she stepped from the doorway and swept past me with a little laugh. A *forced* one.

"Jeez, you two, get a room already," she muttered, her high heels clicking across the porch and down the steps. "Guess I'll go greet the *guests* since you're obviously too busy sucking face."

I watched her go, frustration a tight knot in my chest, then shoved aside my pride and went after her. It took everything in me not to whirl her around and demand she tell me what was bothering her. Because something definitely was, and it was *killing* me. Did she regret coming to my bedroom this morning? Did she regret *us*?

I needed to know, even if she said yes and tore out my heart.

But now was obviously not the time. Alphas from around the world were approaching us, many of them accompanied by their entourages. Several had mates but not all, and a few had come alone, but most had brought at least a few of their most dominant pack members. Jagger was already conversing with a mated pair from Alaska, and Vi was heading toward one of the alphas that had contacted us about a missing female a few days ago.

After a moment of hesitation, I decided to give her some space, choosing to converse with an alpha not too far away. We'd been doing this political dance for years, and Vi had done enough research on each alpha that we knew just how to speak to them. Many of them had been friends with Anthony and Charlotte Rivers during their rule of Midnight Pack, but we couldn't forget that none of them had come to our aid last year.

Werewolves tended to stick close to home, and packs didn't often mingle. Still, they'd failed us in our hour of need, forcing us to accept help from the most unlikely of sources—the royal vampire family. Without them, Kolton might not have found Nora and Luca in time. Midnight Pack could have fallen without our unexpected new allies, and we had every intention of calling on their help again if the werewolf community chose to turn their backs on us once more.

"Is it true that Violet was almost taken?" Alpha Abernathy from Washington state asked me. Word of the abductions had definitely spread, and as I used my heightened hearing to eavesdrop on a few other conversations, it was all anyone was talking about.

"Yes," I confirmed, keeping an eye on Vi as I spoke. "Twice, actually, but they failed both times."

The middle-aged male's eyes widened, and he started questioning me about who "they" were.

"Alpha Rivers will be sharing the details on that soon, but I can at least assure you that no one involved in the kidnappings will be present tonight."

He seemed relieved to hear that, but as more and more alphas arrived, the crowd's restlessness increased. They wanted *answers*, and it was clear that we were the only ones who had them. At the realization, unease settled in my gut. We had answers, but we still didn't know where the missing females were being kept. If no one else knew where they were, it meant that we probably wouldn't find them anytime soon.

My eyes went to Vi again, a fresh wave of protectiveness surging through me. When I found her speaking to a tall male with dark hair, light brown skin, and twinkling hazel eyes, my mind emptied. Rudely excusing myself in the middle of a conversation, I strode toward her before I could check myself.

Whiskey, who'd been rather quiet today, encouraged me onward, growling, *Don't let him take your female again.*

I won't, I assured him. Not this time. Not without a fight.

"I really am sorry," she was saying to him, her back to me as I approached. "You were right. You were right about everything. I shouldn't have—"

Stiffening at the sound of my approach, she whirled rather abruptly. The second she saw it was me, the fear in her eyes dissipated. "Jeez, Griff. You scared the hell out of me."

Her words were lightly spoken, but I knew they were just a front. She'd been terrified that I was a hunter about to snatch her away. Slowing, I watched her carefully, giving her ample time to pull away as I eased into her personal space and slid an arm around her. She immediately melted against me, and I grew weak with relief. Still, I stood tall, firmly pulling her back against my chest as I faced her ex-boyfriend.

"Reid," I said by way of greeting, trying hard not to growl the word.

I was glad he'd ended their relationship, but he'd still hurt her. My protective instincts were demanding I seek retribution, and Whiskey settled back down, assured that I had this under control.

"Griff," the quarterback greeted back, studying me and Vi a moment before adding, "Looks like you got what you wanted."

"Looks like I did," I replied, splaying my hand on Vi's stomach.

At the possessive move, he shook his head with a small laugh. "Don't worry, man. She's all yours. She was only ever yours to begin with."

Vi's heart skipped a beat, but she didn't comment.

The need to stake my claim started to fade, but I kept my hand right where it was all the same, feeling less on edge the longer she was pressed against me.

With an almost wistful smile, Reid stared at us for another beat, then said, "I should go. My uncle wanted to introduce me to some more alphas. He'll be stepping down and initiating me into Lunar Falls Pack as the new alpha once this football season ends, so I have a lot to learn in a short period of time."

"Oh, wow, Reid. I'm so happy for you," Vi exclaimed, and I could tell she truly meant it.

"Thanks," he replied, giving her one of his signature smiles.

As he turned to go, Vi suddenly pulled away from me. "Reid, wait."

My instincts flared up again, and Whiskey sat up in a panic, but I forced myself not to react as she rushed forward to grab Reid's hand.

"I-I really am sorry about what happened," she said as he turned back to her. "I was hoping that maybe . . . that maybe we could still be friends?"

Now that's our smart wee lass, Whiskey purred in contentment, settling back down again.

Reid stared at her, then smiled again and replied, "I would like that."

With a relieved sigh, she hugged him. He hugged her back, and the urge to tackle him to the ground reared up. But the hug was over a second later, and with a little wave, Vi turned from Reid and came back to me.

Me.

I felt a sudden need to kiss her in front of everyone, to let every single male here know that Vi belonged to *me.*

Surprised by the possessive thought, especially when it wasn't entirely true, I didn't see the male with wavy dark blond hair approaching Vi until it was too late.

"Little Violet!" he sang, scooping her up to twirl her around.

Instead of trying to break free, Vi broke into a grin. "Mace! Fashionably late, as always."

"You know it!" he said with a laugh, then stopped twirling to nuzzle her neck and groan, "God, have you always smelled this good? I should have eaten before coming here because I'm suddenly *starving.*"

At that, my vision turned red. It was like a switch in my brain flipped, flooding my entire being with rage.

Bellowing a roar, I pulled Vi from my brother's arms and shoved him. *Hard.* Hard enough to send him crashing to the ground and rolling across the lawn.

"Griff!" Vi cried, but I could barely hear her over the pounding in my ears. I lunged for him again, only for a powerful pair of arms to hold me back.

"*Stand down,*" a familiar voice barked, but I continued to lunge for Mason, out of my mind with fury.

"He touched her!" I thundered, yanking my arms free of Kolton's hold, only for another pair of arms to join in. Even though I knew I couldn't overpower Kolton and Jagger combined, I still fought, my control in shambles at my feet. "Vi is mine. MINE."

"GRIFFIN!" a female voice shouted, with such desperation that I paused. "Griff, *please*. Please don't do this!"

When her words ended in a sob, the red haze disappeared. I blinked to find Vi standing before me, her face streaked with mascara.

Just like that, all of my anger left me.

"Vi," I rasped, reaching for her. Kolton and Jagger let go of my arms, and I quickly gathered her against me. She pressed her face to my chest, her tears soaking through my shirt in seconds. I held her tightly, trembling with the need to carry her far, far away from here.

No one said a word for several long moments. The air was deathly quiet, and I realized too late the sin I'd just committed.

But I suddenly didn't care.

Mason never should have touched her like that.

If he ever did it again, I'd *kill* him.

CHAPTER 25

VIOLET

I'd seen Griff mad at his brother before, but not like this.

Something was wrong.

He was shaking, holding me so tightly that I could barely breathe. He almost seemed *feral*, which didn't make sense. This was Griff. Griff didn't lose control like that.

But he had. He'd completely flipped out.

At an *Alpha Meeting*, no less. Physical altercations weren't allowed at these meetings. If anyone broke the rule, they were automatically banned from all future events.

Even so, it wasn't the repercussions that had brought me to tears. Not even his anger. It was the panic I'd seen in his eyes, the *fear*. He'd been frantic when his brother had snatched me up. He was still frantic, his arms like a steel wall of protection around me, keeping everyone and everything away. Almost as if . . .

He's terrified that someone will take you away from him like the hunters almost did, Sable finished the thought for me.

Yeah. That. It was a feeling I knew all too well, a feeling that I'd been struggling with long before the hunters came into the picture.

"Griff, it's okay," I spoke to him in soothing tones, sliding my hands around him to rub comforting circles on his back. "He's not going to take me. No one is."

He shuddered against me, his heart continuing to loudly thunder. "You're mine. You're *mine*," he said, the words muffled against my hair.

"Okay. Okay, I'm yours. But we're safe here. You can let go."

"Mine," he repeated, his heartbeats gradually slowing.

"Yours," I assured him, coaxing him to loosen his grip. When he did, I shifted in his arms to face the deathly silent crowd.

Normally not a self-conscious person, the mix of curious and critical looks made me feel naked, and I heard more than one person try to catch a whiff of my scent.

They were searching for answers too, most of them familiar enough with Griff to know that he wasn't one to make a scene. A *violent* one, at least. And especially not at an Alpha Meeting where violence was a huge breach of trust.

I could see them forming conclusions, all of them wrong. Even if they could smell that we'd had sex recently, Griff and I weren't newly mated. He hadn't even claimed me. If he had, most here would at least understand the reasoning behind his outburst, but once they figured out that wasn't the case, they'd banish him from the meeting. For *life*. His reputation would be ruined, and they might even question his place as Kolton's third in command.

I couldn't let that happen. I had to *protect* him. So, before I could think better of it, I said loudly for all to hear, "Griff isn't to blame for this. He was only trying to keep me safe. We just got back from being hunted by rogue males, and the trauma of that is still fresh on our minds."

No one spoke for several long moments, and I thought for sure my words had fallen on deaf ears. Just as I was about to lose hope, Alpha Abernathy said, "Rogues? Are they the ones who've been kidnapping females?"

I flicked a glance at Kolton. When all he did was slowly nod, relief filled me. Bolstered by his approval, I stood taller and answered,

"Yes. There are several of them, but we don't know how many or where they're keeping the females. We do know that they're only targeting unclaimed hybrid females and that they plan to use them for breeding."

"*Breeding?*" a female alpha from Germany gasped.

Just like that, the attention shifted from Griff's indiscretion to the troubling news. Shouts erupted from the crowd, several expressing their outrage. Not every pack had female hybrids, but kidnapping *any* female from her pack to be used for breeding was something every pack leader feared.

As Kolton stepped forward to address the crowd's concerns in more detail, Nora came to stand beside me and Griff. Griff's arms tightened around me again, then relaxed when he realized it was her.

Leaning over, I quietly murmured in her ear, "Do you think they'll kick him out?"

"I don't know," she whispered back, then added, "But it might be a good idea for him to excuse himself. Just for a little while until we get things sorted out."

I immediately hated the idea, even as I agreed with her.

Before I could say anything, Griff said, "I'll take a walk. I have my new phone if anyone needs to reach me."

As he let go of me, I immediately missed his warmth. Turning around, I grabbed his hand before he could leave and softly said, "Griff, wait. I'm . . . I'm sorry."

I didn't know what I was apologizing for specifically, only that I was sorry. About *everything*. He wouldn't be in this situation right now if it wasn't for me.

Watching a fresh tear track down my cheek, he reached up and gently wiped it away. "Do me a favor, Vi," he quietly replied, remorse heavy in his voice. "Don't let him touch you again."

Knowing who he was referring to, I nodded, then reluctantly let go of his hand so he could turn and walk away. As I watched him leave, Nora slid an arm around me, and I gratefully accepted her comfort.

"You okay?" she continued to whisper as Kolton finished telling our guests what we knew about the rogues.

No. I was definitely *not* okay and neither was Griff, but now wasn't the time to pour my heart out. Our guests had already seen me cry, and I couldn't afford to reveal any more weaknesses. Mason was looking at me far too intently, his brown eyes so similar to Griff's that I couldn't hold his gaze.

I was an alpha female, and before Nora had joined the pack last year, it had been up to me to keep things running smoothly. I'd spent the past seven years supporting Kolton and making sure other packs only saw his strengths. Which meant that I'd had to be strong as well, even when I'd wanted to break into a million pieces.

"I'll be fine," I quickly reassured Nora, adding a smile when she gave me a skeptical look. *Later*, the look said, and I nodded in agreement, almost relieved that she hadn't believed me.

Because it was getting harder to stay strong. If I kept going like this, something was going to give, and I was pretty sure that something would be my sanity.

The meeting went on for hours, each alpha wishing to weigh in on how best to find the missing females and confront the rogues responsible. Almost all of them wanted justice, their reactions promising compared to the last Alpha Meeting. Apparently, the thought of females being used for the sole purpose of breeding angered even the most neutral pack leaders.

But as the evening wore on, my restlessness increased. Griff hadn't returned, and I was beginning to worry. I couldn't text him, though. I'd left my new phone in the house. Knowing that I'd messed things up even more between us by assuring him I was *his* only added to my misery.

No matter how hard I tried, I couldn't seem to *stop* messing up. I'd done and said things this past week that I couldn't take back, and our friendship was going to suffer because of it. *Griff* was going to suffer.

How could I do that to him? Why was I so freaking *selfish*?

Lost in my own self-deprecating thoughts, I almost didn't notice the crowd beginning to disperse, a sure sign that the meeting had ended. It had concluded in our favor, and no one had brought up Griff's indiscretion. I should feel relieved, but the only thing I continued to feel was an incessant restlessness. An *itch* just beneath my skin that I couldn't scratch.

"You okay?" Nora asked again, noticing that I couldn't seem to hold still.

"Yeah, I'm just gonna take a little walk to clear my head," I replied. When she gave me another dubious look, I added, "I won't go far, promise. Just to the front gates and back."

Not waiting for a response, I turned and strode across the lawn at a fast walk. Cars were pulling through the roundabout and leaving the way they'd arrived, but I didn't pause to wave goodbye, too focused on walking along the narrow road. But the longer I walked, the stronger the itch became, making my face break out in a cold sweat.

What the hell?

My confusion vanished a few steps later when a familiar sensation pulsed through me. It was so strong that I doubled over, nearly twisting my ankle in the process.

Struggling to breathe through the pulsing wave, I waited for it to pass before biting out a curse.

You've gone into heat, Sable needlessly told me, and I sharply swore again.

It was too soon. My last heat had only been three months ago.

Another wave hit, forcing me to accept that I was indeed going into heat—and *fast*. Heat flushed through my body, making me uncomfortable in my dress. A trembling had already begun in my arms and legs, and I came to an abrupt halt, knowing that I had to make a decision while I could still stand.

Call for Griff, Sable urged me, and the heat flared in response to his name.

As it settled between my legs, I squeezed my eyes shut with a groan. It would be so easy, *so* easy to call for him. He would come without hesitation, and that was the problem. I couldn't do this to him again. I *wouldn't*.

Waiting for the second wave to pass, I straightened, my mind made up. But as I turned to head back toward the garage, a silver Rolls-Royce stopped beside me.

"Hey, little Violet. You all right?"

Biting back another curse, I made a split-second decision. One that I'd probably regret, but I was desperate, and I tended to do stupid things when I was desperate.

"I need a ride," I replied to Griff's brother, trying to walk normally as I rounded his car and pulled open the passenger side door. The second I slid inside and shut the door, Mason groaned loudly and tightened his grip on the steering wheel.

"That better not be what I think it is, Vi."

"It is. Just go, okay? You owe me after what you pulled earlier, and I promise you won't have to endure it for long. I have a place not too far from here where I can take care of it."

"By *yourself*?" he asked incredulously.

"Mace, just *go!*" I all but shouted, fisting my hands as I felt another wave hit me.

"*Hell*, Vi, that's strong," he groaned again but thankfully stepped on the gas. As he pulled through the gates and left the estate behind, he asked, "How come you're not calling for your famous quarterback boyfriend to help you?"

"What, are you keeping tabs on me now?"

"No, but I watch sports, and you made the news more than once."

"It's . . . We broke up."

"Ah," he said, then added, "Guess that explains why you're having sex with my brother again."

Despite the pulsating pain eating away at me, I turned my head to glare at him. "If you knew, then why in the hell did you *greet* me that way earlier?"

"Ah, Vi, don't be mad at me. You know I like to get a rise out of my baby bro. I didn't know he'd almost lost you to those bastard rogues only a day ago."

"Yeah, well, what you did was still mean and spiteful. You're an alpha and have your own pack now, so I don't understand why you keep trying to knock him down."

A muscle feathered in his jaw. "It's complicated between us."

Snorting, I faced forward again. "Well, it's complicated between me and Griff too. Which is why I'm taking care of my heat alone."

Mason was silent for a beat, then had the audacity to say, "You don't have to, you know. I help a few of the unmated females in my pack with their heat and will gladly help you with yours."

"Mason O'Neal, you did *not* just say that!" I snapped, shooting him another withering glare. At the same time, my core heated, uncaring who was offering to help. All it cared about was getting *attention*, and an alpha male was willing to do just that. Frustrated with my skanky libido, I said, "Pull over and let me out."

"Okay, jeez! I take it back! Forget I said anything."

With a huff, I grumbled, "I refuse to be a consolation prize in your pointless brotherly feud."

"I know. You made that perfectly clear seven years ago. But Griff's the one who attacked *me*. There's no love lost on his end either."

"Are you *that* dense, Mace? He used to look up to you before you started picking stupid fights all the time."

"That's funny. I've only ever seen him look up to his *idol*—no offense to your brother."

"That's because you're *blind*."

"Well, guess that makes two of us."

I flicked him another glare. "What's that supposed to mean?"

"It means that my brother is in love with you and has been for a very long time, but here you are, running away from him."

"I'm not . . ." Sudden horror gripped me. I looked down at the snake tattoo on my arm, just as a fresh wave of pain streaked through me. Only this time, it was different, like I'd stuck my finger in a *light* socket. "Mother of—!"

A string of curses belted from me, and I curled forward, clutching my stomach as nausea roiled in my gut.

"What's wrong? *Vi!*" Mason stomped on the brakes, and I hit my head on the dash. "Screw this. I'm taking you back."

"No, don't!" I cried, trying and failing to hold back tears. "He's . . . I can't. I can't do this to him again. He deserves *better*."

"Vi, I can't afford to make an enemy of your brother. If something happens to you on my watch, he'll challenge me, and we all know how *that* will turn out."

"Oh, get *over* yourself, Mason," I sobbed, continuing to clutch my stomach in agony. "We can't help it if we're hybrids. Griff wasn't *trying* to steal your place in the pack. The sooner you accept that, the sooner you can move *on* with your life."

"And what about you, huh?" he quickly retorted. "Maybe you should let go of my brother so you can move on with *your* life."

"I'm *trying!*" I screamed, shaking so badly that my teeth clacked together.

Loudly cursing, Mason threw the car into park and reached over to unbuckle my seatbelt.

"What are you doing?" I asked, stiffening when he started to rub my back. "*Mason.*"

"Trying to *comfort* you, okay? I know I'm not Griff, but he's not here right now, so—"

His words were drowned out by the sudden squealing of brakes. When he swore again, I tried to straighten, but the pain was too much, and a whimper burst from me.

A second later, something ripped the driver side door clean off its hinges and yanked Mason out. Another second, and I heard a fleshy *thwack*, followed by an agonized groan. When I caught a flash of bright blond hair in the darkness, I started to move but not before Griff managed to punch his brother several more times.

"Griff," I moaned, practically falling out of the car in my haste to reach him. "Griff, *wait.*"

He continued to hit Mason, his blazing yellow eyes filled with so much fury that my heart stopped.

He was going to kill him. He was going to *kill* his brother. And that wrecked me. That broke my heart into a billion little pieces, because it was happening. My nightmare was becoming reality.

I was *destroying* him. I'd caused this to happen. *Me.*

And I couldn't take it, not for one more second. So I broke. I broke and broke and broke, falling to my knees with a howl. It tore from my lungs, a wail of endless pain.

It was happening. I was tearing apart yet *another* family.

Griff would never be the same after this. He'd never forgive me, not this time, and I'd lose him forever.

It was happening. My worst nightmare was unfolding before my eyes, and there was nothing I could do to stop it.

Utterly broken and defeated, I curled up on the ground and finally let the darkness have me. There was no point in staying strong anymore. No point in fighting.

I'd ruined the life of the most important person in the world to me.

I didn't deserve to live anymore, and so I gave up. I finally did what I should have done seven years ago and—

"Violet! Come back to me. I'm right here. I've got you, baby. I've got you."

Arms lifted me. Cradled me. Rocked me. Held me so tenderly that another keening howl fled my lungs.

"No. No, Griff, don't. Leave me. *Please.*"

"Never. I'm not letting you push me away again, Vi. Not this time."

"It's all . . . It's all my fault. I did this. You . . . You killed him, because of *me.*"

"Mace? I didn't kill him, Vi. I wanted to, but I couldn't. I heard your cries, and I stopped. Look at me, baby. He's alive. Nothing is your fault."

"*Everything* is my fault," I sobbed, struggling to breathe as another hot wave pulsed through me. It hurt, but at least I didn't feel like I was being electrocuted anymore. The magic inside the snake tattoo must have settled down now that Griff was here.

But it was a reminder of yet another of my failures. Just one more reason why I didn't deserve him.

"Leave me," I tried again, flinching when I felt his hand cup my hot, tear-stained cheek. "You deserve . . . You deserve better."

"Let me decide what I do and don't deserve," he tightly replied.

"I'm worthless."

He sucked in a sharp breath through his teeth. "Violet Jane Rivers, you take that back." When I didn't say anything, he pressed his forehead to mine and quietly groaned, "You're breaking my heart, Vi."

"I know," I whispered back. "That's why I need you to let me go."

CHAPTER 26

GRIFF

It hurt to breathe.

Worthless? The love of my life thought she was *worthless*?

I couldn't even fathom the word. Couldn't understand how we'd reached this point. How she'd come to feel this way about herself.

Had I been missing the signs all along? Had I been so blinded by my love for her that I'd failed to see how *lost* she was?

Worthless.

That word could never describe the woman in my arms. She was strong and capable, loyal and kind, bold and fearless. But, apparently, she didn't feel that way about herself.

"Look at me, Vi," I repeated, trying to keep the pain out of my voice. Trying to sound calm when I was drowning in panic. "Please, look at me."

She finally did, and what I saw in her tear-filled eyes would have brought me to my knees if I wasn't already sitting down.

Defeat. Pure and utter defeat.

"You are not worthless, do you hear me?" I told her, willing my voice not to shake.

She stared at me, her gaze dull and lifeless, then said, "I never should have told you I loved you."

The words were like a punch straight through my sternum. It felt like my insides were falling out of the gaping hole where my chest had been, but I managed to say, "You don't love me?"

Her lip quivered, and she cried out, "I *do* love you. I love everything about you. I love the way you comfort me and make me laugh. I love your scent and smile and stupid hair. I even love it when you freaking *tease* me. You're kind, caring, attentive, and you're my best friend in the whole wide world. Even one second apart from you is pure agony. I feel like who I used to be when I'm with you. You make me feel *whole* again."

Speechless. I was *speechless*. She felt all of that for me?

Her words elated me as much as they confused me. She *loved* me, but . . . "You make it sound like loving me is a bad thing."

"It *is*, because I can't stay away from you. I've tried. God, I've tried so hard to just be your friend. But every time you're there for me, the lines blur, and I can't push you away."

"I don't understand. Why would you want to push me away?"

"Because I'm *using* you!" she shouted and choked back a sob as her heat flared up again, leaving her skin hot and sweaty beneath my touch.

"Vi, you need relief," I said, both for her sake and mine. The scent of her pheromones was heavy in the air, and my body was buzzing with adrenaline, desperate to answer its call. "Let me help you."

A crazed laugh left her. "See? *See?* I confess that I'm using you, and you don't even flinch. I'm bad for you, Griff. I'm needy and clingy, and because you're so *nice*, you let me treat you like a . . . like a *plaything*. Like my own personal security blanket. But that's messed up. You deserve so much better than that. You deserve someone sweet and innocent like Desirae."

"But I don't want Desirae or any other female. I want *you*, Vi. So go ahead and use me. Do whatever you want with me, because I'm yours, and that's never going to change."

Her lip quivered some more; then she stubbornly shook her head and whispered, "You're only saying that because of Whiskey. Because of how *he* wants you to feel."

Sudden fury whipped through me. In a flash, I had us both up on our feet. Vi gasped as I yanked her against me, firmly gripping her nape so she had no choice but to face my anger.

"Violet Jane Rivers," I said in a deathly soft voice, "I'm going to say this once and only once. I am *not* Arrow. I would never betray you. Never hurt you. Never *leave* you. What I feel for you is real, not something my familiar is forcing me to feel. So if you want me to let you go, then too bad. I'm not going anywhere. And if you walk away from this again, then you should know that I intend to follow you. I'll push and push and push until you have no choice but to believe that my love for you is *genuine*."

Fresh tears coursed down her cheeks, but I didn't wipe them away. If she wanted my comfort, then she would need to *ask* for it. I was too hurt to accept anything less. Too incensed that she'd compared me with Arrow. I knew he'd wounded her deeply and had shaken her confidence when he'd so readily rejected her after discovering that Sable was a demonic spirit, but to assume that *I* would treat her the same way pierced my very soul.

Angry, Whiskey spoke in my mind.

I know, buddy. Me too.

Angry at us for not noticing.

That gave me pause, and I was forced to admit the same. I should have seen the signs. I should have realized how deep her pain went. I was the pack healer—it was my *job* to notice.

After an unbearably long moment, she finally spoke again. The words were hushed. Barely a whisper. Vulnerable in a way she'd never allowed herself to be before. And every single one of them gutted me.

"I'm poison, Griff. I destroy everything I touch. I had one job—to support and strengthen my family—and I failed miserably. Because of that failure, my dad died and my mom broke. Melanie spent her childhood without a mother. Kolton was forced to become alpha before he was ready. I destroy families. I *break* them. And it's only a matter of time before I break us too. It's why I can't be yours. It's why I have to deny my feelings, because if I give in to them, I'll end up destroying the one thing I can't live without. You."

She might as well have shot me in the heart point blank with a silver bullet. I could barely stand under the weight of her confession, a burden that she'd forced herself to carry for way too long. I'd known she blamed herself for the fallout with Arrow, but this was so much deeper than that. She blamed herself for *everything*, and I couldn't take it anymore.

"Leave, Mason."

My brother had been quiet during the heart-wrenching exchange, but I was all too aware of his continued presence.

"Griff, I . . ." he started.

"*Leave*," I snapped, unable to focus on anything but Vi at the moment.

When I heard his car start and slowly pull away, all of my attention went back to her. Studying her distraught face, hard resolve filled me. Soft words hadn't helped me get through to her in the past, so it was time for a new tactic, one that would either break her . . . or heal her. I was desperately hoping for the latter, but either way, I couldn't let her continue on like this anymore, stuck in a limbo of self-flagellation.

So I did what I never did with her. I called on every ounce of my dominant nature and wielded it to put her in her place. To *challenge* her. She thought she could destroy us? Well, I was going to prove her wrong.

"Do you trust me?" I asked her, firming my grip on her neck so she couldn't look away.

Fear flickered in her eyes, but it only hardened my resolve more.

"Vi, do you *trust* me?" I demanded. *Pushed.* Forcing her to face her insecurities. When she finally bobbed her head, just once, I said, "Then trust in my love for you. Trust that it's strong enough to withstand any storm. It won't break, and you can't destroy it."

"Griff..."

"I'm not finished, Vi. If I make you feel whole, then I want you to use that. I want you to use *me.* Nothing would satisfy me more than seeing you restored to who you used to be, and if I'm the instrument that helps you heal and regain your confidence, then I feel honored. Taking care of you fulfills me. Your pleasure is my pleasure, your happiness my happiness. So *use* me, Vi. Tell me what you need. I'm not asking—I'm demanding. I should have demanded you tell me years ago, but—"

"You."

I blinked, certain I'd heard wrong. "What?"

"You, Griff. I need *you.* All of you. I'll never need anything more."

I stared at her, letting the beautiful words sink in.

Then I lowered my head and crushed our mouths together.

CHAPTER 27

VIOLET

I couldn't believe that Griff was kissing me after everything I'd said.

I thought for sure he would see the wounded, insecure shell I'd become and want nothing to do with me. But, by some miracle, he was still here. He was *kissing* me like I was his last saving grace. Like I was his beginning and end. His *world*.

"Trust me," he breathed against my mouth, and I clung to the words for dear life, needing to believe them more than I'd needed to believe anything.

With each passing second, my heat grew more and more intense. It became hard to stand, and when I whimpered, Griff swept me off my feet and into his arms.

"Trust me," he breathed again, his mouth still hot against mine as he carried me toward the family truck he'd arrived in.

He'd parked it haphazardly on the shoulder, the road dark and deserted this time of night. When he walked past the passenger door and proceeded to open the back door, I knew he didn't plan to move it anytime soon, which was fine by me. All I cared about was him and the way his touch and words were making me feel.

Loved. He made me feel *loved*.

I didn't even have to pretend to believe it this time. He was *making* me believe it. Each kiss burned away more and more of my doubts and fears, filling me with a certainty that what he said was true. That I could trust in his love. That it wouldn't break over time.

That I couldn't *destroy* it.

Tears of abject relief rolled down my cheeks, and he paused to kiss them away, continuing to whisper against my skin, "Trust me. Trust me. Trust me."

I kissed him back, letting him feel my love for him in return. Tentatively at first, then with growing courage.

Climbing inside the truck, he laid me on the backseat and shut the door. Soon, the cab was filled with the heady scent of arousal and the sounds of our labored breathing. Sweat beaded my forehead and settled between my breasts, making me itch to tear off my dress. Before I could, Griff broke the kiss to utter another, "Trust me."

Burning with need, I peeled open my eyes to meet his. "I do. I do trust you."

That was all he needed to hear. Without taking his eyes off me, he slid both hands to my thighs and lifted up my skirt. When it was around my waist, he hooked two fingers into my panties and slowly pulled them down. It became hard to breathe, my eyes glued to his as he continued to tug on my underwear. Lifting one leg, he removed my high-heeled shoe, then did the same with the other. His hands went to my underwear again and slowly resumed their torturous downward path.

I thought I would die. I thought I would *die* from anticipation.

Seeing my desperation, a slow grin curled Griff's lips.

"I hate you," I said in a quivering breath, maintaining eye contact as he scooted backward and knelt on the floor beside me.

"You love me," he corrected, grinning wider when I whimpered in response.

"Yes, I stupidly love you. I stupidly love everything you're doing to me, and I don't want you to stop," I breathlessly said, whimpering again when he slid the underwear free and tossed them on the floor.

"Then be a good girl and place your legs on my shoulders," he purred, and that was nearly enough to make me come.

I immediately obeyed him, propping my head up against the door so I could better watch what he was doing. Sliding his hands up my thighs again, he gripped them tightly and slowly lowered his head.

"Oh God, oh God, oh God," I panted as his face disappeared beneath my skirt. When I felt his warm breath feather over my throbbing pussy, I started to hyperventilate.

He was inches away. *Inches.* But he paused to quietly groan, "Your scent is everything. I'll never get enough."

"Griff, please," I begged, my legs starting to shake. "Please, I need you. I need—"

His tongue licked my clit, and I loudly cried out as pleasure roared through my body. His fingers were magical, but his tongue . . . Oh, his tongue was wickedly good at making me feel naughty things. I saw stars as he applied just the right amount of pressure to my overly sensitive center, swirling his tongue in a way that had me gasping for breath.

Random stuff flew out of my mouth, most of it singing his praises. When my pleasure started to build, I gripped the seat cushion and door handle for dear life, panting so loudly that it sounded like I was in labor.

He burrowed his face deeper between my thighs, adding even more delicious pressure. My legs squeezed his head in response, but he pried them back open so his tongue had full access to my pussy. Every time he flicked it, I cried out, the sensation driving me closer and closer to orgasm.

"Griff, Griff, Griff," I started to plead, my body buzzing with so many intense feelings that I was about to burst from the pressure.

In response to my chanting, his tongue went wild, lashing across my clit so rapidly that I fell over the edge in a mindless scream. Wave after wave of pulsating pleasure pounded through my body. I let it sweep me away, closing my eyes in utter rapture. When I finally came down, I opened my eyes to find him watching me with a self-satisfied smile.

"I'll never grow tired of watching you come," he said.

"Never?" I panted, still trying to catch my breath.

He paused to watch me some more, then quietly replied, "You're my past, present, and future, Vi. I don't want this with you just today. I want this every day. I want forever with you."

All the air left me in a rush. With my legs still propped on his shoulders, I whispered back, "I want forever with you too."

He looked at me like I'd just handed him the moon.

"Then let me claim you."

My heart stopped. "Claim? Like *claim* claim? As in, you bite my neck and mark me, leaving your scent beneath my skin to let other males know that I'm taken?"

"That you're mine, yes," he replied with a small laugh.

Oh. Oh, wow. He was really serious about this.

But was I ready? Could I accept that he actually wanted *forever* with me?

"I'm scared," I admitted, allowing myself to become vulnerable once more. "If I screw this up and lose you, I won't survive."

He searched my face, then lowered my legs to sit on the seat beside me. "Come here," he said, and I didn't hesitate to straddle him as he pulled me onto his lap. Tucking a wisp of hair behind my ear, he said, "I get that you're scared of losing me. You lost your parents, and your family was forever changed. But you didn't cause that to happen, Vi. You're not a failure, you're not poison, and you're not worthless.

In fact, I never want to hear those words come out of your mouth again. We all mess up, but there's no way in hell I'll ever leave you."

"But what if—"

"No buts," he interrupted firmly, and I couldn't help but be aroused by his dominance. "You're Violet freaking Rivers, and you're worthy of love. Say it."

I almost rolled my eyes, but when his stern look intensified, I said, "I'm Violet freaking Rivers, and I'm worthy of love."

"Good girl. Now, say it again like you mean it."

"Griff—"

"*Say* it."

"I'm Violet *freaking* Rivers, and I'm worthy of love!" I shouted, and he grinned a mile wide. Something loosened in my chest, and I found myself grinning back at him. "God, Griff, I've been such a freaking mess."

"A *beautiful* mess," he corrected, staring at me with such open adoration that my heart happily fluttered. "You think Arrow took away who you used to be, but I still see that same girl. She's right here, strong and brave and perfect for me in every way. I'll never let you go, Violet Jane."

Tears once again filled my eyes. I couldn't believe this was actually happening, that this was *real*. It was terrifying, but I truly believed he meant every single word.

Which was why I said without an ounce of hesitation, "I want you to claim me."

Joy sparked in his eyes. "Are you sure?"

"I've been sure for years. I just didn't let myself believe that I could have this with you."

"But you believe it now?"

I laughed, surprised that I could honestly say, "Yeah, I do. I really do. Thanks to you."

He gave me a cheeky grin. "You're welcome."

"This is going straight to your big ego, isn't it," I said.

"Of course it is. I'm feeling quite full of myself at the moment."

"Griff?"

"Hmm?"

"Shut up and claim me already."

He laughed, even as I felt him harden beneath me. Heat flashed through my body once more, making me wetter than I already was. His pants were going to be ruined after this, but the thought of marking him with my arousal completely turned me on.

Situating myself more fully on top of his growing erection, I swept my hair back to expose the claiming spot between my shoulder and neck. "Mark me good now," I told him in mock seriousness. "I don't want anyone getting confused about who I belong to."

His eyes flashed bright yellow. "Don't worry, baby. There'll be no confusion when I'm done with you."

The roughness of his voice pleasantly scraped over my skin, making me shiver with anticipation. I tipped my head to the side, satisfied when I felt him tremble. He reached up and feathered his fingers over the claim spot almost reverently, then leaned forward and nuzzled the spot.

More anticipation spiked through me, and I arched against him, encouraging him to continue. His trembling increased, and he began to place gentle kisses on the spot. When they grew harder and more urgent, another wave of heat rushed through my body, my anticipation through the roof.

Unable to keep silent a moment longer, I whimpered, "Bite me, Griff. Please, bite me. I want you to. I need you to—"

He sank his canines into my neck, and I stiffened against him with a sharp gasp. The pain was unmistakable, but the knowledge of what he was doing filled me with a heady sense of pleasure. My eyes rolled shut, and I moaned, sliding both hands into his hair to encourage him deeper. His canines elongated, going deeper than I thought possible, and my mouth opened in a silent cry.

As my body flooded with an intoxicating mix of pain and pleasure, fresh arousal saturated the air. With a groan, Griff gripped my hips and ground himself against me. Each thrust brought me higher and higher, intensifying my need for him. Blindly reaching between us, I fumbled to undo his buckle and zipper. When his erection sprang free, I eagerly ran my hand up and down its silky length. He jerked against me with another groan, and I felt the tip swell beneath my fingertips.

Desperate to feel him inside me, I lifted up and positioned him at my slick entrance. Before I could sink on top of him, he abruptly thrust his hips up, impaling himself balls deep inside me. Shocked at how fast he'd filled me, I gasped out his name and struggled to breathe. Before I could fully adjust, he did it again, pushing my hips down at the same time. As he hit an ultra sensitive spot deep inside, euphoria pulsed through me, and I gripped his hair with a loud cry.

"Yes! Do it again. Oh, yes, *yes*. That's so good. *So good.*"

He set a punishing pace, clearly as intoxicated with the moment as I was. He drove into me over and over again, so deeply that I gasped with each thrust.

He was claiming me, all right. Claiming me in every way possible. And I *loved* it.

The moment was perfect, and I was deliriously excited to have countless moments just like this one in my future. As the pleasurable tension in our bodies reached a breaking point, the air inside the truck thickened and fogged the windows. It was like being inside a sauna—or that steamy car scene in the *Titanic* movie. Just for the hell of it, I planted a hand on the glass behind Griff's head and left a wet print.

Moments later, his thrusts grew frantic, and I couldn't hold on any longer. A scream tore from my lungs, and I spasmed all over his cock, squeezing it to kingdom come. As his own release barrelled through him, he wrenched his canines from my neck and roared, crushing me to him.

The orgasm went on for longer than usual, and I stayed seated on top of him to prolong it even more. When my body continued to blissfully buzz instead of coming down, though, I whimpered, "Griff."

"I know," he groaned, breathing heavily. "I—"

He abruptly jerked inside me again, orgasming for a second time. Feeling the hot stream of come jet inside me, I fell over the edge again with a blissful moan. He continued to pant, his body clearly still in the throes of ecstasy, and it was then that I realized something was different.

"Griff."

"I know, I know. But I can't . . . I can't stop it."

As if to prove his point, his cock swelled impossibly huge, pushing at my walls until they stretched to accommodate him.

"Ah!" I cried out. Not in pain but in *pleasure*. His engorged length felt almost ribbed now, and it made my pussy spasm with excitement.

"Violet," he groaned out, letting his head fall back against the seat. "If you keep doing that, I'm gonna come again."

Finally understanding what was happening, I blurted, "You have a knot. You're *knotting* me. Since when do you have a knot?"

"Since right now. Claiming you must have awakened my alpha gene."

"Your alpha . . ."

Holy crap, Griff was an *alpha* now? He'd always been more dominant than a beta, but without the ability to knot, he'd never been classified as an alpha. I'd heard of this happening to males, of course. Griff's brother hadn't become an alpha until he'd left Midnight Pack and formed his own.

But Griff? An *alpha*? What was Kolton going to think? As soon as I had the thought, I knew it wouldn't change anything between them. Griff was loyal to a fault, and he would never challenge my brother for the pack alpha position.

Relaxing a little, I decided to test the knot's hold on me by wiggling my hips. When it stuck to me like superglue, I blinked in surprise. "Oh, wow. So *that's* what it feels like." Lifting my skirt to peer between us, I asked, "Does it hurt?"

"No, it feels incredible. And every time you—"

I clenched my walls around him, and his knot jerked inside me, announcing his third orgasm. As he let out a loud groan, my own body spasmed with excitement, filling me with bliss.

"Oh," I gasped out when I could breathe again. "Yeah, that feels amazing."

"Mmhmm. I can understand why Kolton likes to knot Nora so much now."

"Can we not talk about my brother's knot? Like *ever*?" I said, trying and failing to scowl when Griff laughed. "He's gonna be so pissed that the truck smells like sex."

Griff laughed again, and I couldn't help but join him. "Good thing the seats are leather."

"He'll probably still fumigate it. More than once."

As he continued to laugh, I leaned forward and snuggled against him, resting my head on his shoulder. He cupped the back of my head with his big hand and held me close, releasing a contented sigh.

We stayed like that for a long while, resting in each other's arms while his knot slowly softened.

Only to go another round the second my heat flared up again, this time without our clothes on.

When I was finally spent and satiated hours later, Griff had knotted me dozens of times. He definitely seemed proud of his newly improved appendage, and I'd made certain to tell him what a good boy he was. It wasn't until I was safely wrapped in his arms and drifting off to sleep that I realized how quiet Sable had been the entire time.

Speaking through our connection, I told her so, adding, *I thought you'd be howling for joy.*

I don't need to, she answered me, then said words I would never forget for as long as I lived. *I'm at peace, because your eyes are finally open and you can see what's been in front of you all along. Your soulmate.*

CHAPTER 28

GRIFF

I almost couldn't stand how deliriously happy I was.

Vi was *mine*, truly mine.

Every inch of her smelled like me, and I took great satisfaction in knowing that any male who approached her would scent my unmistakable claim.

She was taken. By *me*.

After an entire night of making love, Vi's heat had faded enough that it was safe for me to drive again. I'd texted Kolton that we would be back later today, but it was still too soon for me to be around other males, especially now that my alpha gene had awakened. Most packs didn't have more than one alpha male, but Kolton knew I wasn't a threat to his position. Not in a million years would I challenge him and put his family in danger—a family that was now mine in every way possible.

As I drove toward town on cloud nine, Vi's stomach growled again. I grinned, raising our joined hands to kiss her knuckles. "Don't worry, babe. You'll have all the food you want in a few minutes. I bet you're starving after all the knotting and orgasms I gave you."

Instead of rolling her eyes at my comment, she said, "I could seriously eat a whole cow right now. Knotting definitely burns more calories."

I barked a laugh. "Well, we can fuel up at Joe's Burgers, then spend the rest of the day burning more calories. The others aren't expecting us back until dinner."

She bit her lip but couldn't quite hide a smile, letting me know that she was as excited about the idea as I was.

Don't forget to give me a turn. I want to test out the new peen on my beloved, Whiskey reminded me, and I choked on another laugh.

Vi threw me a quizzical look. I opened my mouth to tell her what Whiskey had said, but her eyes suddenly rounded in horror. "Griff! Watch out!"

I turned my head just as something plowed into the truck's side. The world exploded in a shower of glass and shrieking metal, and pain lit up my body. Before I could see what had hit us, my airbag deployed, punching me in the face. I lost sight of everything around me, but I could feel the truck careen off the road and into a ditch. We went airborne, flipping over and over, glass raining around us.

As suddenly as it all began, we ground to a jarring halt. Only, nothing felt right. My seatbelt was cutting into my shoulder, and all the blood was rushing to my head. With my ears ringing from the violent crash, it dawned on me that we'd landed upside down.

"Vi," I groaned and reached for her, then realized I was still holding her hand in a death grip. I squeezed her fingers, but she didn't squeeze mine back. "Vi, speak to me. *Violet.*"

I turned my stiff neck to check on her and caught movement just beyond her broken window. Military style boots stopped in front of her door, and a split second later, the door was ripped from its hinges.

A growl burst from me. Whiskey immediately came to my aid, and my claws shot out, allowing me to quickly slash through my seatbelt. The second I fell onto the truck's ceiling, I scrambled to protect Vi.

But before I could reach her, something hard struck my temple.

I tried with all of my might to stay conscious, but when another blow viciously pounded into my skull . . .

Everything went dark.

CHAPTER 29

VIOLET

Fire and ice burned in my veins.

It felt like I was being boiled alive from the inside.

At first, I thought the truck had caught on fire and was roasting me like a marshmallow. But when I managed to crack open my eyes, there was no fire and no truck.

Instead, all I saw was a small concrete room.

I tried to move, and debilitating weakness stole over me, one that had nothing to do with my heat.

When I realized what it was, my heart fluttered erratically.

Silver. I was being exposed to *silver*.

Panicking, I tried to move again, but my body wouldn't budge. I glanced down and immediately understood why.

I was strapped to a freaking table. And I was *naked*. Several leather straps secured my arms and legs, while two wider straps kept my chest and pelvis from rising off the metal surface. At least my feminine bits were mostly hidden by them, providing me some dignity.

Sable. Sable, wake up, I urged my familiar, pulling at the restraints. They weren't silver, but *something* was causing me pain.

Sable awoke with a startled yelp and immediately started to help me. We wiggled and twisted, but even our combined strength couldn't break the straps.

Fear trickled through me, and I wondered where Griff was.

When my mind went straight to the worst case scenario, I quickly shoved the thought away. No way was he dead. I would know. I would know in my *soul* if he was.

After a few minutes of useless struggling, I fell back against the table, my strength all but depleted. They must have injected me with something, because I felt weaker than a newborn calf. After another few minutes, faint voices reached me, and I stopped breathing to listen.

"It must have just happened. We didn't know."

Dread shivered up my spine. I *knew* that voice.

"And you didn't kill the male responsible?"

"We didn't have time. There was traffic, and a few humans witnessed the collision."

The unfamiliar-sounding male swore, but I clung to the words like a lifeline. If they were talking about Griff, then he was still *alive*. Despite my precarious position, just knowing that Griff was okay instantly made me feel better.

Seconds later, the door to my tiny room unlocked and opened with a loud metallic shriek, and two males entered. At the sight of Hitman, Sable growled, and I let the sound rumble from my throat.

His face was expressionless as he took me in from head to toe like I was a slab of meat; then he turned to his companion and said, "I still want her."

Fresh panic fluttered in my chest, but I bared my teeth at him and spat, "I'm already *taken*."

The other male clucked his tongue, but his expression was far from disapproving. In fact, his bright blue eyes sparkled in a way that immediately put me on edge. He was *pleased*.

Unlike Hitman's pale complexion and short black hair, this male had deeply tanned skin, a neatly-trimmed beard, and longer dark hair that was graying at the temples. He was probably twice my age but still handsome, and he most *definitely* knew it.

"You've been quite the challenge to secure, Miss Rivers," he said to me, sweeping his gaze over my body in a way that immediately made me want to claw his eyes out. "It's unfortunate that a male has claimed you, but we've worked too hard to let you go now. I'm Atticus Bane, by the way, the head alpha of Rogue Pack. And this is Ivan, my second. He's been wanting to claim you as his mate for months now, but that has yet to be decided."

"I've earned her, Alpha," Ivan said, still staring at me like I was a possession.

"Calm yourself, Ivan. I'm not challenging you for her. Yet," Atticus responded with a sly wink at me. "Every male in the pack is given an equal opportunity to claim a female, as you know. If you still want her when it's time for The Claiming, you can make your intentions known then."

"I've already been claimed, old man," I flatly said, gratified when the little grin on his face vanished. "One of your own told us that you only kidnap *unclaimed* females, right before we locked him in a cell and threw away the key. Oh, and Rogue Pack is a stupid name."

Pompous dick, Sable muttered under her breath.

"Also, my wolf thinks you're a pompous dick," I added, willing a smirk onto my face despite my pain. "As do I."

Not smiling now, Atticus replied, "I'm sorry you two feel that way. We only wanted to take unclaimed females because it would be easier for everyone involved."

"Easier for who?" I demanded with a disgusted lip curl. "Easier for you and your pack of rejects to justify your deplorable actions? Do you actually think females *want* to be claimed and mated by complete strangers? To essentially be used as *broodmares* in order to grow your derelict pack? You violently snatched them away from their homes. You're treating them like *property*."

He didn't say a word during my impassioned speech, his face unreadable. But when I paused to take a breath, he suddenly moved toward me. Sable growled again, and we strained against the straps once more. Atticus stopped beside me to watch my fruitless struggle, then leaned over me and planted his hands on either side of my head.

I ceased struggling to give him my best death glare and snarled, "Don't. Touch. Me."

A grin slowly curled his mouth, and he leaned closer to purr in my ear, "I see now why my second wants you so badly, even with another male's scent all over you, polluting the deliciousness of your heat. Your fierce spirit is intoxicating, but I'm looking forward to breaking it. Once it's molded to my will, you'll do whatever I tell you to do. And if you don't, you'll find out just how *derelict* the males in my pack can be."

With that, he pulled away, but not before stroking a finger down my cheek. I turned my head to bite him, but he snatched his hand out of reach with a quiet chuckle.

"Ivan, see to it that Miss Rivers receives another dose of silver. The longer she refuses to submit, the longer her suffering will be."

With that, he turned and left the room, leaving me with Hitman— aka, Ivan. As the black-haired male pulled something from his pocket and approached me, I started to shake.

"No, don't. Please, don't," I said, staring in horror at the syringe. The needle wickedly flashed as he removed the top and stopped by my side. I opened my mouth, but before I could say more, he grabbed my bicep and plunged the needle full of liquid silver into my flesh.

The pain was instant, streaking through my veins like lava. Unable to escape it, all I could do was release a bloodcurdling scream. Even when Ivan left and I was alone again, I continued to scream, lost in a sea of pain and misery.

CHAPTER 30

GRIFF

"Griff. *Griff!*"

As darkness lost its grip on me, the first thing I did was lash out. My fist solidly connected with flesh, and I was rewarded with a pained grunt.

"What the hell, Griff? Wake up!"

I threw another punch, but an arm blocked me this time. As my blurry vision began to clear, a familiar face materialized before me. In a flash, I tackled him to the ground and shouted, "Where is she?"

"Get off me, man. I don't know!" my brother shouted back.

Yanking Mason up by his shirt collar, I brought his face so close to mine that we were nose-to-nose. "Tell me what you did with her, or you're a dead man," I said, my deathly soft tone promising violence.

Something flashed in his eyes, something that looked a lot like fear, but he replied, "Jeez, Griff, snap out of it. Do you seriously think I would take Vi from you?"

"You've tried before."

"That was seven years ago, and I was *desperate*. What happened yesterday had nothing to do with that. She was in heat, confused about you, and needed a ride. I swear nothing else happened."

"*Then where is she?*" I roared, shaking him until his teeth rattled. All I remembered was someone reaching for her before everything went black. I must not have been unconscious for long, because I was still in the ditch with the flipped-over truck and the police hadn't arrived yet. But it was a busy enough intersection that they'd probably be here soon, which meant that I needed to wrap this up fast.

It was hard to think straight, though. Vi was gone. Someone had *taken* her from me. And the only one here to question and take out my anger on was my brother.

"Answer me!" I barked, shaking him a second time.

Whiskey's desperation intertwined with mine, and Mason's eyes widened as he no doubt saw my irises flash bright yellow.

"I swear I had nothing to do with it, Griff," he said, raising his hands placatingly. "By the time I got here, they were already gone. When I found you still in the truck with blood everywhere, I thought they'd killed you. I thought they'd killed my baby brother, and I never . . . I never made things right between us. I've been such a dick to you all these years and made your life hell, and . . . and I'm *sorry*, okay? I'm just . . . I'm sorry."

Stunned that he'd apologized to me, something he'd never done before, I simply stared at him. Without a word, I let go of him and stumbled to my feet.

"We need to go. The cops are here," I said, hearing the wail of sirens in the distance. As he picked himself up, I added, "I need a ride back to the estate."

"Sure thing," he replied, his voice devoid of its usual snark.

"Why are you even here?" I questioned as we made our way out of the ditch. A few humans had stopped to check out the accident, but I didn't pause to reassure them. I no doubt looked half dead with blood coating my face, neck, and hair. Whoever had knocked me out probably intended to cave in my skull, but I had an exceptionally hard head.

"I never left, actually," Mason admitted, and I shot him a sharp look. "Hey, I almost got you kicked out of the Alpha Meeting and unknowingly triggered your PTSD. I didn't enjoy being beat up by my little brother, but I understand why you did it. You and Vi have been through a lot together, and I felt bad for making your trauma worse."

"So, you decided to stalk me?"

Scoffing, he slid into his Rolls-Royce on the driver side—now doorless, thanks to me. As I did the same on the passenger side, he replied, "No, I was trying to act like a responsible big brother for once. After all the talk about the rogues, I was worried they would hunt you down while Vi was in heat, so I parked my car about a mile away to keep a lookout. I even called Kolton and told him where I was so he wouldn't have to worry that you two were out here alone. Unfortunately, I fell asleep about an hour ago. By the time I woke up, you two were gone."

I didn't respond, comparing the words to the male who'd persecuted me more than helped me over the years. His story made sense, but a scarred part of me still questioned his motives. He could have easily contacted the rogues and told them where we were. He'd always liked Vi, but if it meant getting under my skin, he wasn't above using her. He'd tried pursuing her seven years ago when he'd known how I felt about her, after all.

I couldn't just forget two decades of abuse simply because he'd apologized.

As he started the engine and left the crash site just as the cops arrived, I fished in my pocket for my phone. Relieved to find it in one piece, I quickly called Kolton and told him what happened. He remained calm despite the dire news, but I knew he was as terrified for Vi's safety as I was.

"Contact our allies," I said, reining in my panic so I could focus on what needed to be done. "I know how to find Vi and the other missing females."

"How?" Mason asked, unapologetically listening in to our conversation.

Instead of answering him, I grinned. Not a pleasant grin, but a dark one. A grin filled with malice and deadly intent.

"They never should have taken her," was all I said. "They have no idea what hell they've just unleashed."

CHAPTER 31

VIOLET

I lost track of time. I didn't even know what day it was.

Without access to a window, I had no idea if it was morning or night.

As the hours ticked by, I grew weaker and weaker from the silver, but also from my lingering heat and empty stomach. At one point, I couldn't hold my bladder anymore and wet myself. Sleep came in fits and starts, but I mostly stared up at the ceiling with silent tears tracking down my face as I tried over and over to shift.

After hours of trying, though, I was finally forced to admit defeat. The dose of silver Ivan had given me had effectively weakened my supernatural abilities, including my ability to shift at will. Sable was currently curled up inside me, comforting me as best she could. At least I could still speak to her, which made me feel less alone.

Despite the awful situation, there was no way in hell I would submit to these bastards. If they wanted to claim and breed me, they'd have to do it by force. I shivered at the thought, then quickly focused on something else. Griff immediately came to mind, and I allowed myself to replay the beautiful moments we'd shared just before I'd been kidnapped. Fresh tears leaked from my eyes and into my hair, but I held on to those memories for dear life, letting them carry me away from this nightmare.

I was starting to drift off again, utterly exhausted from the pain I was in, when a sound at the door jerked me fully awake. Expecting

Ivan or his prick alpha to enter, I was shocked to see a slim female with medium brown skin and a pixie haircut slip into my room.

"Desirae?" I said, certain the pain was making me hallucinate her.

She was wearing a white tunic-style outfit and looked unharmed. But it was hard to see in the room's dim lighting, especially now that my abilities had been impaired. As she came closer, though, I spotted something around her neck. It was metal and looked like a . . .

My throat closed.

A collar. She was wearing a *collar*.

"Desirae, what's happening?" I pressed as she approached me with her face downcast.

"I'm sorry, Vi," she whispered, flicking me an apologetic look before focusing on the floor again. "I'm not allowed to answer your questions."

What the hell?

I lifted my head as she came nearer, finally noticing what she held in her hands. "Desirae, no," I said and started to fight against my restraints again. "Whatever that is, keep it away from me."

"I'm sorry," she repeated, her hands shaking as she lifted the collar. "I'm allowed to tell you that any attempt to remove this collar will trigger the needles embedded in the metal. Each needle is filled with liquid silver and will be injected into your skin before you can stop it."

Okay. That sounded extremely unpleasant.

When she inched forward, aiming the torture device at my neck, I snarled in warning. A frightened squeak left her, and she almost dropped the collar.

"I'm sorry. I'm really sorry, Vi, but if I . . . if I don't put this on you . . ." Her breath hitched, and tears slid down her cheeks.

Seeing the terror in her eyes, I stopped struggling. "Desirae. Desirae, look at me." When she did, I gently said, "Will they hurt you if I don't cooperate?"

Sniffling, she nodded.

My heart sank. "Okay. It's okay, Desirae. Do what you came here to do. I won't stop you."

A relieved sob left her, and she quickly secured the device around my neck. As it locked into place, I immediately felt its chilling weight. Before I could adjust to the feeling of being collared like a dog, Desirae got to work unbuckling my leather restraints. Adrenaline shot through me, and I dared to hope that she was helping me escape.

My hopes were dashed a moment later when she quietly said, "I'm allowed to tell you that any attempt to escape will be met with punishment, not only for yourself but for the other females. Your collar will be activated and so will all the others. This includes any attempt to shift or use magic."

Okay, these bastards seriously needed to die. Fury trembled through me, but when the last restraint fell away, I didn't try to escape. I couldn't. Not when my actions would hurt every single terrified female trapped in this hellhole.

Clearly relieved that I wasn't going to make a run for it, Desirae silently helped me down from the table. As my legs turned to jelly beneath me, she slid under one of my arms to carry most of my weight.

"The bathhouse isn't far," she tried to assure me, wrinkling her nose a little as she said it.

Realizing how potent I must smell, I muttered, "Sorry. When you gotta go, you gotta go."

"It's not that. You just . . . You're still in heat, and I can smell . . ."

"Griff? Yeah, I saw you eyeing him last week. Sorry about that."

She abruptly came to a stop. "A week? It's only been a *week?*"

Hearing the misery in her voice, my heart went out to her. Who knew what horrors she'd endured over the past several days. She was already a submissive omega, so the rogue's torture techniques must be extra traumatizing for her.

I opened my mouth to tell her that our pack was doing everything in its power to rescue us, but the metal door to my room suddenly squealed open. As Ivan's broad form filled the doorway, I tensed, my fight or flight instincts kicking in. He stared at me coolly, taking in the collar around my throat before nodding at Desirae.

She ducked her head and started to move, practically dragging me in her haste to leave the room. As we passed by him, I openly glared, wanting him to see just how much I despised him. He didn't react. Not emotionally, anyway. All he did was raise the rifle in his hands, reminding me without words that he held all the power.

I bared my teeth defiantly, then allowed Desirae to lead me down a dimly-lit hallway. Ivan's gaze was like a brand on my back as he followed us, his heavy boots thunking against the cement floor. We passed a few doors that looked similar to mine, making me wonder if they held more kidnapped females. And then we passed through a wide entrance with no doors into a large room sporting an indoor pool.

Only, when I looked closer, I could see steam billowing from the water, and the pool seemed relatively shallow.

A bathhouse, then. A *public* one.

There were benches and cubbies along the walls, but there was no one in the room. Well, except for us.

"Scrub her hard. She still smells like sex," Ivan said from the entrance, making me stiffen. Did the dude seriously think I would want him to claim me with an attitude like that? Then again, he probably didn't care what I wanted.

Pausing at a nearby bench, Desirae let go of me and started to remove her clothing. I blinked in surprise but didn't question her. Not with creepy Ivan still watching. When she was naked, she grabbed a shower caddy from one of the cubbies and a long-handled scrub brush, then nudged me toward the pool.

"I have to wash you now," she explained, flicking a glance at Ivan as if to seek his approval. Anger stirred in my belly. Not at her, but at the males who'd so thoroughly broken her. They'd stolen her innocence, and I knew all too well how that felt.

As I slipped into the pool with Desirae and she began to wash me, I let my thoughts drift to the male I'd shortly been betrothed to nearly eight years ago. For the sake of Midnight Pack's future, I'd been willing to marry Arrow Pemberton, the son of a powerful alpha from Maine. My parents had been so proud of my willingness to strengthen our pack ties, oblivious to the fact that I was about to destroy everything.

But, as I had the thought I'd allowed myself to believe for way too long, Griff's words came back to me.

"You didn't cause that to happen, Vi. You're not a failure, you're not poison, and you're not worthless."

I wasn't a failure. I wasn't worthless.

I was Violet *freaking* Rivers, and one sociopathic male—or several—couldn't take that away from me. And when all of this was over, I would remind Desirae of that as well. They might have stolen her innocence, but she was still sweet and kind. She didn't have to lose that, and I would help her see that just as Griff had helped me.

That's my girl, Sable murmured. *Stay strong. Our boys will come for us.*

I glanced at my arm, at the snake tattoo that magically bound me and Griff together. I had no idea where I was, but Griff had found me once before with the magic's help. I hadn't willingly tried to leave him this time, so it wasn't causing me pain, but the sight of it alone gave me comfort.

Combined with Sable's confidence, I let myself relax as Desirae scrubbed every inch of my skin until it turned red. Ivan continued to watch us from the entrance, but I pretended like he wasn't there, giving him my back. If he thought I would be cowed into submission by the fact that a strange male was watching me bathe, he was dead wrong. The creeper could watch all he liked. He could even get off on it for all I cared.

This place wasn't going to break me, and I would do everything in my power to protect the other females stuck in here.

I was given that opportunity only an hour later when Desirae and I left the bathhouse to meet up with the other females for dinner. There were a dozen of us, all hybrids and under the age of thirty. All unclaimed, except for me. We all wore the exact same outfit like a freakish cult—or inmates. The room looked like a prison cafeteria and felt like one too. Male guards stood at every exit, making sure we didn't leave the room. Every time one of us talked, a male would clear his throat, and all of the females would quickly stop.

Fear. They were being ruled by *fear*.

Every time one of them flinched, my anger grew. These were powerful hybrid females whose confidence had been weakened. They were lost, a feeling I'd allowed to define me for way too long. But not anymore. I would no longer shrink away from what scared me. No longer let fear *control* me. I needed to remind these females of how strong and capable they were.

But how?

As we all sat down at a long metal table with our trays of food, an idea came to me. Quickly checking that the guards weren't watching, I flattened my mound of mashed potatoes and used my fork to write, *Where are we?*

When I nudged the girl's leg beside me to get her attention, she saw my message and let out a soft gasp. Everyone froze to look at her, so I hurriedly coughed to cover up the noise and took a sip of my water. After a moment of silence, I tried again. She shook her head, but I persisted, pointing to the message.

"Please," I whispered, the sound barely a wisp of air.

She tightly clenched her own fork, then dug it into her mashed potatoes and hastily wrote, *Alaska.*

Alaska? How the hell had they transported me all the way across the country? They must have kept me sedated with silver for the long journey.

With the time zone difference, that meant I'd probably been here less than a day, even if it felt like several had passed. No wonder Desirae had sounded so miserable that she'd only been here a week. I hadn't seen a single window in the place, making time drag impossibly slow.

Despite the news that I was so far from home, I erased my message and wrote a new one. *How many?*

The girl glanced at me in confusion, so I threw a pointed look at the guards. Understanding, she wrote back, *30.*

I nearly choked on my mouthful of meatloaf. Okay, more than I'd thought. Taking them all out was definitely going to be a challenge.

As I tried to come up with an escape plan, the girl across from me suddenly sniffled. I looked up just as she swiftly wiped the tears off her face. Looking at the others, I noticed several other morose expressions, and many of them had barely touched their food. Understandable, considering the situation, but something else seemed to be bothering them.

Nudging the girl beside me again, I wrote, *What?*

When she saw me glance at the others, she hesitated before writing back, *The Claiming.*

Oh crap.

When?

Tonight, she replied.

Who?

All.

ALL? What kind of creepy event was this? I probably didn't want to know, but it looked like I was going to soon enough.

As the girl across from me shed a few more tears, I couldn't help but whisper, "Don't worry. I won't let any of them touch you."

Her eyes fluttered up to meet mine, and I gave her my most confident smile.

When a male cleared his throat in warning, I rolled my eyes and muttered, "Suck it, dickface."

Several gasps lit up the room. Whoops. Guess I'd been a little too loud.

Sable snickered, clearly pleased with my sassy mouth despite the situation.

A hush fell over the table as heavy footfalls stomped toward us. Oh boy, I was in trouble.

Worth it, Sable said.

I agreed, but the other females were staring at me in horror like I was about to die a grisly death.

Feeling the male storm up behind me, I raised my water glass and took a casual sip. In the next second, he knocked the glass from my hand and grabbed a chunk of my hair, forcing my head back.

"Want to repeat that?" he growled in my ear, clutching my hair so tightly that tears of pain filled my eyes.

Blinking them away, I crooned, "Why? Are you hard of hearing or just not used to being called a dickface?"

He let go of my hair, only to backhand me across the face. My head flew to the side, and I bit my tongue. But as blood filled my mouth, I ignored the pain and turned to spit it out.

Onto his boot.

He released an enraged growl and raised his hand again, but before he could hit me a second time, a commanding voice said, "Stand down, Jensen."

Dickface—aka, Jensen—turned and snapped to attention. "But, Alpha Bane, she was talking back. You said—"

"I know what I said," Atticus interrupted, and I turned my throbbing head to watch him approach. His eyes were on me, and they had that pleased look again. Stopping a few feet away, he said to Jensen without taking his eyes off me, "Escort the females back to their dorm room. They need rest before The Claiming tonight."

As one, the females all rose from their seats and shuffled toward Jensen. I followed suit, only for Atticus to hold up a hand and say, "Not you. Ivan will take you back to your holding cell and administer another injection. You haven't yet learned to submit and, therefore, aren't ready for The Claiming."

As he gestured for Ivan to come get me and turned to leave, desperation made me blurt, "Wait!" When he paused but didn't turn around, I quickly added, "I'll behave. I'll *submit*."

The words tasted bitter in my mouth, but I refused to take them back. The girls needed me, and being strapped down with fresh silver in my veins would make me useless to them. If I had to submit in order to help them, then I would gladly do it.

Atticus slowly turned to face me again, but I could tell right away that he didn't believe me. I broke eye contact and lowered my head, *showing* him my submission. But that wasn't enough for him, unsurprisingly. He might be a creep, but he wasn't dumb.

Stepping toward me until he was only a foot away, he quietly ordered, "Get on your knees."

I immediately obeyed, dropping to my knees at his feet and keeping my face downcast.

He clucked his tongue, but it wasn't a disapproving sound. He was *pleased* to see me this way. As he bent down, I stayed perfectly still, even when he placed his mouth near my ear and purred, "This is exactly where I want you to be after I claim you tonight, spitfire. On your knees before me, sucking my dick."

As he straightened, I almost hurled up my meager dinner all over his shoes. So many angry retorts came to mind, but I savagely bit my tongue to keep them inside. He left then but not before telling Jensen to take me to the dorm room as well. As I rose to my feet, I managed to catch Ivan watching his alpha leave. Normally expressionless, there was no mistaking the *fury* in his eyes.

Despite the humiliation I'd just subjected myself to, I perked up. Ivan clearly hadn't expected Atticus to challenge his verbal claim on me. I could use that against them. I could use that against them *all*.

There was a reason why dominant unmated males often got kicked out of the pack. They were volatile when challenged, especially when it came to females. But this pack was entirely made up of possessive, testosterone-driven males.

Each and every one of them was a powder keg about to explode.

A wicked smile slowly curled my lips.

I could use that. I could *definitely* use that.

CHAPTER 32

VIOLET

I gently touched my collar for the umpteenth time, even though I knew I wouldn't find an off switch.

The metal was smooth on the outside and tight enough around my neck that I couldn't wiggle my fingers under it. If I wanted it off, I'd either have to break it—and risk triggering the needles hidden inside—or find the device that controlled it. I was currently thinking about the latter option, certain that one of the males had a remote control that could deactivate the collars.

Or activate them.

I needed to find out who had it if we had any hope at all of escaping during The Claiming. Once the collars were off, we could shift again, giving us the upper hand. The males outnumbered us by far and had weapons, but if the collars were off, we had a fighting chance.

I just had to convince the other females that submitting wasn't the only option. Problem was, they probably didn't realize my little stunt in the cafeteria had been an act. I'd have to do damage control first and quickly. We needed to all be in this together for an escape to work. If even one female panicked, it could spell doom for us all.

We were currently in the communal bathroom across from the female dorm room, preparing for bed. Jensen stood at the entrance, but with the sound of running water and flushing toilets, I decided to make my move.

"Remote," I whispered to the blonde girl using the sink beside me. I'd chosen her after watching how she carried herself in the cafeteria earlier. I didn't know if she was an alpha female, but she certainly wasn't an omega. She still had fight in her despite the abuse she'd endured. When she glanced at me, I lowered my toothbrush to tap on my collar. "Where?"

She peeked at Jensen before whispering back, "Atticus."

"No talking," the surly male barked. She flinched, but that didn't stop her from miming a chain around her neck with a device attached to it.

Thank you, I mouthed back, then resumed brushing my teeth in silence.

Only when we were shuffled across the hall to a dark room full of cots did I dare to speak again. Using the sounds of creaking springs and shifting bodies to mask my words, I turned to the girl nearest to me and breathed, "Escape. Tonight. Pass it on."

She gaped at me with terror in her eyes, but there was something else too. Something that hadn't been there before now.

Hope.

I gave her an encouraging smile, and after only a moment's hesitation, she turned to the girl next to her and relayed the message. Every time one of them spoke, I coughed or cleared my throat to mask their voices. Jensen openly glared at me from the doorway, but I ignored him.

When the last female delivered my message, I finally settled against the thin mattress and shut my eyes. I didn't sleep, though. I was too busy plotting, too busy worrying about the worst case scenarios, too busy hoping that *Griff* would arrive just when I needed him.

He will. Your mate will come for you, Sable whispered as if she too was afraid of being overheard.

Mate. I liked the sound of that. *Loved* it, actually.

Letting my mind picture his smiling, handsome face, a face I knew better than my own, I relaxed my tired body and waited for the inevitable.

For The Claiming that would either free us . . . or doom us all.

Hours later, just as I was starting to drift off, a bright light flooded the room.

"Time for The Claiming, ladies. Get up, get up," Jensen's booming voice said. I sat up and squinted, trying to adjust to the bright light. The other females did the same, and even though my senses weren't fully back, I heard more than one heartbeat start to race.

They were terrified of what was to come, and rightfully so. My own heart had picked up speed despite my steady resolve, old feelings of inadequacy threatening to distract me. My plan could utterly fail, and I could end up hurting these females more than helping them, but I wouldn't let that fear stop me from trying. They needed the strength and support of an alpha female, and I would fight like hell to protect them from these bastard males.

As we lined up and shuffled from the dorm room, still wearing our collars and matching tunic outfits, I noticed that Jensen kept looking at Desirae. When she passed by him, he suddenly grabbed her arm and breathed in her ear, "You're mine."

I was moving before I could check myself, boldly wedging my body between theirs. Jensen looked startled, then angry. He bared his teeth at me, but before he could say anything, I said, "You can't stake a claim on her yet. The Claiming hasn't started."

At that, fury contorted his face. "Why, you little—" he began, raising his hand to no doubt strike me. I held my ground, staring him dead in the eye.

Right before he could hit me, a deep voice from behind him snapped, "Don't touch her."

Jensen stopped. Just barely. Still glaring at me, he replied to the other male, "It's a mistake including her in The Claiming tonight, Ivan. She should be kept in seclusion until her spirit is broken like all the others."

"That isn't your decision to make," Ivan shot back. "So unless you want me to report this little incident to our alpha, I suggest you keep your thoughts to yourself and stick to doing your job."

Jensen continued to glare at me, but I could sense that some of his ire was now directed at his second in command. Seizing the opportunity, I gave him a little smile and crooned, "Better listen to him, dickface. He outranks you by far."

His face flushed scarlet, the veins in his neck and forehead protruding. Despite the murderous look he was giving me, Sable snickered under her breath.

You go, girl.

My smile widened, and Jensen slowly turned purple. Before he could explode like an overripe watermelon—or kill me—Ivan muscled his way between us and grabbed my arm. As he dragged me into the hall out of harm's way, he grumbled, "Stop causing trouble."

I blinked at him innocently. "Yes, Alpha. I mean, Ivan. Forgot you weren't in charge for a second."

Something dangerous sparked in his eyes, but I didn't shrink away from it. He wanted me, and I had to pray that meant he wouldn't report this little incident to Atticus and get me sent back to isolation. If he did that, he wouldn't get a chance to claim me tonight, and I could tell he desperately wanted to leave his mark on me before his alpha could.

So instead of diffusing the situation like an omega would, I stepped closer to him and whispered, "Hope you're on your A-game tonight. Wouldn't want someone *else* to claim me before you can."

A growl rumbled from him, and he jerked me closer until my chest bumped his. I allowed the contact, knowing that it would further stoke his need to claim me. As I heard him inhale my scent, I held perfectly still. He undoubtedly smelled Griff's claim, but there was another scent just beneath that, a scent that drove both unmated and mated males wild.

My heat.

It wasn't as strong anymore, but the pheromones were still dancing in the air, tempting even the most stalwart male to give in to his baser instincts.

Firming his grip on my arm, Ivan breathed the pheromones in for another moment before rumbling, "Mark my words. You will be mine."

I didn't comment. I didn't need to. He'd played right into my trap, and I was inwardly cackling with glee right alongside Sable.

You're absolutely wicked, she chortled. *I love it.*

Keeping a straight face was nearly impossible, but I managed not to smile as Ivan released my arm and gestured for me to follow him down the hallway. The other females fell into line behind me, Jensen bringing up the rear. When we reached the end and a door buzzed, allowing us to pass into a stairwell, adrenaline shivered up my spine.

Were they letting us above ground? Dare I hope that they were letting us go *outside?*

That would definitely make it a lot easier for us to escape. Once we were topside, I could focus all of my efforts on getting our collars removed. The plan hinged on Atticus, though, so I replayed all the scenarios I'd spent the past several hours concocting, making sure I had solid backup options in case my original plan fell through.

When Ivan took us up a flight of stairs, my hope grew, but when he opened a door to the outside world and the first thing I saw was *snow*, my heart blipped to a halt.

Snow in Alaska this time of year could only mean one thing. As I stepped into it with my bare feet, breathing in fresh, cold air for the first time in what felt like forever, my fears were realized with a single glance.

A mountain. We were on top of a freaking *mountain*.

Dismay settled in my gut, but I straightened my spine anyway and forged ahead, knowing that the other females were counting on me to stay strong. Being on top of a mountain wasn't ideal, but with our collars removed, we would be stronger, *faster*.

We could still do this. We *had* to. I wouldn't accept any other outcome.

Our boys will come for us, Sable reassured me.

I knew they would, but our time was running out. The Claiming was happening *now*, and I couldn't wait for them to rescue us. No way was I letting these terrified females be claimed and mated against their will. It was up to me to save them. There was no other option.

A few snow flurries struck my face, the chilly wind teasing my hair and bangs. If I was human, the cold would no doubt have me shivering and blue within seconds. But despite the silver still lingering in my veins, my werewolf DNA kept me toasty warm, including my bare feet.

"Come, females. Your destiny awaits," a loud voice boomed from up ahead. The females behind me crowded in close, their hearts pounding like jackrabbits. We could all sense it, could all hear the dozens of excited heartbeats just around the bend.

The entirety of Rogue Pack was waiting for us.

Sure enough, as Ivan led us to the front of the ugly cement

building, at least thirty males were standing in the snow, each of their faces hungry for what was to come.

In front of them all was Atticus Bane, and his expression lit up at the sight of me. Bile climbed up my throat, but I forced it back down and scooted a little closer to Ivan. Atticus saw, and I watched with satisfaction as his eyes darkened.

When we were still several yards away, Ivan stopped, and so did we. The males ahead shifted on their feet, clearly impatient for The Claiming to start. After a few more moments of tense silence, Atticus took a step forward and said, "My fellow rogue brothers, I know you've been eager for this moment for a long time. With no females to call our own, our existence has been lonely and rife with tension. Our needs have gone unmet, our desire for connection and family denied. But today, we finally have hope. Today, we become a *true* pack."

Dozens of males howled in reply, raising their faces up to the night sky. The sound was so feral that goosebumps erupted over my flesh.

Atticus lifted his hands to quiet them down and continued, "I'm aware that we currently don't have enough females for the entire pack, but the strongest among us will claim their mates tonight. After The Claiming is complete, we'll seek out more females until everyone here has a mate."

More excited hoots and howls echoed through the air, along with a jubilant stomping of feet. The females behind me cowered, scared witless by the males' hungry response.

Disgusted by their primal display, I took my own step forward and loudly said, "Why kidnap hybrids?" Complete silence descended over the crowd. Every hair on my body stood on end as dozens of unmated males paused to look at me, but I plowed ahead anyway.

"You could have pursued willing females. There are hundreds of them all over the world looking for mates. So why take hybrids? Why *us?*"

Reading Atticus's growing obsession with me correctly, instead of punishing me for speaking out, he rewarded me with a response. Still, there was a clear warning in his eyes as he replied, "I thought that part was obvious. We've seen the power hybrids wield and want to populate the world with more of you. Imagine how great Rogue Pack will become once we've sired hundreds of new hybrids. We'll be the world's most powerful pack, and there won't be a single werewolf who would dare turn their back on us."

Before I could process his horrific words, he added, "One day, Miss Rivers, you'll thank us for this incredible opportunity. We're changing how werewolves see us outsiders. Together, banished rogues and hybrids will become the new superpower, but we'll need a strong alpha female for that to happen. After tonight, I'm hoping that female will be you."

I stiffened, all too aware of what he meant. He wanted me to be his mate and rule beside him, dangling the proposal before me like it was a prize. But I knew all too well what his *real* intention was—to bribe me into cooperating so the other females would follow suit.

Sick to my stomach by his twisted vision, I couldn't help but say, "You know hybrids aren't created that way, right? The celestial beings inside us *choose* who to share their spirits with. Just because the parent is a hybrid doesn't mean the child will be gifted a spirit at birth."

I thought for *sure* this would pop his delusional bubble, but all Atticus did was smile a little and reply, "Either way, every single male here is willing to take that chance. The mere hope of siring a hybrid is enough to make them try several times over. I myself am willing to sire dozens of children if it means becoming the father of even one hybrid."

As hunger burned in his eyes, hunger for *me*, an overwhelming need to run trembled through my bones. I couldn't imagine what the other females were feeling, but if I didn't act soon, I was going to lose them. They would panic, and my flimsy escape plan would crumble to dust.

So, despite the terror filling my own veins, I stood taller and said, "If it's power you seek, then you need to earn it."

He cocked his head to the side in curiosity. "I'm listening."

Holy crap, I didn't think he would go for that. He must *really* want me as his alpha female.

All too aware of Ivan standing still as stone beside me, I said, "I don't know what your plan is for this claiming tonight, but if your pack's goal is to claim and mate the females here, then a traditional hunt is the only way to earn that right."

Just as I thought, excitement rippled through the pack of males. It was in their DNA to hunt and chase their prey, and that included their pursuit of a mate. Now that I'd planted the idea in their heads, they wouldn't be able to resist it.

Sure enough, the hunger in Atticus's eyes deepened. "Go on."

"The females are given a head start. The males must wait until they can no longer see them before giving chase. If the male catches a female and she submits, then he's allowed to claim her."

The males rumbled their eagerness, clearly on board with the plan.

"But there's one problem with that plan," I continued, and the males fell silent. Pointing at my collar, I said, "If we run, we trigger our collars. Where's the challenge if we're all on the ground, writhing in pain?"

Aaaand I'd said the magic word. *Challenge.* Every dominant male loved a challenge, and calling them out for cheating kicked every single one of their inflated egos.

"Where's the challenge, indeed?" Attitcus mused, watching me closely as he tugged on a chain around his neck and revealed the attached remote.

My heart skipped a beat, but otherwise, I didn't react. So close. *So close.* All he had to do was push the button and unlock the collars. Sable rose up as much as she was allowed, preparing to take over the second the collar fell away. She yearned to sink her claws and fangs into every single male here, especially Atticus, but I'd seen the pile of weapons stacked behind them.

One silver bullet to the heart could kill me. My need for vengeance was strong, but my need for survival was stronger. Once we were free of the collar, Sable and I would have to ignore our instincts and flee. It was the only way we could lead the other females to safety.

Toying with the remote for several torturous moments, Atticus finally said, "Unfortunately, removing your collars gives you too much power, and we have no intention of losing any females tonight." I watched with dismay as he tucked the remote back inside his shirt. "Don't worry, though. The collars won't be triggered so long as you stay within the five mile perimeter surrounding the compound. There are traps just beyond that, so I highly suggest you don't try to escape. And don't forget that any attempt to remove the collar, shift, or use magic will result in an extremely painful silver injection."

With each word he spoke, my plan crumbled more and more. We were *helpless* with the collars on, especially with the ever-looming threat of the needles.

As I watched our only leverage slip away, I blurted out, "No weapons, then."

Atticus lifted an eyebrow at me.

"It's only fair," I pressed. "The females aren't being allowed weapons, so the males shouldn't have any either."

Atticus stared at me hard, no doubt calculating the risks—and wondering what I was up to. I stared right back, lifting my chin a notch.

After a few moments, a smile slowly spread across his face. "Deal," he purred. "My men will wait to begin the hunt until every female is out of sight. Without weapons. Let The Claiming begin."

My breath seized in my lungs.

His smile turned downright wicked. "That's your cue, ladies. I suggest you all run."

CHAPTER 33

VIOLET

I ran like the wind, my feet barely touching the snow-covered ground.

Determination fueled me, along with a heavy dose of terror.

Worried that the other females would panic and scatter, I barked, "Follow me!" before taking off down the mountain. So far, it sounded like they'd obeyed me, but they barely knew me. Once the males started to pursue us, their fear would override common sense.

The second we all disappeared from sight, dozens of eerie howls lit up the night.

The chase was on.

Several females cried out in fear, but before they could bolt, I snapped, "Stick together!"

I led them farther down the mountain, frantically searching for a spot where we could make our stand. When I finally found a relatively flat open clearing, I ignored my instinct to keep running and skidded to a halt.

"No! We have to keep going!" one of the females cried, pushing past me.

I grabbed her arm and spun her around, shouting, "Stop! If we keep going, we'll reach the boundary and trigger the collars. The best thing we can do right now is stay together and fight them."

"Fight?" another female shrieked. "We're outnumbered and *weak* with these collars on. Fighting is useless."

"No, it's *not*," I argued, whirling to face the others. "We're still strong. Still capable. Still fierce female werewolves. We're not helpless, and we're not submitting to these feral bastards without a fight. There's too many of them and not enough of us. Use that *against* them. Make them fight each other for you. Make them *kill* each other. All I need to do is get that remote. Once I've deactivated our collars, the males don't stand a chance. You know this. You're freaking hybrids, so *act* like it."

Every single female stared at me in utter terror, sounds of the ravenous male pack closing in fast. I wouldn't blame them if they tucked tail and ran right now, if they took their chances alone instead of agreeing to a flimsy plan that could get them killed. These males were stark raving mad, and who knew what they would do if the females didn't submit.

I desperately wanted to flee myself, but I knew it wouldn't get me anywhere. This was our only chance. We had to *fight*.

As the ground started to rumble, the sound of stampeding footsteps almost deafening, Desirae stepped forward and said, "I'm with you."

Hope fluttered in my chest. I glanced at the others, and one by one, they all said the same thing.

"I'm with you."

"I'm with you."

"I'm with you."

Giving them all a grateful smile, I replied, "Then stand your ground. Fight with everything you have. And remember . . ." I turned to face the approaching males. "Atticus is mine."

Seconds later, several males burst through the trees and into the clearing. Spotting the females in the center, their stances far from submissive, they skidded to a halt in confusion. Several more arrived and did the same thing, clearly not expecting the females to be standing their ground.

As I saw Atticus and Ivan start to push through the throng, I let a grin stretch my lips. Crooking my finger at them in a taunting gesture, I crooned, "If you want us, come and get us, boys."

Dead silence fell over the clearing. It was so quiet that I heard a snowflake land on my nose. And then . . .

The world erupted into chaos.

In a flash, the males rushed forward and collided with the females. Growls and screams echoed through the clearing. A male plowed into me and almost took me down, but I used the momentum to reverse our positions. As he hit the ground, I landed on top and immediately lit into him with all of my pent-up rage. After only two punches, I knocked him out cold.

I was immediately up again, but before I could engage another male, a cry for help distracted me. Not too far away, I spotted Desirae. A big male had her. A *familiar* male. She cried out again as Jensen yanked her head back and savagely bit into her neck just below her collar.

At the sight of him forcing a claim on her, fury flooded me. I raced forward and jumped onto his back, snaking an arm around his throat. I squeezed and squeezed, clinging to him with all of my might. He released Desirae with a roar and tried to buck me off. I wound my legs around his waist and held on, ignoring the pain as he yanked and clawed at my arms.

He abruptly threw himself backward and landed on top of me. The move knocked the wind out of me, and my grip loosened. He jerked his head back and hit my cheek, making me see stars. My grip loosened even more. Just as I was about to lose, his head violently snapped to the side. The blow came again and again, pounding into him like a battering ram. Sobs reached my ears, but the hits kept coming until Jensen finally went limp.

With a grunt, I shoved him off me and reached for the sobbing girl.

"Desirae, stop. *Stop.* It's okay. I've got you."

She clung to me, shaking uncontrollably. Werewolves were fighting each other everywhere I looked. A few females were holding their own, teaming up to drive the males back. Several more looked ready to bolt but valiantly held their ground. Blood and carnage littered the white snow, and I saw more than one male rip into another male as they grappled over the same female.

My plan was working. The males were *fighting* each other.

Now, I just needed that stupid remote.

As I had the thought, my eyes collided with a broad, black-haired male several yards off. I stood up with Desirae and pushed her behind me to face Ivan. His pupils were dilated, his gaze wholly locked on me. At the feral way he was looking at me, I mistakenly took a step back. *Retreated.* Like prey.

He surged forward, shoving male after male aside in his haste to get to me. I planted my feet and squared off with him, a growl of defiance burning my throat. Sable bristled, ready to aid me as best she could against the male determined to claim me. Feet away from reaching me, another male barrelled toward him with a roar.

Barely taking his eyes off me, Ivan twisted around and grabbed Jensen by the head. Using his forward momentum against him, Ivan savagely jerked Jensen's head sideways and snapped his neck. I flinched at the awful cracking noise but continued to hold my ground, watching as Jensen collapsed to the snow dead.

Ivan started toward me again, bloodlust sparking in his eyes— only for another male to step into his path and draw him up short.

Immediately recognizing the dark-haired male, I froze, barely daring to breathe.

"Step aside, Alpha," Ivan growled, hyped up on his recent kill. "She's mine to claim."

"She's too alpha for you, Ivan," Atticus growled back, his voice nearly as feral as his second's. "I need a strong alpha female like her to carry my heirs."

Eww, gross. No way was I having babies with that old creep.

"Ivan," I called, saying his name like a plea. Like I wanted *him* to claim me.

That one word might as well have been a kill switch. Just like that, their brains switched off and they became mindless animals. The two males let out bellowing roars and charged each other, clashing in a powerful display of brute force. Snow and blood sprayed as they attacked each other like rabid beasts, their intentions crystal clear.

Only one of them was walking away from this fight alive.

I watched their every move, shielding Desirae any time they got too close. Bones cracked. Clothing ripped. I watched and watched. Waiting. Hoping. One move. One little move would change everything. So close. *So close.*

When the fight dragged on and on, both males equally matched, my patience thinned. I had to end this. Females everywhere were crying out for help as they began to lose their fight against the males. There were too many of them, and even though half of them were fighting each other, the winners would move on to claim their chosen females next.

Unable to wait another second, I wailed, "Ivan!"

Just as I'd hoped, he paused to look at me. One move. One little move.

Atticus immediately took advantage and punched a hole straight through Ivan's chest. Ivan's eyes were on mine as they filled with stunned disbelief. Atticus ripped his hand back out, removing Ivan's heart in the process. The life in Ivan's eyes instantly vanished, and he toppled over sideways, hitting the snow with a muffled thud.

Before I could feel guilty for what I'd done, Atticus dropped Ivan's heart and turned to face me. His blue eyes were impossibly bright, glittering with victory. Covered in Ivan's blood and breathing heavily, he slowly stalked toward me. Dread skated down my spine, but I held my ground, refusing to run.

Desirae whimpered out my name, but I waved her back. This was between him and me. The only way I was going to save these females was to let him get close. *Really* close. And close he came, striding right up to me to yank me against him.

"I won," he said in a guttural voice, still juiced up from the fight. "You're mine to claim now."

Ignoring the nausea swirling in my gut, I lowered my eyes in submission and whispered, "Then claim me."

A growl of satisfaction rumbled from him, and he gripped my nape to force my head back. Squeezing my eyes shut so I couldn't see his face, I went pliant in his arms, fully submitting to him. Excited that I was willingly giving myself up to him, his arousal saturated the air. I almost gagged but managed not to react. A second later, his mouth was on my neck, nuzzling and nipping me.

Then he struck.

His canines sank deeply into my flesh, marking me in the exact same spot where Griff had. A howl of dismay rose up inside me, doubling in volume as Sable joined in. She didn't try to stop it from happening, though, because she knew. She knew that this was the only way.

The only way to *stop* him.

As he pulled me even closer, groaning as he sank his canines deeper, I made my move. Quick as a snake, I grabbed the chain around his neck and yanked.

"Desirae!" I shouted and tossed her the chain containing the remote.

Atticus jerked his canines from my neck with a growl, but it was too late.

My collar unlocked with a click, and I yanked it off, throwing it to the ground.

As I did, an earth-shattering roar cleaved the air. Atticus's eyes widened, and we both looked up just as something fell from the sky. Like a shooting star, it hit the ground with a resounding *boom*. As the impact trembled through me, I started to laugh, realizing that it wasn't a star at all. It was a man—a *werewolf*—with spiky blond hair.

My laughter turned to sobs, tears of relief rolling down my cheeks.

My best friend. My *mate* had arrived.

CHAPTER 34

GRIFF

I hit the ground hard, the thin layer of snow absorbing some of the impact. Seconds later, four more booms shook the earth.

As Kolton, Jagger, Mason, and Reid straightened from the fall, I was already moving. I'd seen her from up above. Seen the male bite into her neck. And I'd nearly lost it. The four other males in the helicopter had to stop me from jumping out too soon and blowing our cover. A few more helicopters were on their way, but I hadn't been able to wait any longer.

The magic that bound us together was thrumming loudly, practically shouting that I'd finally reached my destination. Reached *her*. But I wasn't quite there yet.

Several feet still separated us, and I quickly ate up the distance, my sights solely set on her. All around me, chaos ensued, but I didn't pay it any heed. The others would take care of it.

My mission—my *only* mission—was her.

As I raced toward her, Vi cried out my name and stumbled forward. I picked up speed, my heart in my throat as she came nearer and nearer. A few more feet, and we collided. I immediately crushed her to me, holding her impossibly tight. When I felt her warmth seep through my clothing, I cried out in relief and crashed to my knees in the snow.

Her body shook against mine, her tears saturating my shirt. I finally let my own tears fall, the nightmare I'd been trapped in for the past day slowly fading away. Rocking her in my arms, I whispered over and over, "I got you, baby. I got you."

I allowed myself to rock her for another few moments, but when several more booms shook the ground, I rose to my feet and tucked her against me. A quick glance around the clearing showed that many of the rogue males had scattered like cowards, not willing to face the growing army of alphas.

"Don't let them reach the compound. They left their weapons out front," Vi said, and I was so relieved to hear her speak that my knees weakened again.

"Kolton," I called and quickly relayed the message. Several alphas from different packs took off after the retreating rogues, including my brother. The rest stayed to fight the males still in the clearing. Many had already been killed, though, probably from fighting each other or the females. A few females were injured, but I couldn't see any dead ones.

Noticing that Desirae had been bitten too, I watched as Reid slowly approached her. She was gripping a device in her trembling hands, but when he held out a hand toward her, she dropped it and hurried over to him.

As he enveloped her in a hug, Vi hummed and said, "That could work, actually."

I glanced down at her in surprise. "Are you *matchmaking* right now?"

She shrugged. "Maybe." Then, "Your entrance was a little showy, don't you think?"

I cracked a smile. "We needed the element of surprise. There are traps and alarm systems all around the perimeter. It's like Fort Knox up here. Bill Andrews and several other SCA operatives are dismantling them right now. Good thing you were all out here tonight. Rescuing you was almost too easy."

Vi scoffed. "That's because the other females and I already did most of the work. We were just about to shift and gain the upper hand right before you arrived."

"Are you saying you didn't even need rescuing?"

She shrugged again. "Not really, but I'm still glad you're here."

As she tipped up her face to smile at me, I wiped away a lingering tear on her cheek. "I was so scared," I whispered.

"Me too," she whispered back, her chin quivering.

I lowered my head to softly kiss her lips, and she sighed against my mouth.

A throat from nearby impatiently cleared. "All right, you two. We're still not done here," Jagger said. "What do you want me to do with this dirtbag?"

I glanced up and immediately locked eyes with the bastard who'd bitten Vi. Now that she was safe, my fury from earlier returned with a vengeance.

Kill him, Whiskey said with finality.

As much as I wanted to tear him limb from limb for marking *my* mate, I glanced down at Vi again and said, "It's your call."

She looked over at the male and tapped her chin in thought before saying, "Toss him in a cell and let him rot for all I care. He's a slimy worm and doesn't deserve to see the light of day again."

The male pulled his lip back in a silent snarl. "I see now why you have such a mouth on you, spitfire. The males in your life never taught you to heel."

Oh, he did not *just say that. Let me at 'im*, Whiskey growled, fighting with me for control.

I almost let him take over, beyond furious now. My eyes must have started to glow yellow, because the male suddenly lost some of his bravado, his gaze wavering.

"Say what you want, old man," Vi spoke up before anyone else could. "Your pack is gone, and you won't be mistreating females ever again. Your short reign of terror has ended."

He was noticeably trembling now, and when he saw Kolton approaching our group, he looked at me and barked, "I claimed her. She smells like *me* now, not you. If you want her back, you'll have to fight me for her. Fair is fair."

"Gladly," I replied, letting go of Vi so I could whip off my shirt. "I accept your challenge. Give me your best shot, gramps."

Whiskey howled with glee, surging up so quickly that fur erupted over my chest and arms.

The male's eyes widened, unmistakable fear flickering in their depths. I grinned at him, revealing my lengthened canines.

"Show off," Vi muttered under her breath, and my grin broadened.

"This fight needs to be *fair*," the male said, clearly starting to lose his nerve. "Fight me as a man, not as a beast."

"*Fair?*" Vi snapped, taking a step toward him. As she did, I noticed that several of the other females had come closer to watch the spectacle. Whiskey puffed up his chest, pleased to have an audience. "Was it fair when you tore these females from their homes? Was it fair when you put collars on them and threatened them with violence to force their submission? Was it fair when you sent a feral pack of males after them to claim and *rape* them?"

At that last part, I couldn't hold back a growl. Stepping forward, I pulled Vi back against me, needing to feel her before I completely lost it and took the male's head off.

"No, Atticus," she continued, drawing more and more females over with each bravely spoken word. "You don't deserve fair after all that you've done. So either face my mate—my *alpha* mate, by the way—or run like the coward you are. If you choose to run, we'll give you a head start. But the second you're out of sight, we're coming for you. How's *that* for fair?"

When she was finished, one of the females loudly cheered. Another joined in, and soon, they were all hooting and hollering, even Desirae.

Vi glanced at them with a wide smile, then turned back to Atticus and said, "That's your cue, old man. Fight or run. The choice is yours."

He stared at the teeming crowd, not a single one of his pack members in sight. Took one last look at me. And then . . .

He turned tail and bolted.

CHAPTER 35

VIOLET

It was thrilling running with so many hybrids.

The second Atticus was out of sight, the clearing lit up with the sound of breaking bones. Within seconds, massive wolves of varying color dotted the snow. Even Burgundy, Desirae's dark brown wolf, had shifted and was clearly eager to pursue Atticus. There were fifteen of us in all, and it was a glorious sight. None of the wolves had opted to shift into their true forms, but we didn't need them to.

There was no way that Atticus could outrun us. The hunter had become the hunted, and the irony of the situation made me howl with glee.

Sable released my howl, and as it echoed through the trees while we ran, the wolves behind her excitedly answered the call. It was a terrifying sound, and Atticus was no doubt wetting himself right now.

In no time, we caught up with him, but the pack decided to fan out and bring him down slowly. He needed to feel the fear that we had felt. To experience how terrifying it felt to be hunted. We chased him for miles, ever-so-slowly tightening the circle. He ran and ran, helpless against so much power.

A power he never should have messed with.

A loud *snap* suddenly cleaved the air, and Atticus fell with a cry.

Sable slowed to a trot, approaching him cautiously. When I saw a flash of silver in the snow, I barked a laugh. *He fell into one of his own traps! Ah, poetic justice.* The other wolves closed in, watching Atticus writhe on the ground in agony. After several long moments, I said, *Guess we should help him.*

Just a little bit longer, Sable softly whined.

We're not evil, remember? I chastised.

Fine, she said with a sigh.

She stepped forward, but Whiskey brushed against her, clearly wanting to help. Together, they approached the fallen male, pausing to shift their front paws into clawed hands so they could pry the trap open. As Whiskey grabbed the male's injured leg, Atticus reared up, a syringe tightly gripped in his hand.

The needle was headed directly for Whiskey's neck, and Sable immediately reacted.

Faster than I could blink, she lunged forward and bit Atticus's head clean off. As blood spurted into her mouth, I wailed, *Gross! Drop it, Sable. Drop it!*

She spat it out into the snow with a sheepish whine. *Oops.*

OOPS? That's all you have to say for yourself?

As I continued to scold her, Whiskey made a noise that sounded a lot like a laugh.

Ugh! You two are impossible, I groaned.

Sable didn't respond, too busy making googly eyes at her mate. The more he laughed, the more she preened, clearly delighted with his approval.

Okay, you two are officially in timeout, I firmly said, nudging her to shift back.

Whiskey leaned over to lick her muzzle clean, but as soon as he was finished, both wolves relinquished control. Shadow and Onyx did the same, and soon, Griff, Kolton, Jagger, and I were staring down at Atticus's decapitated body and head.

"He looks much better this way," Griff observed after a silent beat. He let out an *"Oof!"* as I elbowed his ribs.

"Efficient," was all Jagger said.

"Well, one less bad guy for the SCA to lock up," my brother said, clearly not at all upset by the outcome.

Neither was I, but I could still taste Atticus's blood in the back of my throat.

"I need to do something," I abruptly said, turning to face Griff. "Something I should have done a long time ago." Then, before I could lose my nerve, I said, "Griffin Hayes O'Neal, I want to claim you as my mate."

Griff gaped at me like he'd heard wrong. "Claim me? What, like right now?"

"Yes."

His brows practically disappeared into his hairline. "Here? Next to a dead body and in front of everyone?"

"Yes."

So romantic, Sable sighed.

Griff suddenly grinned a mile wide. "Hell, *yes*, you can claim me. And if there's anything else you wanna do while you're at it, I'm totally down with it. We're naked, after all. It would be a shame to waste this golden opportun—"

"Griff!" Kolton and Jagger barked at the same time.

Several of the wolves still surrounding us snorted and shook their heads, making Griff laugh.

I watched him with a little smile, beyond grateful that he'd chosen me of all people to spend his life with. Not just for now, but forever. And I couldn't wait even one more second to choose him in return.

Standing on tiptoe, I wrapped my arms around his neck before whispering, "Griff?"

"Yeah?"

"Shut up and let me claim you."

His expression softened, and the amount of love I saw shining back at me took my breath away. Without a word, he tilted his head to the side, exposing his vulnerable throat to me. Submitting. Allowing me to take what was mine.

And so I did.

EPILOGUE
1 Month Later

VIOLET

"Griffin Hayes O'Neal, get your butt up here!" I yelled at the top of my lungs.

The front door slammed shut, and I heard feet hurry up the stairs, taking them two at a time. As the bedroom door burst open seconds later, I swallowed a giggle.

"Vi, I'm here. What—?"

I slowly stepped out of Griff's closet, and the panicked look on his face quickly morphed into shock. When I leaned against the doorframe and struck a provocative pose, his jaw slackened and he dropped the paper bag in his hand. It thumped on the floor, drawing my gaze downward.

My mouth immediately began to water, but I forced my eyes back to Griff's and said, "Sorry it's not what you envisioned." I placed my hands on my bare stomach and sensually dragged them up to my breasts. Cupping them through the purple lace material, I added, "At least *these* are bigger too."

He gaped at me with an adorably lost expression, watching me fondle myself.

Hiding my smile, I asked, "Did you remember to get three this time?"

He slowly blinked, then made an unintelligible sound.

Realizing his brain had left the building, I dropped my hands with a huff. "Seriously, Griff. If you messed up my order, you can forget this little peep show. We need to leave in a few minutes, and I'm absolutely *starving*, so—"

"Your breasts are—" he started, then shook his head and corrected, "Your burgers are all there."

I beamed at him, rushing forward to give him a chaste kiss on the lips. "Thank you, husband."

He grunted, still struggling to form syllables after seeing me in my newest lingerie. Modeling for him was our thing now. Every time I did it, his response was the same. He immediately turned into a drooling mess, unable to do anything but stare at me. I loved the attention, but the delectable smells wafting from the paper bag at his feet were currently distracting me.

Bending over, I picked it up and hurried to the bed. Griff continued to watch me, his gaze no doubt glued to my backside covered in nothing but a tiny thong. I quickly robbed him of the view, though, sitting down to dive into the bag. Eagerly unwrapping one of the quarter pounders, I took a monstrous bite. A blob of ketchup plopped onto my bare thigh, but I was too busy chewing and moaning in pleasure to care.

"Being pregnant is *exhausting*," I mumbled around my mouthful of juicy beef. "I'm barely three weeks along and can't stop eating. Did you know I had *three* breakfasts this morning?" Knowing his brain still needed time to reboot, I went on, "I think I'm showing already. Did you see the bump? Who knew that you'd get me pregnant with the first knot. I mean, I'm not complaining. I love that we're going to be parents soon. But I would have liked to be a newlywed a little bit longer, you know? Maybe do some traveling first. Griff?"

He blinked again.

"You forgot to ask for napkins."

He blinked a few more times and finally came out of his coma to say, "You're definitely bigger." When I stopped chewing to glare at him, he hastily amended, "Your boobs, I mean. They're . . . Wow. Can I touch them?"

He stepped toward me, but I immediately put him in his place with a look. "We already talked about this, Griffin. Peep show before we leave, sex when we get back."

"Ah c'mon, babe. Just a quickie? Two minutes tops, I promise."

I snorted, but when he came toward me again, I didn't stop him. "Okay, fine, but I'm going to eat while we do it."

"I can work with that," he said and hurriedly unbuttoned his jeans. "Just don't choke on your burger when I make you come."

That would be hilarious, Sable mused, and I had to agree. After being kidnapped, I'd expected our lives to return back to normal. But only a week later, I'd discovered that I was pregnant. A week after that, Griff and I got married. We'd held the wedding and reception in the backyard, the exact same place where Kolton and Nora had been married. Only Midnight Pack had attended the ceremony, but Griff had surprised us all by inviting a special guest to the reception.

His brother.

They still had a long road of healing ahead of them, but after Mason had helped rescue me and the other hybrid females, Griff was doing his best to make amends. Mason was *ecstatic* to be an uncle, and he'd already showered his future niece or nephew with several gifts.

On top of all that, I'd kept in touch with the females who'd been kidnapped, and we'd formed a trauma support group. We'd only met up twice so far, but today would be the third time. I was especially looking forward to this meeting, because I'd been helping Reid plan something special for the occasion all week.

He and Desirae had grown close over the past few weeks, so close that he was already prepared for the next step. Once we all arrived in Boston, I was taking the girls shopping and finding Desirae the *perfect* outfit. Next was hair and makeup, then the game. After the Rebels won—and they would—Reid was going to pop the question in front of the *whole* stadium.

Normally, I'd think three weeks was too soon for a couple to be getting engaged, but they were absolutely smitten with each other. His easygoing nature paired beautifully with her gentleness. They were *perfect* for each other.

Kind of like me and Griff.

Our lives had changed so much this past month, but I'd never been happier. I was fulfilled in every way possible, and I couldn't stop smiling.

"What?" Griff said, looking down at his erection. "Do you think it's getting bigger like your boobs? I've heard that can happen during pregnancy, kind of like sympathy morning sickness."

I burst out laughing. "That is *so* not a thing, Griff. Your dick is the same size it's always been."

"Except when it's knot," he said with a wink. "Get it?"

I rolled my eyes with a groan. "We *definitely* don't have time for that. I told Desirae we would pick her up in twenty minutes."

"Guess we'd better get started, then," he purred, reaching a hand down to run it up my thigh. Pausing at the blob of ketchup, he swiped at it and sensually licked it off his fingertip.

My core immediately tightened, reminding me that my increased appetite for food wasn't the only side effect of this pregnancy. I was also ravenous for sex, morning, noon, and night. If I spent the next three months doing nothing but eating and having sex, I'd be one happy pregnant woman.

Unfortunately, I had a full day ahead of me, and if I didn't get going soon—

Griff abruptly flipped me over onto my stomach. As I hit the mattress, I scrambled to hold on to my burger. I really had meant it when I said I'd continue eating while he banged me. As I took another bite, he slipped a finger under my thong strap and tugged. The action stimulated my clit, and I instantly grew wet. Griff inhaled my arousal with a pleased rumble, then snapped the thong in two as if it was floss and tossed it aside.

I rolled my eyes at the neanderthal move but grew even wetter. "One pair, Griff. I would like to wear just *one* pair more than once."

"Where's the fun in that?" he crooned, gripping my thighs to spread them open. Before I could swallow my mouthful of food, he thrust his cock inside me with one smooth stroke. Always shocked at how good it felt to have him fill me up, I literally almost choked on my burger.

Sable snickered, and I silently growled at her to butt out. We had rules about this stuff now. When Griff and I were getting frisky, our familiars weren't allowed to intervene. Same went for when Sable and Whiskey did the deed. Their time was their own, and so was ours.

Hey, boundaries were important.

When Griff started to thrust, my appetite for food quickly vanished. Another appetite took its place, and it was equally hungry. Tossing the burger aside, I gripped the comforter and moaned He slid a hand up my spine, and with a flick of his wrist, my top disappeared as well. Leaning forward, he slipped his hands beneath me and cupped my breasts. When he pinched my nipples, I gasped, the hard peaks more sensitive than usual.

As my head came off the bed, he burrowed his face in my neck and nuzzled his claim spot. He freshly marked me at least once a week, but I couldn't blame him. He'd almost lost me, and I'd almost lost him. We were still reassuring each other every day that this was real. That we were together, whole and safe.

Every time he claimed me, it cemented in my mind that I was his. He wanted me. *Loved* me. And that would never change.

As his thrusts grew more urgent, he reached down and touched my clit. The added stimulation had me panting, each movement pushing me closer and closer to the edge. When he suddenly bit his claim spot, sinking his canines in deep, pleasure exploded through me and I loudly cried out his name.

My walls spasmed around his hard cock, and he jerked inside me with a muffled groan, spilling his release. With his canines still in my neck and his fingers between my thighs, I rode the incredible high, completely blissed out.

I was about to ask him to go again, just one more time, when a groan reached my ears. A groan that was *definitely* not Griff's.

"Seriously, guys? You didn't even close the door!" Brielle complained from the—oops—open doorway. "I almost let Melanie in."

"I smell burgers!" Mellie piped up from the hallway. "Can I have one?"

"Whoa, squirt, you do *not* want to go in there," a new voice said, this one Jagger's.

"Why not?" my little sister whined. "Vi's in there."

"Yeah, but so is Griff. It's just like when Kolton and Nora are in a bedroom together. No rugrats allowed."

"I'm not a rugrat!" she pouted, then suddenly squealed as Jagger no doubt picked her up to carry her far, far away from here.

When Brielle firmly shut the door and padded away, I whispered, "Sure you want to make this room a nursery?"

Griff removed his canines from my neck and chuckled. "I'm sure.

We can move into the new house at any time, but I want you to be ready first."

I smiled, beyond grateful that I had a mate who knew when to push . . . and when not to. Now that Griff's alpha gene had awakened and we were starting a family of our own, Kolton and Nora thought it would be a good idea for us to have our own place. I'd panicked at first, still recovering from being taken away from my family, but when they'd explained that the new house would be built on the Rivers estate property, I'd gradually warmed up to the idea.

For now, though, we would stay in the big house. There was no pressure to move out, but our house would be there waiting for us when I was ready for our next chapter.

Five minutes later, Griff and I were presentable enough to leave his room. As we headed downstairs with my burger bag clutched in my hand, I saw Brielle in the foyer down below and mouthed, *Sorry.*

She waved off the apology with a good-natured laugh, but I saw the way her eyes darted to the left. Before I could confirm who'd caught her attention, Sable purred, *Those two have so much pent-up energy, they're going to explode if they don't bang it out soon.*

Jagger walked into my line of view a second later, and I forced my expression to remain neutral. It had taken lots of cajoling, but I'd finally weaseled the truth out of Nora a week ago.

Brielle and Jagger were soulmates.

Jagger had found out months ago, but Brielle still had no clue. Even so, their connection was obvious to me now. I'd promised Nora that I would keep the secret, a secret that she'd promised Jagger she would keep from her best friend, but that didn't mean I couldn't do a little prodding.

I'd seen the way they looked at each other—when the other wasn't looking, of course. A bond like that couldn't be denied forever, and with them still living in the same house, something would eventually give. I'd known Jagger for most of my life, and he'd always been a mystery when it came to females, but maybe it was time to poke the lone wolf. Hell, *I'd* needed poking, and I was so grateful to everyone who'd helped nudge me and Griff together.

Leaning into him a little more, we reached the ground floor and were met by several familiar faces.

"Aww, you didn't have to see us out, everyone," I said, taking in each precious face. Seeing my niece and nephew in Kolton's arms, I hurried forward to pepper them with kisses—even though I'd done so less than an hour ago.

I hugged Kolton next, and he murmured against my hair, "We don't want to take a single moment for granted."

I knew exactly how he felt and hugged him a little longer—just in case. I turned to Nora next, snorting when our bellies bumped. "Yep, it's official. We're definitely blowing up like balloons."

She laughed and pulled back to inspect both our stomachs. "I still say you're farther along. I'm just showing faster because my body's already done this twice."

I side-eyed my brother, muttering, "You really need to put your sperm on ice after this. Three babies in one year is a lot."

Griff loudly guffawed and pulled me back against him. "Who's to say *we* won't have three kids in a year, babe? Now that I have a knot—"

"Not again," Jagger groaned from behind us.

"What kind of knot?" Melanie piped up.

"More grandbabies?" my mother excitedly said at the same time.

Laughing, I hurried to hug the rest of my family and proclaimed, "If these males have their way, this entire house will be filled to the brim with babies."

As I finished hugging my mom, I sneaked a glance at Jagger. He practically looked *green*. Sable chortled, more than happy to observe the growing drama now that our own had been sorted out.

Mark my words. Those two. Epic fireworks. It's only a matter of time.

Smiling at her remark, I rejoined Griff, content when he slid an arm around my waist and pulled me close. As we opened the front door to depart, Kolton said, "Keep her safe, brother. Keep them both safe."

Griff turned to his best friend and gripped his shoulder, pulling me a little closer as he replied, "I will, brother."

And he would. He'd do *anything* to keep his mate and unborn baby safe. There wasn't a doubt in my mind that he'd always, always be there for us.

No matter what.

ALSO BY BECKY MOYNIHAN

WOLVES OF MIDNIGHT
Midnight Vow
Midnight Claim
Midnight Queen
Midnight Hunt (spin-off standalone)
Midnight Bond (spin-off standalone)

A TOUCH OF VAMPIRE
Shadow Touched
Curse Touched
Fate Touched
Sun Touched (spin-off standalone)
Forever Touched (spin-off standalone)

THE ELITE TRIALS
Reactive
Adaptive
Immersive

GENESIS CRYSTAL SAGA
Dawn till Dusk
Fall of Night
Stars till Sun

ACKNOWLEDGMENTS

Aaahhh, I think childhood friends to lovers is my new favorite trope! I swooned so hard writing this story. The teasing, banter, and yearning had me kicking my feet! Thank you to everyone who encouraged me to give Griff and Vi their own book.

This isn't goodbye to our werewolves, though. The final book in this series will be Jagger and Brielle's story, eeee! They're going to be absolute fire, I know that much.

Thanks a bunch to my incredible beta readers—Melissa, Allie, Morgan, and Kate. I value your feedback so much!

To my ARC readers new and old, thank you for taking the time to read and review for me! Your enthusiasm for my stories means more to me than you know!

And to every single one of my readers, you've changed my life in so many ways, and I hope my characters and stories leave a mark on you as well!

BECKY MOYNIHAN is a bestselling, award-winning author of paranormal romance and urban fantasy. Her books include the A Touch of Vampire series, Wolves of Midnight series, The Elite Trials series, and the co-written Genesis Crystal Saga.

When she's not writing, you can find Becky curled up on the couch in her North Carolina home, binge-watching shows and sipping Mountain Dew.

To stay up to date on new releases, sign up for her monthly newsletter: www.beckymoynihan.com/newsletter

www.ingramcontent.com/pod-product-compliance
Lightning Source LLC
Chambersburg PA
CBHW021536250626
47154CB00006BA/2138